AFTER ALICE DIED

AFTER ALICE DIED

Margaret Bingley

PIATKUS

Copyright © 1986 by Margaret Bingley

First published in Great Britain in 1986
by Judy Piatkus (Publishers) Limited of London

Reprinted 1986

British Library Cataloguing in Publication Data

Bingley, Margaret
  After Alice died
  I. Title
  ISBN 0 86188 531 7

Typeset by Phoenix Photosetting, Chatham
Printed and bound in Great Britain by
Mackays of Chatham Ltd

For my husband, whose patience
and encouragement are beyond belief.

Prologue

Prologue

At two a.m. Allan Firmager stumbled into his bedroom, fumbled with his shoe laces, nearly strangled himself with his tie and wondered what bloody fool had invented stag nights. Whoever it was the name was very apt considering the manner in which he was staggering round the room. With a final lurch he fell onto the bed and closed his eyes.

The dream seemed to come immediately. It was one of those peculiar dreams where you imagine that you are awake; certainly Allan felt awake as he sat up and looked round his room. It had suddenly turned very cold, and switching on his bedside lamp he glanced across at the window. There, standing by the curtains, was the most beautiful girl he had ever seen.

She was below average height with delicate bone structure and a cascade of golden hair that gleamed with a silvery sheen as it tumbled to her shoulders. Slowly, she turned to face him, and he gazed into a pair of incredible violet eyes that dominated the face and seemed to penetrate his innermost soul.

As he continued to stare she lifted a small hand and ran it through her hair, giving her head a slight shake as she did so in an apparently unselfconscious gesture of invitation. If she hadn't been surrounded by such an aura of cold he would have reached out and touched her, but instead he kept still, shivering more violently now.

Keeping her eyes fastened to his, the girl began to unbutton the cream camisole top that she was wearing, and as the buttons opened so her full, ivory-coloured breasts were gradually revealed to him. With one final shrug she shed the camisole entirely, and it slipped from her shoulders. He looked at her pale pink nipples, already erect, and his throat tightened. She stretched herself, arching her body towards him, and this time he did reach out and his fingers touched her breasts as lightly and as carefully as he could manage.

3

To his relief her flesh was warm. He pushed the duvet off and knelt on the top of the bed, lowering his mouth to her nipples and flicking his tongue over them until he heard her give a strange moan of contentment deep in her throat. Encouraged he fastened his hands round her tiny waist and began to unbutton her skirt. She let him continue until he finally felt the velvet skin of her thighs, and then all at once she gave a gentle laugh and with a swift movement was free of him, standing in the middle of the carpet, still naked from the waist upwards, her eyes shining and her skin glowing.

Unable to let her go after he had progressed so far Allan began to move after her, but she shook her head and drifted back to the window, buttoning her camisole top as she went. Now he could feel the cold again, and he stood halfway between the bed and the beautiful girl, incapable – as sometimes happens in dreams – of taking a step in either direction.

'Don't go!' he pleaded. 'I want you. Don't leave me.'

She smiled. 'But I have to. After all, tomorrow you marry Julie.'

'You mean I'll never see you again?' His voice was thick with frustration, and even in his dream he knew a moment of despairing impotency as she started to drift away from him.

'Oh yes,' she reassured him gently. 'Marry Julie and we'll be together for always.' She began to fade, her outline less clear, the image blurring.

'Don't go yet. Stay a little longer.'

'I can't; it isn't possible. Remember, once you marry Julie we'll never be parted again.' The last few words were faint and lingered in the air after her physical shape had vanished.

Her departure released him and he stumbled back to his bed, his mind in complete turmoil. He had never desired a girl so much in his entire life, and marriage to

4

Julie was suddenly the last thing on earth that he wanted.

In the morning, when he awoke, he wondered what strange subconscious thoughts had caused the dream. Probably the realisation that all beautiful blondes were out of reach now he thought wryly. As for the girl, she looked a little like one of Julie's fellow nurses whom he'd seen once or twice at parties and dances. He'd never spoken to her, but it appeared she'd left quite an impression on him. Well, this was one dream he wouldn't tell his future wife about. It was scarcely an ideal prelude to their lifelong union! With a laugh he climbed out of bed, and then moaned as the headache struck.

Grateful for an afternoon wedding he showered and dressed before giving his duvet its usual shake. As he did so, the scent of the dream-girl's perfume filled the air. His mouth suddenly dry he backed away from the bed towards the window where, as he remembered it, she had stood waiting in the dream.

There, lying on top of the deep brown carpet, he found one single strand of ash-blonde hair. With trembling fingers he picked it up and placed it on the palm of his hand. Immediately her voice echoed round the room. 'Marry Julie and we'll always be together,' she said, her voice curiously pure and passionless.

His hand shook violently and he continued staring at the hair as though hypnotised by it. 'Remember,' she continued, 'do as I say and we'll never be parted . . . never be . . . never . . .' Her voice became fainter and fainter until it faded into oblivion. Slowly, the hair began to disintegrate on the palm of his hand, until with one final shimmer it too vanished.

Allan stared disbelievingly at his empty hand. The smell of perfume had vanished now, and complete normality had been restored to the room. It had to be the alcohol he thought, and repeated the words aloud, as though this had the power to make it true. Alcohol, he repeated defiantly. Anyone might hallucinate after mixing their drinks with such foolhardy abandon. Yes, it was the drink. After all, what other explanation could there be?

Chapter 1

Julie Pask awoke at seven a.m. on the morning of the 22nd December, slipped out of bed and was promptly sick into the basin. Being a pregnant bride rather took the edge off the big day she decided as she studied her reflection in the mirror.

The face that looked back at her was oval in shape with a closely fitting cap of small, petal-like curls in a deep shade of auburn that can never be achieved from a bottle. She had the perfect creamy complexion that usually accompanies such hair, and this – coupled with the soft golden-brown of her expressive eyes – made her a highly striking young woman.

She smiled at her solemn expression, and immediately a small dimple appeared in her chin; a dimple that Allan had found irresistible right from their first meeting. At the thought of Allan her eyes sparkled and the sickness was forgotten.

Slipping on her dressing-gown she waited quietly at the top of the stairs, listening to all the hustle and bustle going on below as her mother organised the buffet. Finally, satisfied that everyone – even her eight-year-old sister Jill – was busy she went along to Russell's room and tapped lightly on the door. 'Come in,' he muttered, sounding more like a sulky fifteen-year-old than a man of twenty-five.

She entered to find him lying on his bed, arms crossed behind his head, staring blankly into space. He glanced at his sister for a moment, his expression unreadable, then nodded his head towards the window.

'So you're really leaving our little cocoon and joining the human race?'

'I think it might be best – for all of us.' Her voice was light, casual.

'Meaning yourself.'

'Meaning all of us. Mother, Father, you and last but not least, yes, me.'

She sensed that he wanted a scene and tried desperately to avert it. Nothing must be allowed to mar today. Surely one perfect day wasn't too much to ask? Most brides could take if for granted. Just this once she wanted to be like other girls again; as she had been before, many years ago.

'Father knows nothing. Mother spends her life avoiding reality. That only leaves you and me.' His voice was petulant.

'It will be easier this way. You know how hard it is at the moment.'

Russell ignored the plea in her voice. When he spoke he sounded sullen again, like a small boy being thwarted. 'You mean you're actually going to marry that creep?'

'I love him, Russell. Why won't you believe that?'

'Because I've always imagined you to have good taste. Allan's not worthy of you. He's shallow, conceited and totally lacking in sensitivity.'

Julie's face flushed. 'How dare you! Anyway, who do you think *you* are to talk of sensitivity?' There was a second of shocked silence between them before Russell turned his face to the wall and curled up into a small ball.

Since his breakdown this was the usual signal for a set-back in his progress. It often heralded weeks of

8

staying indoors, scarcely eating or sleeping, simply sitting looking out of various windows at the people passing by.

'Nothing will change,' she assured him more gently. 'I've been thinking it over very carefully, and I'm sure this will work out best for everyone in the end.'

She waited for a moment, but when Russell only uttered a small whimper she walked away, leaving him alone with his thoughts. At the foot of the stairs her mother was waiting. 'Where's Russell?' she asked anxiously, her hands working nervously at her sides.

'Lying on his bed.' Julie kept her voice quiet, almost placating.

'He isn't . . .? You know . . .'

'Yes; I rather think he's getting into one of his states.'

Mrs Pask looked at her daughter in anguish. 'Really, Julie, this is all your fault. You know how highly strung Russell is: all the arguments recently, they've been very bad for him.' The unfairness of the comment stung Julie into a sharp reply.

'*I'm* pregnant, not Russell!'

'You don't understand your brother at all,' snapped her mother.

'But I do, Mother; believe me, I do.' Their eyes met briefly, and the older woman ignored the silent plea for understanding from her daughter. She moved away, hurrying up the stairs, anxious to talk to her son and if necessary call the doctor, even if it was Julie's wedding day.

Mr Pask came out of his study. 'Russell not quite . . .?'

'He's in bed, having an attack of nerves. As usual Mother's gone to pander to him.' She couldn't conceal the bitterness she felt.

'Good God!' exclaimed her father. 'It's been five years. It's about time that boy pulled himself together.

They should have retained National Service.' He walked away muttering, and Julie thanked heaven for Allan and his love, which would rescue her from this house with its deep, treacherous undercurrents.

For the ceremony she wore a blue woollen two-piece and carried a small spray of artificial flowers. Everything was quiet, and it was all over in ten minutes. In a strange way Julie felt cheated, but under the circumstances a church wedding had not seemed appropriate. Outside sleet was beginning to fall causing Allan to shiver as they stood on the Registry Office steps for the photographs.

Despite Julie's pregnancy, and his personal disapproval of the marriage, once Mr Pask had come to terms with its inevitability he had purchased outright a neat, three-bedroomed semi-detached house for the couple only a few roads away from Julie's present home. Allan had been astounded at such generosity but Julie accepted it with what seemed to him a rather casual attitude.

'He's got loads of money,' she explained, 'and he wants Number One grandchild to have a good home to live in!'

'Even so,' retorted Allan, 'to buy us a house!'

'He's pleased to see me married and off his hands,' she joked.

'That's ridiculous; he was furious when we told him.'

'At first yes; but not later, once he'd thought it through.'

Allan had frowned, remembering the peculiar lecture Mr Pask had delivered about skeletons in cupboards and things working out for the best in life, but he still didn't think that the man had been pleased. Surprised definitely, but not pleased. Not in comparison with his own parents who thought Julie both attractive and sweet natured. Indeed, once or twice his mother had implied that Allan wasn't good enough for such a desirable girl.

'I only hope you can make her happy' she'd told him doubtfully. Yet when he pressed her for an explanation she'd merely shaken her head and walked away. He was no cosseted, worshipped only child.

Finally the guests were gathered back at Julie's family home, helping themselves to minute sandwiches, sausage rolls, cheese dips and the usual unsatisfying buffet snacks. The talk was cheerful and no one looked happier than the bride and groom. They cut the cake together, smiling again for the photographer.

As Jill, full of self-importance in her blue velvet dress, handed round slices from the bottom layer Julie's mother whisked the top layer away. 'For the christening,' she murmured to Julie, who smiled at her mother's excitement over the forthcoming grandchild.

She followed her out, and Allan turned to speak to the guest standing by his left elbow. Her face was half-turned away from him, but she wore an attractive peach-coloured dress that flared from beneath the bust and he wondered who she was. He couldn't remember seeing her at the Registry Office.

As she turned to face him he went rigid with shock. It was the girl from his dream. She was smiling, and her violet eyes were sparkling. Grateful that she couldn't know of their erotic, nocturnal lovemaking Allan handed her a glass of champagne.

'I'm sorry, but I don't know your name,' he apologised as he waited for her to take the glass. She smiled again, but her arms stayed by her sides.

'Don't you drink?'

One or two of the guests began to cast sideways glances at him. Embarrassed he reached for her hand, only to discover with stunned disbelief that there was nothing there. There was no flesh for him to touch. His hand had gone straight through hers, causing her to vanish while he remained frozen in a ridiculous posture with one extended glass of champagne and a free hand stabbing at empty air.

Fortunately Ben, the best man, came to his rescue.

'Something wrong, Allan?'

'No, why?'

'You seemed to be talking to yourself!'

'No one else is interested in what I have to say! Weddings are obviously for the bride, the groom doesn't count.' They both laughed, and after a few moments Ben moved off. Immediately the girl reappeared, making her way out of the room towards the kitchen. Allan followed like a sleepwalker.

Julie and her mother both glanced up from where they were carefully wrapping the cake and looked enquiringly at him. The girl stood at Julie's shoulder and watched Allan with an unblinking stare.

'Are you going to get changed, Julie? We should set off soon.' To his relief his voice sounded perfectly normal.

Julie smiled. 'Yes, of course. I hope the hotel's warm and friendly. It seems a strange way to celebrate Christmas.'

'It was your idea. You said it would make a memorable honeymoon.'

'I know, and I'm sure it will. It won't take me five minutes, darling.' Allan watched as she hurried away. The beautiful girl glided gracefully behind her, casting one brief glance back at Allan before she disappeared.

While Julie was gone he thanked her mother for all her help.

'It was my pleasure, Allan. We must make the best of things, and I hope you'll be very happy together.' She didn't appear over-optimistic, but her social manners were always impeccable and she didn't seem aware of how stilted she sounded.

Hearing a door close above, Allan went to the foot of

the stairs to watch Julie come down. She had changed into a grey wool coat with a fur collar and hem, and grey suede boots completed the outfit. He thought again how lucky he was to have her, and watched with pride as she descended the steps, her left hand resting lightly on the banister rail.

All at once his eyes widened in shock as with a silver shimmer the dream girl materialised, drifting silently down behind the new bride. Then she pounced. Her hands shot out and with immense force she pushed Julie between the shoulder blades, her face fleetingly distorted with rage. Allan saw the look of stunned amazement on his wife's features as she tried desperately to keep hold of the banister, but the push had been powerful and unexpected. As Julie teetered on the stair her fashionably high-heeled boots twisted and with a scream of fear she pitched head first down into the hall.

Alerted by the scream guests crowded out to see what had happened. She lay on the carpet, her right foot twisted awkwardly beneath her and her mouth contorted with pain. Allan ran forward and went down on his knees beside her.

'Are you badly hurt? What happened? Darling, say something.' She looked at him, her face white and tense. There were tears in her eyes as she fought for self-control.

'I thought . . . it felt as though . . . my foot must have caught . . .' Disjointed fragments of sentences issued from her mouth, and then she gave a louder cry of pain and Allan stood up in alarm.

Mrs Pask took one look at Julie and ran to the telephone. Allan crouched next to her again. 'Your mother's telephoning for help,' he assured her. She nodded and took hold of his hand, squeezing it tightly.

As they waited, Allan looked back up the staircase. The girl was still there, standing on the third step holding something out to him. Something she wanted him to see. She moved nearer and there was a strange smell. Not her perfume, not a scent that he had ever encountered before, but he didn't like it and all at once he didn't want to look at her beautiful face.

Julie gave a louder whimper and gripped his hand even more tightly. He wondered what was hurting her so badly. Apparently realising that he wouldn't look at her the girl moved until she too was crouching beside Julie, but on the opposite side to Allan to that he was forced to look directly into her eyes. She held out her hands to him and whispered softly. He bent closer to Julie. Small hands moved between the young couple. 'My wedding present,' the blonde whispered, and now the smell was stronger. Reluctantly he looked at her outstretched hands. There, lying in a pool of blood and matter, was a tiny but perfectly formed foetus.

With a strangled cry Allan tried to pull away but Julie held him tightly and there was no escape. The dripping mass was pushed closer until he felt that his face would become smeared with the blood and slime surrounding it, but just as his head started swimming with the fear and horror the girl and her ghastly present disappeared.

An hour later a young doctor explained to Allan that despite all their efforts his wife had lost the child she was carrying. He remarked later to a colleague how well the husband had coped, little realising that he had simply confirmed something that Allan already knew.

When he was finally alone in the house that was to be his and Julie's first home he sat down and wept. He wept for Julie; he wept for the child; but most of all he wept for the horror that had entered his life and which he knew instinctively had not yet finished with him.

When he awoke alone in the double bed the next morning he thought immediately of Julie as he had last seen her; half-asleep from medication but trying to smile

14

when he had to leave. He wondered how she felt, knowing that her accident had come too late: a week earlier and there wouldn't have been a wedding. Julie could have continued with her career, just as she had always wanted. If she was bitter she hadn't shown it last night, but he was afraid it might become obvious over the next few months.

He felt grateful for the central heating, remembering his childhood winters and the teeth-chattering mornings when he was dressing for school. Making his way down to the kitchen he prepared toast and coffee then seated himself on one of the high stools he and Julie had chosen the previous week.

He knew that the girl was there before she materialised. Not only could he sense her watching him, there was also the drop in temperature and the smell of perfume, but he refused to turn his head. Let her make the first move, he thought, force her to speak first.

There was a rustle of petticoats and then she was with him, perched on the breakfast bar, shapely legs swinging bare and brown from beneath an orange linen dress. She smiled, but didn't speak.

'What do you want? Why did you push Julie yesterday?' he asked at last. She didn't reply, gave no sign that she had even heard, instead she examined her tanned legs carefully.

'Why are you always dressed for summer?' he demanded, searching for some clue as to who she was and where she had come from.

'Because that's when I died. It's my favourite time of year, summer.'

'Was,' he corrected her. 'It *was* your favourite time of year.' She raised her eyebrows in surprise. 'You don't sound very pleased to see me. Don't you want me any more?' Her voice became coaxing and childlike.

'*Want* you? What kind of a man do you take me for?'

She wriggled closer to him, letting one arm brush against the sleeve of his pullover. 'How unkind! I thought you liked me.'

'Yesterday you killed my child and injured my wife. How the hell can you expect me to be pleased to see you?' She gave a peal of laughter. 'What an innocent you are! That wasn't *your* child. There will be other babies, babies that really are yours. You should be grateful to me. Think how annoyed you would have been if you'd ever discovered there was a cuckoo in your snug little nest.'

'Not mine?' he repeated disbelievingly. 'Whose was it then?' She poked the tip of her tongue between her lips and thought for a moment. 'I'm not going to tell you.'

'That's because you can't! You're lying. Why? Who the hell are you? and why have you attached yourself to me? I don't need you; please, go away and pester someone different.'

Although the words were bold enough inside he felt sick and terrified. As he had spoken he had noticed the violet eyes darkening, and he realised that she was seething with fury. He waited with some trepidation for her response.

The girl turned her face away, hiding her features until she had regained her self-control, only then did she turn back to him.

'It doesn't matter why I'm here. You'll just have to accept it. After all, there's nothing else you can do.'

'I can call in a priest. Ask him to exorcise you. That's what they do in films.'

She giggled. 'How sweet! I'm afraid that it wouldn't work. Besides, would you really be able to talk to anyone about me?'

'Yes.'

'Despite the ridicule?'

'Well . . .'

16

'I thought not! It would be a terrible waste as well; we're going to have some lovely times together you and I.'

'We most definitely are not. I've got a wonderful wife, I don't need you to give me lovely times.'

'You can't say that. You don't know enough about me. Don't you want to make love to me?'

'No.'

'I think *you're* lying now. How is your wife?'

'In a lot of pain, and heartbroken about the baby.'

'The baby wasn't needed any more.'

'Needed? By whom?'

'Anyone. It had served its purpose. Once you were married it became surplus to requirements.'

'You're unbelievable! Doesn't Julie's suffering mean anything to you? Don't you feel in the least bit remorseful?'

'She'll live. I'm dead; why should I pity her? No one pitied me.'

'When?'

She jumped lightly down to the floor and walked round the room. Allan watched her nervously. 'It's all very small isn't it? I'd hate to live here. I never could bear being cooped up in small rooms.'

'Good; then perhaps you'd like to move on to a larger house. Julie and I like this one, and that's all that matters.'

'It's so touching the way you talk about her! Julie this and Julie that. Romantic love! I find it rather nauseating myself, but I know it's always been popular.'

'Don't you dare sneer at me. I've loved Julie for nearly two years now, a fact you'd know if you were as clever as you claim, and I can't get over my good luck in persuading her to marry me. She's beautiful, open, cheerful and very loving. Not qualities that you seem likely to be acquainted with, but I happen to rate them very highly.'

'What a little prig you are! Not that I mind. Basically you're all the same, if you did but realise it.'

'Who do you mean by "all"?'

'Men of course. They're my speciality. I never got on very well with women.'

'Fancy that!' he said dryly. The girl didn't answer, instead she stood at his elbow with a hand resting lightly on his shoulder.

'Don't you think *I'm* beautiful too?'

Her touch seemed to burn, but around her the air was still bitterly cold. Allan shuddered. She looked thoughtfully at him, then returned to the breakfast bar and began to unfasten the buttons down the front of her dress.

Allan fought desperately against the temptation of looking at her, but the blatant air of sexuality that now filled the room began to take effect and despite his good intentions he found himself glancing from the corner of his eyes as she slowly exposed the creamy skin of her throat and breasts.

Despite the fact that she was so small the flesh was full and irresistible; his hands reached out against his volition and as his fingers closed on her warm, womanly curves so his anger evaporated. The girl smiled, but this time there was no mockery behind the smile, it was a smile of pleasure and welcome. Like a man in a trance he moved until he was close enough to press her entire body against his, and although he didn't they both knew that the desire was there.

The girl parted her lips and let a small sigh escape while her eyes grew heavy and sensual as his hands roamed more and more urgently over her. After a few moments his touch grew more demanding; he was less the supplicant, more the aggressor and the only emotion that showed on his face was plain, basic lust.

This was something that the girl understood. She took

18

hold of his right hand and jumped lightly to the ground. After the briefest of hesitations he led her towards the stairs.

He was breathing heavily now and almost pushed her into the bedroom. In a matter of seconds his clothes were in a heap on the floor, and he lay on the bed watching as the girl slowly and provocatively removed her own garments.

By the time that she was finally naked he felt that he was ready to burst with pent-up desire. The air was no longer cold, instead it was warm and relaxing. Daintily she came to the bedside and looked down on him.

She saw his swollen penis, his glazed expression and she smiled a slow, secret smile of satisfaction. This was always the best moment, the moment before they gained their objective. The moment when, for a few glorious seconds, they were completely in her power.

Lying beside him she rolled her body onto his so that her long, golden curls brushed his chest and shoulders. Delicately she licked his skin, her tongue darting in and out like a cat lapping at milk. Allan put his hands in her hair, loving the feel of its silky smoothness, the smell of shampoo that lingered there.

She seated herself across his thighs and groaning he tried to manipulate her so that he could enter, but she wasn't ready to relinquish her power so swiftly and evaded him.

For over half an hour she played with him, covering every inch of his body with tongue and lips. Time and again she brought him to the very edge, only to draw back leaving him half-crazed with frustration.

Finally, when she knew that he was unable to wait any longer, she straddled herself on top of him and as he entered her began to move in a slow, sensuous rhythm that he attempted to quicken by pulling her hips towards him, but she would not be hurried. All at once he felt the

19

tension in him building to a tremendous height. It felt as though his entire body might explode and with a shout of triumph he climaxed, his body shuddering violently.

The girl sat quite still, her expression cool and remote. She watched his head thrashing from side to side, his face swollen and red, and she despised him as she had always despised men at that final moment of release.

Opening his eyes he pulled her close, making her lie on his chest and stomach with her head resting in the hollow at the base of his throat.

'I have to go now,' she murmured. He tightened his grip. 'Not yet. Stay a little longer.' He couldn't see the anger in her eyes and she kept her voice soft. 'I have to go. I shall come again.'

Allan smiled. 'I shan't let you go!' Carefully she lowered her mouth to the sensitive flesh where her head had been resting and bit savagely with her tiny, pearl-like teeth. He gave a cry of pain and threw her off. 'Why did you do that?' he asked in disbelief, watching a small trickle of blood run down his chest. 'How am I supposed to explain it to Julie?' It was the first time he had thought of his wife since the lovemaking began.

The girl was at the window now, her form fading slowly. 'That's your problem,' she laughed. 'When I say I'm going I mean it. That's lesson number one, my darling. Next time we'll . . .' Allan sat up, vainly straining both ears and eyes, but there was no longer anything to be seen or heard. His visitor had gone.

Exhausted and with leaden limbs and aching muscles he walked over to the dressing-table mirror. As he had feared two tiny puncture marks and a dry trickle of blood stood out starkly against his white skin.

Now that the ecstasy was over he felt sick and unclean. Going into the bathroom he ran a scorching hot bath and scrubbed remorselessly at his body. He had to be clean before he could visit Julie. But no matter how hard he

20

scrubbed his body his sense of self-disgust could not be erased.

There was still over two hours left before visiting time, and he wondered how to keep himself busy until then. Deciding that some coffee might help him to feel more human he made a pot and took his cup into the living-room where he sat down in his armchair and – despite his good intentions – began to replay the sexual encounter in his head.

It was the sound of the doorbell that broke the spell. On the step stood a very pale, worried-looking Russell who mumbled something unintelligible then brushed into the house without any invitation. Allan was surprised. His brother-in-law had always been abrasive and slightly hostile towards him, and he wondered what could have prompted the visit.

'Anything to drink in the house?' Russell asked abruptly.

'Only tea or coffee I'm afraid.'

'I'll have to settle for coffee then. Two sugars please.' Allan silently complied, then sat waiting for an explanation.

'I've been to see Julie,' Russell blurted out after taking a brief swallow of the liquid.

'But I was told to wait until this afternoon. Why did they let you in? *I'm* her husband.'

'We all know that! However, she kept asking for me. The doctor was worried and they rang me up.'

'They should have sent for *me*.'

'Don't you listen? She didn't want you; she wanted me.' He sounded almost triumphant, and Allan felt a surge of dislike. He had hoped that after the wedding he might get to know Russell better, but it now appeared that his brother-in-law had no intention of allowing any such thing. Anxious not to increase the hostile atmosphere himself he forced a calm response. 'Fair enough.

21

What did she want?'

Russell was looking round the room, his eyes searching the corners and glancing out of the windows. He looked tired and tense.

'Sorry?'

'I said what did she want?' This time Allan couldn't keep the edge out of his voice.

Russell moistened his lips with his tongue. 'It didn't make any sense. I told her it was shock, but she kept insisting that she was telling the truth. I couldn't disprove it, I wasn't there at the time. You were, you saw it all. Perhaps you can put her mind at rest.'

'I don't know what this is about,' said Allan, uncomfortably aware of the pounding of his heart, 'but since Julie knows where I was yesterday and therefore realises that I can help why did she ask for you?'

Russell looked strangely apologetic. 'She imagines that you won't tell the truth. I promised not to discuss it with you, but I can't think what else to do.'

'What did she say?'

'She told me that she didn't trip on the stairs; she's certain that someone pushed her.'

The hairs on the back of Allan's neck prickled and he began to sweat. He struggled to express the right amount of astonishment that the statement should have produced. It was difficult, and he wasn't entirely sure that he succeeded.

'Who? he asked incredulously. 'Who does she think pushed her?'

'I don't know. *Did* you see anyone?'

He stood up, turning his back on Russell. 'Am I supposed to take this seriously? Do I really have to answer?'

'Yes.'

'Very well: I did not see anyone on the stairs apart from Julie, who twisted her ankle and fell. It looked to

22

me as though her heel caught on a loose piece of carpet.' The lie almost choked him.

Russell sighed. 'Well, that's it then. I might as well push off.'

'Did you seriously imagine for one moment that I was going to say yes?' queried Allan with an attempt at a laugh.

'No, I didn't. What I really wanted was your reaction to the question, and I got it.'

'Fine. I take it I'm to keep this a secret when I see Julie?'

'Yes, please. You think she's mad don't you?'

'Of course not! It sounds like concussion to me.'

'Does it really?'

'Yes.'

For a moment Russell seemed about to speak again, but then his shoulders drooped. 'Have it your own way,' he muttered. 'I'm off.'

His visit left Allan even more uneasy and troubled than before. He longed to see Julie again, to hold her hand and plan their future and laugh at all the silly things that amused them. That was reality, and he vowed never again to betray his wife however great the temptation. Once he had her home with him he would be safe. He only hoped that the hospital weren't planning on keeping her there too long.

Chapter 2

Julie was lying flat on the bed when Allan arrived. She looked curiously young and vulnerable. All at once he remembered the very first time they met. She had been sitting alone in a corner of a crowded living-room with exactly the same defenceless air about her.

However, once they began talking he found her lively and amusing. They saw each other often after that, and it was only occasionally that she would become lost in some private, isolated world of her own. It was this complexity of character that kept him interested; that and the fact that for the first time in his life he was the pursuer.

Even after they knew they were in love Julie remained reluctant to commit herself to marriage, and but for the unplanned pregnancy he was still not certain that she would ever have become his wife. Looking at her now, pale and exhausted, he silently vowed to make certain that she never regretted her decision. A vision of the dream girl floated unbidden into his mind, and he quickly crossed the floor of his wife's room.

At the sound of his feet she gave an exclamation of pleasure and stretched out her arms. He sat beside her, holding her tightly. 'I'm so sorry,' he whispered, 'so very, very sorry.' He wasn't only talking about the accident, but there was no way that Julie could know that, and she was touched by the fervour of his words.

'A fine start to our married life!' she said lightly. 'That's what vanity does to you. I ought to have settled for lower heels on my boots!' No mention of anyone pushing her Allan noticed. He wondered if Russell had invented it. Somewhere in Russell's past there had been a breakdown, and even now Julie described him as mentally unreliable; possibly he had been voicing some neurotic theory of his own, in which case there was nothing for Allan to worry about.

'I'm sorry about the baby, Julie,' he murmured. 'I know you didn't want to get married for another year, and now there's no baby but you're still stuck with me for a husband!'

She smiled, her expression tender. 'Silly! I've only ever wanted you for a husband. Besides, what difference does one year make? We'll be gloriously happy, and there will be other babies; although perhaps not just yet.'

He gripped her hands tightly. 'Of course there will. I'm afraid I'm feeling rather low today. I don't know why; you're the one who's ill!'

'It's always more difficult to be the relative than the patient.'

'Well, Russell's certainly very worried about you.'

'Oh?'

'Yes. He called round saying the most extraordinary things.'

Julie's eyes became wary. 'Such as?'

'He seemed to think that you'd been pushed downstairs and wanted to know if it was true.'

'Well, if I had thought that I'd scarcely have asked Russell. He wasn't anywhere near.'

'So you didn't say any such thing?'

Julie's expression softened. 'Of course not, but don't

25

tell him. I'm afraid that ever since his breakdown he gets thrown off balance rather easily. Any minor accident or trauma can set him back. Who does he imagine I think pushed me? If you know what I mean!'

'I've no idea. Probably me; I'm not his favourite person.'

'Well, I know it wasn't you, don't I? I saw you looking up at me. You looked so happy, and I remember feeling elated by the pride on your face. It was a lovely moment.'

'There'll be lots more lovely moments too.'

Julie gripped his hand tightly. 'Do you know, for a fleeting second, just before I fell, you had an almost frozen look on your face. It was weird, as though you had a premonition about it.'

'Did I? All I can remember is feeling so helpless once you started to lose your balance. It was horrible! I'll never forget you lying in the hall; for one terrible moment I thought you were dead.'

'Don't sound so intense! I'm not, and what's more I'll soon be allowed home.'

He sat back from her to see if she was really looking better, and immediately she gave a gasp of fright. 'Allan, there's blood on your shirt! Look, the stain is spreading all down the front of you.'

With fingers that felt thick and clumsy he took off his tie and fumbled with the shirt buttons. It was as he had feared. The small bites that the girl had inflicted on him earlier had re-opened and he was bleeding profusely. Sickened and afraid he pressed a clean handkerchief firmly on them until the seepage finally ceased.

'I should have told you,' he said casually as Julie continued to stare at him in puzzlement. 'Your beloved cat went for me when I tried to push her off the breakfast bar this morning.'

'She probably doesn't like the change of scenery.

Make sure you put some disinfectant on it; animal bites can easily turn septic.'

'Yes, nurse!' They both laughed, and the difficult moment passed.

On New Year's Eve, the doctor decided that Julie was fit enough to go home. She telephoned Allan to give him the good news and he promised to have her clothes there within the hour. After he'd hung up he stood for a moment, thoughtfully absorbing the atmosphere of the house.

The girl had visited him every day while Julie was away, and he had become an expert at sensing when she was there before she showed herself. There was always the feeling of being watched, the sensation of someone standing just out of his line of vision, and sometimes he would turn his head quickly hoping to surprise her. She was never there. He wondered how it was that he could sense her presence. Whatever the reason it displeased the girl. She liked her arrival to be a shock, a complete surprise; his sensory perception irritated her.

It was always after that moment that the scent of perfume would fill the room, and only then would she herself materialise. Allan knew that she was beginning to obsess him. His original feeling of lust and sexual hunger was being replaced by a desire to know her better. To search beneath the brittle, albeit beautiful, surface and find out more about her. So far he had made no progress, and this irked him. Now, with Julie coming home, there wouldn't be any further opportunities.

He was disgusted to find that the telephone call hadn't given him the pleasure he would have expected. The girl had blunted his feelings for Julie. Sickened by his fickleness and confident that he was alone he swore aloud at the situation in which he now found himself.

'It will be different once she's home,' he thought, throwing Julie's jersey and skirt into her pigskin case.

27

'Once we're together I won't have any need for . . .'

The room filled with tinkling laughter. Soft at first it increased in volume until seeming to bounce off all the walls, echoing round and round in his head so that his ears hurt. He clapped his hands over them in a futile attempt to shut out the noise.

Still the laughter grew; peal after peal of light amusement which he was acutely aware also held derision. 'Shut up!' he shouted. 'Shut up and leave me alone. I don't want you. Do you hear me? I don't want any more to do with you. Go away. Just go, and leave Julie and me in peace.'

He hadn't expected his words to have any effect, but to his amazement the sounds slowly died away and at last there was silence. The room was quiet; quiet and watchful. She was there, and she knew that he was aware of it, but she remained invisible and he had to complete the packing and walk away from the house acutely conscious of the hidden eyes following his every move.

'You look terribly tired,' commented Julie in concern. 'Do you feel O.K.?'

'It's all the visiting and housework. I'm only a simple male, and not up to such exertion!'

'Then it's a good job you've had some practice. Since we're both working the domestic chores will have to be split between us. After this you'll find your share quite easy!'

Arm in arm they made their way back to the house that was now their home. Ignoring her squeals of protest Allan carried her over the threshold. 'I intend to start off right,' he joked. 'You have to appease the pagan gods you know!'

Julie clasped her arms tightly round his neck. 'Oh, darling! It's so good to be home at last.'

As soon as they entered the kitchen Allan knew that she was there. Quickly he let go of Julie's hand and

28

moved away as she tried to kiss him. 'I'll make some coffee,' he muttered.

'I'd rather have a kiss!'

He distinctly heard a snigger. 'I thought you were convalescing,' he retorted, and instead of coming out as a teasing comment it sounded snappy and bad-tempered. Julie's face fell and she turned awkwardly away.

Horrified he hurried over and gave her a hug. 'Sorry! I don't know what's wrong with me. Reaction after all the excitement perhaps?'

She gave a strained smile. 'Probably. I'll go and sit down in the other room.' He bent and brushed her lips with his, but very quickly, hoping that the girl wouldn't appear while he was doing it.

For a second Julie looked at her husband in puzzlement, then she gave her familiar grin. 'You're out of practice! We'll have to put that right as soon as I'm fit.'

'It can't be soon enough for me,' he lied valiantly, horribly aware of the lurking shadow watching them both. 'Go on then, you sit down. I'll be with you in a second.'

Alone he waited tensely, but all at once the sense of her presence vanished. He was really alone. Relieved he started to whistle cheerfully, and his colour was better when he handed Julie her cup.

She reached out to take it. As her fingers closed on the saucer so a slender hand reached across her face and tilted the cup, causing the boiling liquid to spill down Julie's arm. She leapt up with a scream of pain, and ran into the kitchen so that she could hold her burnt flesh beneath the cold water tap.

She was biting on her lip in silence, but Allan could see the tears in her eyes and was horrified by the blisters already forming on her arm. 'Hadn't you better go to Casualty, darling?'

'No, I don't think so. It's only a surface burn. Most of it went in my lap. I don't seem to be very lucky since our wedding day, do I?'

'What happened?' he asked. 'Did I let go too soon?'

'Somehow the cup got tilted. I couldn't have gripped the saucer tightly enough. By the way, is it shock or is this kitchen freezing cold?'

Allan swallowed hard. 'It is a bit chilly. I think we need draught excluder round the window. You're terribly pale. Perhaps you'd better go and lie down for half an hour.'

'I think I will. I feel rather wobbly.' As she left the room the girl appeared by the open door and slammed it closed before Julie was out of the way. It caught her on her funny bone and she gave a loud shout. With a feline smile the girl disappeared.

'What's the matter now?' Allan asked, trying to sound puzzled even as his eyes travelled round the room in case the blonde was lurking elsewhere.

'The damned door shut on me. I'm beginning to wonder if we've got a resident poltergeist!'

'Come off it!'

'I'm only joking; it's plain that I'm being clumsy. I probably need to rest.'

'You don't believe in poltergeists do you?'

Julie looked down at the floor. 'Not as such, but I keep a fairly open mind about spirits and so on. More things in heaven and earth etcetera.'

How true thought Allan watching her walk slowly away. Once she'd gone the girl returned and immediately moved close to him, pressing her pelvis against his hips. Taking hold of her by the shoulders he pushed her away. 'Cut it out!' he snapped. 'Leave Julie alone. What's she ever done to hurt you? Isn't my adultery enough? Just leave her in peace.'

'Is it adultery with a ghost I wonder? I doubt it, Allan!'

'I'm not in the mood for stupid jokes.'

She pouted. 'I was only having a bit of fun. No one ever appreciated my sense of humour. You didn't even laugh when the cup tilted, and yet her face was hysterically funny! That look of surprise and disbelief! It was priceless.'

'If that's your idea of fun I'm not surprised no one found you amusing. Now push off, I'm going up to my wife.' Ignoring him she put out her fingers and gently undid the zip of his trousers before slipping her cool fingers beneath his Y-fronts and starting to fondle him.

He stood frozen to the spot, knowing that he must break free and yet weakened by the exquisite sensations she was arousing. With a tremendous effort of will he turned away and did himself up.

The girl's lips tightened in annoyance. 'Go on then, but you'll regret it. I can be quite nasty when people annoy me.'

'What a surprise!' he said ironically and with a quick flouncing movement she vanished. Cold and shaking Allan left the kitchen, seated himself in the lounge and wondered where the hell things went from here.

All at once the telephone started to ring. This time Allan found himself pleased to hear from Russell, and immediately invited him round for the afternoon. 'Bring . . . er, Prudence wasn't it?'

'Prudence has been given her marching orders; I'll come alone, unless you've any gorgeous girls in your now redundant black book who might like to make up the numbers!'

'Is your brother ever serious about his girlfriends?' Allan asked Julie when he went up to the bedroom to tell her about the visit.

'I don't think so. He's too wrapped up in himself.' Her voice was flat.

'I've never heard you criticise him before. I thought

31

you were very close.'

'So we are, but I'm not blind to his faults. Anyway, Prudence always made me feel short and overweight, so I'm not sorry she's gone!'

'Don't start fishing for compliments. You know perfectly well that most girls would give anything for a figure like yours! Talking of which, how long before we can . . .?'

'A couple of weeks I should think. It's horribly frustrating isn't it!'

'I'll put some bromide in our tea!'

Julie was back downstairs when her brother arrived. 'Here you are little sister; some champagne to bring the colour back to your face. Got any glasses?'

'Dozens,' responded Allan, 'but most of them in their boxes. I'll see what I can find.'

Once he'd gone Russell moved closer to Julie. 'Are you really all right? You don't look it.'

'I'm fine. What happened to Prudence?'

'The same as all the others; she didn't measure up.'

'You've got to get over it, Russell. You can't spend your entire life making comparisons.'

'I'm not willing to settle for second best.'

'Darling Russell, you've no choice. You have to put the past behind you. Nothing can alter that, but . . .'

'Here we are,' said Allan, 'in the last box, of course.'

'Naturally! Now, a toast to you both. May you have a long and fruitful union.'

'Ugh!' exclaimed Julie. 'You make me sound like a brood mare. Years of happiness and joy would be more acceptable.'

'Sorry, I'm a realist!'

'A misogynist you mean!'

Russell leant back on the two-seater settee and gazed around him. 'Quite a nice room, really. Of course it will look better once it's fully furnished.'

32

'Stop it, Russell. You know perfectly well it *is* fully furnished.'

'Young Allan likes the spartan look does he?'

'I'm not that young and I don't consider it spartan.'

'Oh well, each to his own taste. When do you return to the slaughter house?' Allan's welcome for his brother-in-law was rapidly evaporating. He glared at the other man, knowing full well that Russell was aware how much he disliked that aspect of his work as a government health inspector.

'Russell! If you're going to be unpleasant then I'd rather you left,' reprimanded Julie crossly.

His face was immediately contrite. 'Sorry, Julie. It's the champagne. It always makes me gloomy, I don't know why. Then, when I'm down, I start remembering Alice.'

Julie glanced at her brother's glass. He had already re-filled it once, and now it was empty again. This he speedily rectified and she gave a small sigh.

'Who's Alice?' asked Allan. No one answered him.

'Are Mum and Dad recovered from the wedding?' Julie asked brightly.

'She always wanted champagne didn't she? I remember her telling me that she'd never marry a poor man because he wouldn't be able to afford champagne. Another affectation, but she could certainly knock it back.'

'She wasn't the only one,' said Julie drily.

'Pity you didn't know Alice, Allan. She was probably your type.'

'Why's that?'

'Because she was everyone's type, that's why!' and Russell laughed harshly.

'Russell!' Allan had never heard Julie sound so annoyed.

Her brother looked vacantly at her. 'Nothing left in

33

the bottle! Never mind, I've got another one in the car.'

'I think we've all had enough,' said Julie, casting a warning glance at Allan.

'I certainly have,' he responded quickly.

'Well I haven't.' Russell left the room and they heard the front door being opened. Julie looked beseechingly at Allan.

'Try and get the subject changed, darling. It's so bad for him to keep harking back to the past. He'll end up in hospital again.'

'I don't understand a word he's saying. Was Alice his one true love or something? Did she jilt him?'

'It's more complicated than that. Sometimes it's difficult to tell love from hate, don't you agree?'

'I've never really considered it.'

'Well, it's true.'

'What's true?' demanded Russell, returning with the second bottle. Allan hesitated. 'Come on, what's the secret? Were you talking about me?' He glared at the couple.

'Of course not. Julie was saying that love and hate are closely related. Mind you, I don't go along with that.'

Russell snorted. 'I wouldn't expect you to. A man who makes his living from watching the slaughter of animals is scarcely likely to be deeply sensitive or aware of the finer nuances of emotion.'

'For the last time I do not make my living out of watching animals being slaughtered! I only go to the abattoir twice a month. In between these visits – from which, incidently, I do not draw any vicarious pleasure – I go to hotels, restaurants, pubs etcetera and safeguard the health of the general public. Perhaps you'd rather do away with health inspectors and experience an attack of salmonella poisoning for yourself? I'm sure it could be arranged. A dirty kitchen, a half-thawed turkey . . .'

'Such an impassioned speech, and all defending what

34

is, basically, a very plebian occupation!'

'Right, that does it! If you can't be civil then perhaps you'd be kind enough to leave.'

'Was I rude? Frightfully sorry! Must be the champagne clouding my judgement.'

At that moment the door from the hall swung gently open; Allan stared fixedly as the girl crossed the room with small, quick steps and perched on the arm of Russell's chair.

This time her hair was piled on top of her head, and she was wearing a long cotton skirt with the printed cheesecloth blouse unbuttoned just sufficiently to show the beginning of the swell of her breasts. As her eyes met Allan's she curved her mouth into a half-smile.

'There's no need to stare!' Russell sounded drunkenly belligerent.

'Sorry, my mind was miles away.'

'You've got one have you?

'Russell!' Julie jumped up in horror. 'Look, Allan's quite right. Why should we listen to your drunken rudeness in our own home. Please leave.'

'Is that a demand, darling sister?'

'If it isn't I'm making it one.' Allan couldn't wait to be rid of their visitor, particularly as the girl was watching and listening to them all with malicious pleasure.

'You'd have liked Alice,' muttered Russell. 'She was a supercilious little madam at times, but you wouldn't even have realised. You're so full of conceit that you'd probably have been flattered by her attention, certain that you deserved it as a reward for your own undeniable good looks and easily deniable charm.'

'I scarcely expect my brother-in-law to find me charming!' joked Allan, trying to lower the tension in the room.

'That's fortunate. It's a pity Julie isn't so discerning.'

'I'll drive you home,' said Allan quietly.

'If you come within twenty paces of my car I'll flatten you. Goodbye, Julie. It's a pity you've been deceived, but I suppose, things being what they were, any port in a storm, as they say.'

'Go home,' she whispered. 'Go home and sleep it off, Russell.'

With one final glare at her husband he went.

Allan gave a sigh of relief. 'Somehow I don't think he likes me!' he laughed, attempting to take some of the strain out of Julie's face.

'In those moods he doesn't like anyone; least of all himself. He's never been the same since his breakdown.'

'Was it very bad?'

'Yes. He withdrew completely from the world. He didn't know any of us and would sit on a chair with his arms wrapped round his body rocking to and fro for hours at a time. It was dreadful to see him. Sometimes I wondered if he'd ever recover.'

'What caused it?' As he asked the girl moved her position, crossing her legs and revealing shapely calves and a tantalising glimpse of the smooth, tanned flesh of her inner thighs. He looked resolutely at Julie. Immediately the girl drifted over and sat beside his wife.

'I'll tell you another time.'

'Why? I *am* family now. I'd like to understand.'

'I don't want you to regret being family; that's why I'd rather wait!'

'But surely . . .?'

'Can we drop it?' She sounded tired. He felt immediately contrite.

'Sorry, darling. Whatever you like.' He started to go over, wanting to kiss her trembling, vulnerable mouth, but at once the golden girl's face contorted into such fury that he checked halfway to the chair. 'I'll clear up the dirty glasses,' he said weakly and saw her smile before she shimmered briefly and then was gone.

36

That night Allan and Julie lay in their bed kissing and caressing. They both knew that complete lovemaking was out of the question, but Julie was always only too happy to bring Allan to a climax and as their passion mounted and she moved her lips down over his chest and stomach he caught his breath in pleasure. This was how it was meant to be: something private and special between two people who were in love, not a frantically hurried coupling based purely on lust and technical skill. He pushed his fingers into Julie's hair as the first tingle began deep inside him and then, without any warning, he heard a harsh tinkle of laughter like ice cubes in the bottom of a glass.

It had the same effect on him as the ice would have done. His erection vanished completely, leaving him limp and foolish. Julie stared in surprise at his body's sudden change. There was an awkward silence.

'Sorry about that. Apparently champagne isn't the aphrodisiac they claim!'

'Obviously not,' she said quietly; but long after Allan was asleep she lay staring at the ceiling, a puzzled frown on her face.

Allan's realisation of his continuous – if non-tangible – lack of privacy remained constantly with him. Night after night he would lie rigid in the double bed, staring into the darkness, aware that the girl was near. He could almost *feel* her eyes upon him, waiting for the perfect moment to reveal herself.

The perfect moment would only be when Allan was sexually involved with Julie, that much was plain, and he defended himself in the only way he could. He left his wife alone.

The weeks passed and Julie's bewilderment increased. By the end of February she was fully fit and back at work, yet still Allan kept aloof. Even in the evenings and at weekends he was strangely reluctant to hold her hand or put his arms about her.

Now and again she tried to instigate their lovemaking herself, but each time she was rebuffed. She didn't feel that she could discuss the problem with anyone as in her opinion that would be disloyal. Eventually, one night in the middle of March when Allan lay stiffly at her side, she forced herself to reach out for him. Yet again he gently moved her hands away before turning his back on her.

She sat up, determined to bring the matter out into the open. 'Allan!' Her voice was tremulous, the tears not far away, and Allan hated the unknown girl for what she was doing to his marriage.

'Yes?' He tried to sound tired but Julie refused to capitulate.

'What's wrong?' she asked.

'Nothing.'

'We haven't made love since our wedding day! There must be something wrong.'

'I'm tired, that's all.'

'Why?'

'I don't know. I'm busy at work; I was worried when you lost the baby; that heavy cold pulled me down: it's probably a mixture of things.'

'Darling, we're young and newly married. You sound like a jaded husband of thirty years standing! Is it me? Is it something I . . .?'

Ignoring the hidden watcher he turned and wrapped his arms round Julie. 'Of course it isn't you! I'm sorry; I honestly don't know what's wrong. Somehow I can't . . . To be frank, I seem to be physically incapable. I want to make love to you, you're very desirable, but something physical must have gone wrong. Perhaps I ought to see a doctor.'

'If we kissed and cuddled more it might help. You know, one thing leading naturally to another. I'm beginning to feel that even touching me is distasteful to you.'

She was starting to cry and Allan wished that he could tell her the truth, but the truth was too incredible. She would either disbelieve him or laugh, and neither reaction would alter the situation.

'That's ridiculous, Julie!'

'Is it? When did you last put your arms round me? Or kiss me goodbye in the morning?'

'I'm holding you now.'

'Only to comfort me like a parent with a child. I want you to make love to me, not treat me as though I were a pet dog!'

While Allan racked his brains for words of reassurance the odour of perfume, sharp and tangy, filled his nostrils. She was very near. Without thinking he snatched his arms away from Julie's body. With a cry she buried her face in her pillow and started to sob.

Out of the corner of his eye he saw a shimmer of light. Turning his head he found her standing by the window with moonlight spilling onto her silken hair.

'Be nice to her,' she whispered as she drifted towards the bed.

'I can't,' he muttered. 'You know why. Please, leave us alone.' Julie was sobbing so loudly that his whisper went undetected.

'Certainly not,' replied the girl crisply. 'I've come to watch. Threesomes can be very exciting!'

'Not to me. Lovemaking should be private. There's a name for people like you, it's voyeur.'

'Is it? How quaint! Don't be so stuffy. Make love to her now, while I watch.'

'I wouldn't dream of it. Besides, thanks to you we're in the middle of a quarrel.'

'You could turn it into an apology. Go on, slip her nightdress off. She's fallen asleep; she won't know.'

Allan checked and found that it was true. Exhausted by emotion Julie was sleeping.

'No,' he reiterated.

'If you don't I'll never see you again.'

'Nothing would suit me better.'

She smiled and stretched sensuously. 'Are you sure? Think of all the things we've done together. How you love to touch me, bury your face in my hair, enter me. Do you really want to lose me?'

'Of course, I've already got . . .' He stopped. Even as she watched he realised the ghastly truth. She was like a drug. The very thought of never holding or seeing her again filled him with anguish and yet he didn't know why: couldn't understand what it was that chained him to her so tightly.

She smiled at the expression on his face. 'Go on them,' she urged. Slowly, his hands clumsy, he started to ease his wife's nightdress off her sleeping body. She stirred once and murmured but remained asleep.

'Put your hands on her breasts,' the girl's voice was full of excitement. Like a zombie he obeyed, his hands seeming to move of their own accord.

'That's right!' She herself was breathing quickly. 'Now, do exactly what I say.'

He didn't know how long he spent making love to his wife's body. It seemed like hours but could have been minutes. The girl instructed, he obeyed and Julie's body responded automatically to his touch while she continued to sleep. It was only at the final moment, as he penetrated her warm, moist entrance, that her eyes snapped open and she gave a muffled exclamation before her body began to tremble and then shudder, thrusting upwards towards him as they climaxed together.

In the distance he heard another, secret, cry of pleasure.

Once it was over they lay quietly together, their naked

bodies still damp with perspiration. 'You are strange!' laughed Julie, but her voice was full of love. 'Did you enjoy doing it like that? Without my knowledge?'

'Yes, it was – I don't know, incredibly erotic I suppose.'

'I'm sorry I missed so much of it! Wasn't it a bit foolish, though? I mean, we don't want children yet do we and I wasn't prepared. Did you use something?'

'What?' He was anxiously searching for the girl's presence, but she had vanished.

'Did you use a contraceptive?'

'Hell! No, I forgot.'

'Never mind, it's a pretty safe time. Goodnight, darling.'

The next day was a Saturday. It was unusually warm for March, and on the spur of the moment Julie suggested driving to the coast, taking a picnic lunch with them. Allan agreed, and for the first time since their wedding they enjoyed an entire, relaxed day in each other's company.

They drove to Beachy Head and after lunch walked hand-in-hand to the top of the cliff path. The sun was bright, but a cool breeze ruffled Julie's curls and Allan took a photograph of her looking beautifully windswept, hands tucked into the pockets of her sheepskin coat.

They giggled over the antics of the gulls, and admired one or two elderly couples who walked past them on the path.

'I hope we'll still be that happy when we're old,' said Julie, her voice strangely wistful.

'Of course we will. Why not? Are you planning to leave me?'

For a moment her mood threatened to change, the light in her eyes flickered and faded.

'Tell me it isn't true!' he cried dramatically, rolling his eyes and lurching toward the cliff edge in mock despair.

Julie bit her lip, but he caught his foot in a pot hole and tumbled to the ground. At once she was giggling again, extending a helping hand to assist him up.

'Idiot! Of course it isn't true. I'll love you for ever and ever.'

'And I love you,' he whispered, pulling her into the safety of his arms. At that moment they were truly happy; happy and confident.

Nine months later their daughter Melissa was born, and both their lives were changed for ever.

Chapter 3

'Isn't she beautiful,' said Allan, his face suffused with love and pride.

'You're biased!' laughed Julie. 'If you'd spent twenty-three hours producing her you might not feel quite so elated.'

'I'm just grateful you're both all right. I'm sorry I left when things got rough but I was in danger of disgracing myself by flaking out!'

'That all right. I'm not even sure what the panic was about.'

Just then a nurse bustled in. 'Time for you to leave Mr Firmager. Your daughter's going to break a few hearts when she grows up by the look of her!'

'Probably! I'll be off, then. See you tomorrow, darling.'

'Right. Don't forget to ring your parents.'

'I shall spend the entire evening ringing people up! All the cricket crowd want to know. You're quite a favourite with them.'

'She was a very popular nurse,' put in the sister as she entered the room. 'Everyone liked your wife.'

'I'm not surprised, I quite like her myself!' After a brief kiss he left, and all the way home had to keep reminding himself that he was now a father.

As soon as he entered the house he knew that *she* was there, and his elation over the birth of Melissa vanished. Feigning unawareness he picked up the telephone and when all the calls were done went straight to the kitchen. In the doorway he stopped dead in his tracks. The kettle was plugged in, two cups were on the work top, and the coffee and sugar jars beside them.

His hand shook as he lifted the kettle, then the sound of the front doorbell made him start nervously and slop water into one of the saucers. He wondered who it could be, and how his invisible golden girl would react. It was the first time he had thought of her as his.

Russell was standing on the doorstep. 'Congratulations! A daddy no less. Now you're really a man!'

'It isn't an honour confined to macho-type males. Rabbits are good at it too!'

'Ah yes, but they have leverets, not sweet little babies.'

'Hares have leverets.'

'What do rabbits have, then?'

'Bunnies!' retorted Allan, and Russell followed him to the kitchen.

'Two cups. You must be psychic! Or are you expecting someone?'

'It was force of habit. Mind you, Sophia Loren did say she might call.'

'I'll drink hers in case the traffic holds her up!' Unpleasantly aware of distant giggles Allan was forced to sit down and make polite conversation, knowing that any moment the girl might appear and try to embarass him.

'What's she like, Allan?'

'Who?'

'Your daughter, of course! Melissa isn't it?'

Allan's face brightened. 'She's beautiful. Not a lot of hair, and her eyes are still screwed up but she's really

44

lovely. She's so tiny it's unbelievable.'

'Doesn't sound like a future Miss World, but there, you never can tell. How's Julie?'

'Fine.'

'Is that all? Fine. You mean she isn't tired?'

'Well, of course she's tired, but that's natural. She looks very well. Do you know, when I put my finger in Melissa's hand she wrapped her own fingers round it.'

'Reflex action.'

'Killjoy!'

'The parents would like you to come to Sunday lunch tomorrow. Is that O.K.?'

Allan paused, suddenly wondering what he would miss by going.

'You haven't got anything planned, have you? They really would like you to come, then later we can all go on to the hospital.'

Allan despised himself for even hesitating. 'Sure! I'm miles away at the moment. Still on cloud nine.'

'I can tell them you'll be there, then?'

'About twelve all right?'

'Excellent. Thanks for the coffee; Sophia will have to make do with the dregs. Cheers for now.'

As soon as his car drove away *she* appeared at the kitchen window. Allan wished that he knew her name or her age, but whenever questioned she vanished, and he no longer tried. She stood watching the direction that Russell had taken for a long time, and when she finally turned to Allan her expression was cold.

'I thought he was never going,' she said petulantly. Drawn yet again by her incredible, inexplicable sexual magnetism, Allan found himself moving to take her in his arms. To his surprise she stepped away.

'I'm not in the mood. I don't feel well.' Her voice was sharp. Certainly her face was pale, with no trace of her usual tan. Once again her clothes were highly inappro-

45

priate for the weather, consisting of brief white shorts and a bright red halter-top.

'I didn't know ghosts could be ill!' joked Allan.

'They can't. I'm not ill in that way. I'm not in the mood for your pathetic love-making, that's all.' Her mouth was tight with temper and her features looked sharp and pinched. For the first time her beauty was diminished.

Her taunt stung him. 'Pathetic? You've never said that before. You've always told me how exciting I was.'

'That's because I knew what you wanted to hear. Julie doesn't exactly moan with ecstasy does she?'

'She's never complained! Anyway, that's quite different. With you it's . . . I don't know . . . so incredibly . . .'

'Dull! I wonder what Russell really thought about the two cups.'

'Dull? Never mind bloody Russell, let's get one thing clear. You searched me out. Right from my wedding night you've kept pursuing me. I've asked you to go, so what's the point in continuing our relationship, for want of a better word, if I'm so inept at the only thing we ever do together?'

'You're not just dull in bed; you're stupid dull. Still, I've made my bed, now I've got to lie in it.'

'Don't be ridiculous. If you're fed up with me then go. I don't need you. To tell the truth I don't even like you. I want you to leave.' Even to his own ears he sounded unconvincing.

The girl flicked her hair away from her eyes and gave a gurgle of laughter. 'Liar! Of course you don't. Fatherhood seems to have made you quite bold.'

Now he thought that he understood. 'You're jealous!' he exclaimed in surprise. 'You're jealous of Melissa.'

'What?' Her violet eyes opened wider than usual and she stared at him with contempt. 'God! I thought I met some fools when I was alive, but none of them compared

46

with you. You're completely clueless!'

'In what way?'

'Forget it.' She yawned and stretched her arms above her head, then entwined her fingers behind her hair and pulled her shoulders back so that her breasts nearly came out of their red cotton covering. Allan tried to look away, but his mouth was dry.

Her eyes followed his. 'Do you want to make love, Allan?'

He shook his head, determined not to give in after her insults. He was also clinging desperately to his sense of loyalty to Julie. How could he betray her at a time like this? The birth of their first child was a unique moment in their lives; he doubted if he could live with his own infidelity, even with a woman who wasn't – in the accepted sense – made of flesh and blood.

'Yes you do. Come here, let me feel your pulse.' He was pulled closer, as though by an invisible cord, and she rested her fingers on the pulse spot before lightly rotating one of them round the palm of his right hand. She was so tiny that he couldn't help but look down at her voluptuous body and his stomach muscles tightened in anticipation.

'Say, please,' she demanded softly. 'Say, please, and then we will.'

Allan was infuriated. 'Go to hell, or wherever you come from. I'm not begging for you. And hurry up, I'm due at the pub in half an hour.'

Without taking her eyes from his she shrugged off her halter top, and then her hands and mouth were everywhere. Without realising what was happening he quickly found himself naked on the kitchen floor with the girl crouching over him.

His hips began to move and she shifted away slightly. 'Say, please,' she repeated. He was frantic with desire. All his good intentions vanished: there was only the girl and her promise of sexual release. 'Please,' he croaked, hating himself even as he spoke.

Immediately she slipped on top of him, taking him up to the heights that only she could manage, and when he finally came he felt as though his body was shattering into a thousand pieces.

Lightly removing herself she stood up and looked dispassionately down on him. 'Your face goes all red and blotchy when you climax. Did you know?' she asked sweetly. Baffled he stared at her.

'What do you really want?' he asked.

'Never mind. It doesn't concern you,' she retorted.

'Of course it concerns me! I'm the poor sod who's obsessed by you.' Immediately he wished the words unsaid for her eyes lit up and a triumphant smile lit her face.

'I know,' she replied pertly, 'however, that's the extent of your involvement. Be content with it; don't try prying into things you know nothing about. Oh yes, and give my love to Melissa. If only she and Julie could see you now!'

With one final peal of laughter she left, leaving him naked, shivering and close to tears on the kitchen floor.

The following day he reluctantly presented himself at the Pask's house for Sunday lunch. After everything had been cleared away Mr Pask decided to take the family spaniel for a walk. 'Anyone else interested?' he enquired.

They all glanced out of the windows. It was a cold, damp December day and Russell didn't hesitate to decline. 'Not me, thanks. I'm going to sit around. Lizzie hates exercise, don't you, darling?'

His new girlfriend laughed. 'That's right, blame me for your laziness. I go to keep-fit and play squash, remember?'

'All right then, *I* don't want to go. Is that better?'

48

'It's more honest,' retorted his father. 'Allan?'

'If you don't mind I'll stay put, too.' Looking thoroughly disgusted with the younger generation Mr Pask and the dog set off alone.

Russell immediately closed his eyes and appeared to fall asleep. Mrs Pask picked up her tapestry work and a basket of coloured threads. 'Why don't you show Allan some of the old photograph albums, Jill? They're quite amusing on a wet day.'

'Only on a wet one? asked Russell. His mother ignored him. Jill hesitated. 'I'm sure Allan doesn't want to look at our albums, Mum. He won't know half the people.'

'I'd like to see them,' Allan assured her. 'I think it's fascinating watching people change over the years.'

'I think we've thrown them out,' Russell put in, his voice bored.

Mrs Pask glanced at him in surprise. 'Don't be silly; I'd never do that. They're in the cupboard in your bedroom, Jill.'

In a couple of minutes her daughter was back. 'Shall I guide you through them?' she offered, putting three heavy albums on Allan's lap.

'I'll look too,' said Lizzie. 'It might be amusing!' She settled herself at Allan's feet and he opened the first one.

There were a lot of photos of Russell and Julie as young children. Julie smiled out at him from every page, her dimple even more pronounced than now, and not once did he see the guarded, remote expression on her face that could make her intriguingly but disturbingly complex. As a child she was plainly permanently happy and open. Russell had been a stocky youngster; it was only in his late teens that he began to change into the lean young man currently feigning sleep on the sofa.

There were holiday photographs, birthday photographs and several of the various family pets. One thing

49

came over clearly. Despite the five year age gap Russell and Julie had been very close. At an age when many boys wouldn't have wanted a younger sister near them Julie was always present. She had even joined in games of cricket and football, and her face was frequently screwed up in an expression of earnest concentration that Allan found highly endearing.

There weren't many pictures of Jill, and Allan queried this omission.

'Don't worry,' responded Russell lazily before his mother could speak. 'Jill's got an album all to herself, hasn't she Mama?'

Mrs Pask smiled. 'We started a proper baby album for Jill, and her pictures still go into that. She's so much younger we treat her more like an only one, I'm afraid.'

'You'll ruin her,' said Russell. 'I keep telling you.'

'I suppose you're wishing you'd had an album all to yourself as well,' joked his mother. 'Even if we'd started one it would have been abandoned very early on. Once Julie could toddle she went everywhere with you.' Russell grunted and kept his eyes closed.

Allan was slowly tiring of the pictures. There were lots of group snaps now. Russell and Julie with friends and relations. Family outings with new faces appearing all the time. He turned the pages more quickly, and then suddenly stopped.

He blinked and looked again, but his eyes had not deceived him. Sitting on a large rock with the sea behind her, blonde curls framing her perfect, heart-shaped face was the girl. His girl. He peered closely at the snap, trying to see the colour of her eyes, but it was impossible to be sure.

Mrs Pask glanced down to see what had caught his eye. 'That's Penzance; Russell and Julie went there for a holiday with some relations. If you turn the page you'll see some more from that year. It was a very hot summer I remember.'

Allan found that his hands were trembling as he turned the page. Scanning quickly down the pictures his eyes fastened on the last photo. It was of five young people sitting in a field. Russell and Julie were there but, for once, they weren't side by side. In between them, her smile revealing the familiar small, white teeth and her eyes clearly a dark violet colour was the girl again. His heart banged uncomfortably against his ribs and he tried desperately hard to keep his voice normal as he pointed towards her.

'Who's that?' he asked quietly. Mrs Pask looked down, and for the first time her hands were still as she ceased work on the tapestry. 'Why that's Alice,' she said calmly. 'One of the children's cousins.'

'She's very lovely. Where is she now?'

Mrs Pask's fingers re-commenced their work and she turned her gaze back to the emerging pattern she was creating so skilfully. 'Yes, she was lovely,' she said at last. 'Probably the loveliest young girl I've ever seen. It was her eyes of course; they caught everyone's attention.'

'Was?' His spine was rigid with tension.

'Yes. She died a few years ago. It was very sad. Unfortunately these things do happen, and life has to go on doesn't it?' She flashed him a tight, bright smile and he could feel the almost electrical atmosphere in the room.

'Come along,' interrupted Russell. 'Isn't it nearly time to visit Julie?' With exclamations and murmurings the group broke up, but Allan was quite sure that he didn't imagine the strange, questioning look Russell gave him when he walked past.

Later he could never recall any details of the visit. All he could think about as he sat by his wife and daughter

51

was that now he finally knew the girl's name and her blood-tie to the Pasks. Alice, he thought. Next time she appeared he would call her by name, and he longed to see the surprise on her face.

That evening he invited Russell to join him at their local pub. After a couple of drinks he steered the conversation round to the family albums, pretending to see resemblances between Melissa and the young Julie.

'What happened to your cousin?' he asked at last, trying to sound only casually interested.

'The albums are full of cousins. Was there a special one that caught your eye?'

'I wouldn't say that. I'm just intrigued I suppose; after all it is unusual.'

'What is?'

'Well . . . a girl dying so young.'

Russell looked down into his glass. 'You mean Alice,' he said after a pause. 'She was special even before she died! Very lovely, beautiful really; strange how such beauty could house a personality as warped and destructive as Alice's.'

The venom in his voice shocked Allan. 'How did she die?' he asked.

Russell shrugged. 'We don't know the details, but it was a swimming accident. It happened about five years ago.'

'Was it in Cornwall, during your holiday?'

'As a matter of fact, yes.'

'Was she alone?'

'Yes. 'Russell certainly wasn't giving anything away thought Allan.

'It must have been a dreadful shock for you all.' He hoped he sounded suitably compassionate.

'I suppose so; it seems a long time ago. To be honest life was much more peaceful after Alice died. She drew all the boys to her that last year, including Julie's idol.

'Oh, it wasn't a serious love affair, not on his part, but fifteen is a vulnerable age for puppy-love. She doesn't talk about it herself; won't speak ill of the dead, all that nonsense, so I'd rather you didn't let on that you know.'

'Naturally. You've all tried to forget her then have you? No regrets for a young life lost; you just buried her memory along with the body. It seems rather callous.'

'Really? Well, it's none of your business is it?' He glared at his brother-in-law, his eyes cold. Hastily Allan became conciliatory.

'No, of course not. I'm sorry. It does seem odd, though. A girl so vibrant, so glowing with . . .'

'How the hell can you say that?' Russell's expression was suddenly sharp, his normal air of casual boredom had vanished. 'Two rotten photos in an album and suddenly you're an expert on Alice.'

'Not at all, I . . .'

'I'll tell you this much. She was a first-class, grade A, self-centred scheming little bitch and thoroughly deserved to die.'

His expression was growing wild, his voice rising. One or two customers glanced curiously at the young men. Allan was intrigued by the reaction, and certain he knew the reason for it.

'You loved her didn't you! You loved her and she let you down.'

Immediately Russell quietened, although his hand shook as he lifted his glass. 'You cretin! I hated her. Do you understand what I'm saying? I hated Alice Reynolds, and so did a lot of other people. Now, can we drop the subject?'

'Of course, but I'm not convinced you're telling me the truth.'

'You wouldn't recognise the truth if you fell over it!' sneered Russell, draining his glass. 'But here's one additional piece of information for you. As I've told you before you're lucky she's dead because you're exactly the sort of gullible fool she used to twist round her little finger!'

Allan wasn't given any opportunity to answer because his brother-in-law promptly barged his way out of the pub leaving him alone to face the staring customers. Quickly he too left.

Chapter 4

Later on – when he understood – Allan realised why Melissa's birth affected Julie so much, but at the time her lack of enthusiasm over the baby plus uncharacteristic bouts of frenzied, despairing weeping were diagnosed as classic post-natal depression, and tablets were duly prescribed and taken.

No one could fault Julie on her physical care of the child, but never once did she hug her impulsively or murmur the endearments that came so naturally to Allan's lips. At times he would try to press the baby on her, and she would passively accept, only to look down at the small features with an expression of mingled puzzlement and fear. All her normal, spontaneous affection seemed to have dried up; even kissing Melissa goodnight she appeared tense, and the gesture false.

Since Alice's identity had been revealed she had failed to materialise, and Allan was extremely grateful. Full of love for Melissa and concern over Julie he had neither time nor inclination for his beautiful, haunting, sensual spectre from the past.

One evening, when Melissa was four months old, he arrived home early. Taking off his coat in the hall he heard odd scraps of conversation and idly wondered who Julie's visitor was. Hopefully some company would have lifted her spirits, which were still very low.

At the living-room door he hesitated, not wanting to intrude without warning. 'You might think you're clever,' Julie was saying wearily, 'but you're not. The trouble is you haven't changed. You still want it all ways don't you?' Allan waited, but there was no reply.

'Why do you have to be so devious?' his wife continued, sounding close to tears. 'Does it amuse you? Is the straight-forward approach too boring? I'm so tired of trying to . . .'

Quickly he opened the door. If Julie was depressed then she needed rescuing. He looked round the room in disbelief. Melissa was lying on her changing mat, legs and arms waving in the air, and Julie was bending over her, struggling with the safety pin. There was no one else present. She turned a flushed face to her husband.

'I didn't hear you come in. Could you give me a hand with this? She won't lie still and I'm afraid of sticking it in her.' Allan remained motionless, blinking in surprise.

'Allan! Hurry up or she'll wet this one before it's on her.'

'Sorry! It's only that when I got in I could have sworn I heard you talking to someone.'

She caught hold of Melissa's ankles and lifted her bottom off the mat, sliding the clean nappy beneath the round, pink buttocks. 'You did: it was Melissa. There isn't anyone else around.'

'It didn't *sound* like Melissa.'

'Quickly, slide the safety piece down. There! Thank heavens that's over. What didn't sound like Melissa?'

'The voice.'

'You heard someone's voice?'

'Yes. Well, actually no, only yours, but I naturally imagined a second party.'

'Melissa isn't very vocal. That's the trouble with babies, they don't participate, which makes for a some-

56

what tedious conversation! You're early aren't you?'

Allan knew that Julie was lying to him, but he couldn't understand in what way. 'What did you mean when you said she was devious?' he challenged.

'What is this? Firmager of the Yard?' she laughed. 'I didn't mean it literally! I was half-talking to myself; it's this annoying knack she has of making a mess of a clean nappy straight away. I'm sure she's deliberately controlling her bowels in order to maximise the washing!'

'But you were talking as though . . . Well, it wasn't baby-talk.'

'I don't believe in baby-talk,' she said, avoiding his eyes. 'There's no one else here. Search the kitchen if you don't believe me! Besides, who would be here at this time in the evening?'

He wandered into the kitchen and out again. Everything was as it should be. For one brief moment he had thought of Alice, but there was no sensation of invisible eyes, no suggestion of perfume in the air.

Julie lifted Melissa into her baby chair. 'Satisfied? Who did you think it was? Paul Newman? I should be so lucky!' Allan felt confused, fleetingly it seemed that not only was Julie lying, she was also secretly laughing at him as well.

Swallowing hard he decided to take a calculated risk. 'I thought it might be Alice,' he said, and then watched her features closely, interested as to what her reaction would be.

She looked at him in incredulous amazement. 'Alice? My cousin, Alice? The one who's dead?' He kept silent. 'You're serious aren't you? You really think I was entertaining a ghost!' Throwing back her head she gave a peal of laughter, her first since Melissa's arrival.

'I suppose I should be pleased to see you amused again,' he remarked, 'although I wouldn't have thought the idea very comical.'

57

Julie wiped her streaming eyes. 'I suppose not. Worrying, but not amusing. I didn't realise you believed in ghosts! My God! Russell said that Alice had caught your interest but I never thought . . . How pleased she would have been if she'd lived long enough to see *you* fall victim to her charms!'

She should have been more stunned thought Allan. She should have been frightened or shocked, but not amused. Her reaction was completely wrong. Not only that, there was now the faintest trace of Alice's perfume in the room.

He stared at his wife uneasily. If she was lying she was doing it very well, more like a veteran than a novice in the art of deceit. He decided to let the subject drop.

'It's all right, I only said it to get a response. To tell the truth I thought it might be Cassie. Ben told me that she often comes round but that you're usually too busy to ask her in. I think she feels rather hurt.'

Julie pushed past him into the kitchen. 'Does she? Well, it wasn't Cassie. Only me and your precious Melissa. The steak and kidney pudding won't be ready for another half hour. Would you like a cup of tea?'

'No thanks. What do you mean, "my" precious Melissa. Isn't she precious to you?'

'Yes, but I think you're more maternal than I am!'

'That was rather uncalled for.'

She hesitated and then pulled a face. 'Yes, you're right. I'm sorry. Why don't you go and talk to her while I see to the vegetables?'

At four months Melissa had fulfilled all her earlier promise of beauty. Her hair was turning a light gold colour and her eyes were still dark blue, with long thick lashes. She beamed at her father and waved her arms up and down.

He bent down and kissed her, loving the smell of milk, talcum powder and baby lotion. She gurgled and kicked

58

her legs so that her heels banged against the wooden supports. At once her feet were still and tears filled the large eyes.

Allan scooped her out of her chair and perched her on his lap. She rested her head against him as he dried her eyes.

'Why's she sitting there?' queried Julie, bringing in Melissa's tea.

'She hurt her feet.'

'I didn't hear her cry.'

'She didn't. She just shed a few silent tears. Brave, like her father!'

Julie smiled faintly. 'Very impressive! Put her back now, she needs feeding.'

'I'll feed her on my lap.'

'She'll mess up your suit. She's into blowing raspberries at the moment.'

'I don't mind.'

'Allan, you really are the limit! Talk about a doting father. Still, if you want your suit spoilt that's your business. Here you are; bowl, food and spoon, and don't blame me when they all end up on your lap.'

She left them and Allan cuddled Melissa tightly. 'There, my precious; Mummy's in a nasty mood today. Daddy will look after you. Open your mouth for Daddy. There's a good girl!'

Melissa looked the picture of contentment as her father coaxed her to eat each tiny spoonful, praising her extravagantly every time she swallowed. He scraped round the bowl and gave her the final helping. Still smiling she opened her mouth, closed her lips over the spoon and began to move it around with her tongue.

Allan bent closer. 'There, Mummy was wrong wasn't she? Melissa's a good girl. A very good, clean baby.' As his face drew level with hers Melissa opened her mouth and spat out the entire spoonful, watching as it splattered over his eyes, nose and mouth. Then, chuckling with glee, she picked up the plate and solemnly placed it upside down on Allan's head before picking up the spoon and jabbing it in his eye.

He gave a shout of pain and tried to remove the bowl from his hair, the food from his nostrils and at the same time ease the ache in his watering right eye. Melissa watched him silently, her eyes gleaming with pleasure as she clapped her hands.

'What on earth's going on in here?' asked Julie, pausing at the sight of her husband stumbling round in circles with apple purée dripping from his hair and face and clutching a handkerchief to his right eye. Briefly her glance locked with Melissa's, and for one fleeting moment a smile touched the child's mouth before Julie broke the contact and went over to Allan.

'What happened?'

'My eye! I think she's blinded me in my right eye!'

'What a dramatic evening you're creating. First, I'm holding a conversation with my dead cousin; now your daughter's blinded you with a plastic baby spoon loaded with apple purée! I warned you she was a messy eater. Go and get cleaned up, dinner's almost ready.'

She sounded more like a nurse than a wife Allan realised, and wished that he could discover a way of changing her back to the lovable, humorous, pre-Melissa Julie.

'She behaved perfectly until the end, then she went berserk!' he complained in annoyance.

'You were lucky, some days she's like that from the first mouthful. Now get changed, and do stop groaning!'

'Are all nurses as unsympathetic as you?' he demanded, but she didn't respond with a laugh, as she would certainly have done in their courting days.

'They've no time for people who make a fuss,' she said crisply. 'You *will* live I promise! As for you, Melissa, you're going into the playpen.' Allan left the room, still nursing his aching eye.

'That was naughty!' chided Julie. Melissa stared at her. 'Very naughty,' she reiterated. Her daughter merely gurgled in reply.

Swiftly Julie picked her up and placed her in the round, mesh playpen. Immediately Melissa sat down and began to throw wooden blocks systematically round the room. With one last glance Julie returned to the kitchen leaving her daughter alone. Without an audience the block throwing ceased and Melissa conserved her energy.

Over their meal Allan's eye began to swell, looking puffy beneath the lower lashes. 'I hope she's better behaved next week,' he commented. 'I don't suppose the vicar will relish a black eye.'

'The vicar won't be foolish enough to give her a chance to blacken his eye. Do you want some apple crumble?'

'I suppose so. There's nothing worth watching on T.V. tonight is there? Perhaps we might get to bed early,' he added hopefully.

'For sleeping purposes?'

'Not necessarily.'

Julie flushed. 'I'm sorry, Allan, but I really don't feel up to it yet. I'm still very sore.' She didn't sound sorry, and Allan felt his temper rising. She was young and highly desirable; he was tired of her excuses.

'Then go to the doctor. Melissa's four months old; how much longer have I got to wait?'

'I remember a time when that wouldn't have bothered you.'

'Well, it does now. Please, darling, go and see the doctor.' He reached over the table and covered her hand with his. His fingers trembled and she attempted a shy smile.

61

'All right, I'll go tomorrow if he can fit me in. Incidentally, we've got new neighbours.'

'What are they like?'

'About our age. She's quite tall with one of those frizzy perms, and he's even taller, dark-haired and handsome in a macho kind of way.'

'Sounds as though you've studied them pretty closely!'

'I have; in between my communications with the dead that is!'

Allan pushed his dessert away untouched. 'Julie, what's wrong? You've changed so much lately. You ought to hear yourself. I'm forever having my head bitten off. Please, tell me what's wrong.'

She bit her bottom lip. 'Somehow I can't . . . I don't know how to explain this . . .'

'At least try.'

'I feel smothered, as though you and Melissa are stifling me. It's different for you, you go out to work.'

'Husbands do,' he said gently.

'I *know* that. I realise it's not rational, but you wanted me to explain.'

'I expect most new mothers feel the same,' he soothed. 'Why don't you get out more? Cassie really likes you.'

'I know, but . . .'

'Julie, you have to make an effort. You're my wife; I love you, and I can't live like a monk.'

Julie flushed. 'I really am sorry about the sex, Allan, but you ought to remember that I never wanted a child so soon. It was your erotic midnight rape that forced me into motherhood this quickly, and quite honestly I wasn't ready.'

All at once he lost patience. 'That's right, blame me!' he shouted, and stormed out of the kitchen.

In the living-room Melissa was sitting quietly in her playpen, and as she turned her face to watch his progress he saw with incredulous amazement that her eyes were no longer dark blue. They were a deep violet.

A cold shiver ran down his spine and his breath caught in his throat. It would be almost incestuous if she looked like Alice he thought in horror, hoping desperately that it was only a trick of the light. Long after he'd gone the child stared thoughtfully into the distance through her dark, violet eyes.

Chapter 5

'I christen this child Melissa, Elaine . . ..' The vicar
droned on, but Allan wasn't listening; he was watching
his beautiful daughter. Clad in a white silk dress she
smiled happily at the relatives standing round the font.
Allan was enchanted by her dainty, small-boned beauty,
and marvelled that he could have fathered such a child.

After the service they all went back to Julie's parents –
since the larger house was more suitable for entertaining
– where a finger buffet had been laid on. Allan's parents
were there, but less enraptured by their only grandchild
than he had expected. Also present were Ben and Cassie;
apart from them everyone else seemed to be related to
Julie. For the first time Allan realised how isolated his life
as an only child had been, and how fortunate he was to
have married into a larger, closely-knit family.

Melissa was handed round from one pair of doting
hands to another, and all the time she continued to smile
and gurgle, as though she were a miniature queen at her
coronation.

'She's really gorgeous!' exclaimed Cassie, who was
one of the godmothers. 'You must be very proud of her,
Allan.'

'I am. She's so good-natured as well. We've been
incredibly lucky.'

64

'*You* certainly have!' exclaimed Ben. 'James was hoping to marry Julie before you came on the scene and whisked her away from under his nose.'

'I know. I feel a bit guilty about it; but as soon as I saw Julie I just knew that I wanted to marry her. Strange really, I'd never thought about marriage as being anything but a trap before!'

'Julie used to tell James that marriage was a legal straightjacket: obviously you affected her pretty strongly too.'

'I don't know about that,' said Allan sadly. 'I often think that if she hadn't been pregnant she wouldn't have married *me* either.'

'What?' Cassie and Ben looked at him blankly, and he flushed painfully as he realised that they didn't know.

'She lost it, when she fell on the wedding day. I assumed that you knew.

'As a matter of fact, no.' Cassie's voice was cold. 'Excuse me, I'd like to hold Melissa.'

'I took it for granted that you knew,' said Allan unhappily. 'It must be the champagne; I'm not thinking properly.'

'Champagne?' queried Russell as he wandered over to the men. 'Did I hear the magic word?'

'Yes, but there isn't any here!'

With a flourish Russell produced a bottle from behind his back. 'Here you are *Daddy*. Now, come along, the photographer wants one of the happy family group. Sorry to drag him away, Ben.'

Julie was already seated on the large settee, Melissa upright on her lap, leaning her golden head against her mother's burgundy-coloured velvet dress.

Allan sat down beside his wife and put a hand on his daughter's lap. 'The other arm round your wife, perhaps?' suggested the photographer. Allan did as he was asked and distinctly sensed the tension engendered by his touch.

What was going wrong with their marriage? he wondered helplessly, smiling a plastic smile. At the start he had been cool, and now that Alice had thankfully left him Julie had begun to change. It was almost as though they were doomed he thought with an involuntary shiver.

The photographer took six shots before allowing everyone to disperse. 'A beautiful child,' he remarked to Julie. 'Incredible eyes. I don't believe I've ever seen violet eyes before. Do they run in the family?'

'Yes,' said Allan, 'and it's my wife who must take the credit. It's been handed down from a cousin of hers.'

'I'd like to meet the cousin!' joked the man, pressing his card into Allan's hand. 'I'll send you the proofs in a week's time. Goodbye beautiful!' and he tickled Melissa under the chin. She laughed, but the rest of the family were silent.

All round the room the other guests continued laughing, talking, eating and drinking, but on the settee no one apart from Allan moved. He glanced around in surprise. The family's faces were set in expressions of shock or astonishment and Mrs Pask refused to meet Allan's eyes.

'What is it? What's wrong?'

'Nothing old chap,' said Russell, but his eyes belied the relaxed tone of his voice. 'Probably a trick of the light, or the flash bulbs.'

'What is?'

'Melissa's eyes. They're not violet at all.'

'Yes, they are. I first noticed them changing last week. What does it matter? I know Alice isn't the most popular of topics in your family, but surely inheriting her eyes isn't a crime?'

Mrs Pask bent down and stared into her grand-

daughter's face. Melissa lifted her chin, her eyes wide
and alert. They were also, without question, violet.
Drawing back as though burnt her grandmother drifted
away towards the food, followed by her husband who
was muttering to himself and shaking his head.

Jill wondered what all the fuss was about. 'I think she's
lovely,' she declared stoutly. 'I'm proud to have such a
fabulous niece. Anyway, surely it's nice to have something left behind to remind people of Alice? Alice was
very beautiful, everyone says that, and now Melissa will
be beautiful too. I wish I didn't have so many freckles.'

'You don't know what you're talking about,' snapped
Russell, and Jill walked away in a huff. This left Russell,
Julie, Allan and Melissa alone. Julie refused to look at
her husband and kept her gaze firmly on the top of
Melissa's head.

'What the hell's the matter?' queried Allan. 'What's
the harm in inheriting violet eyes? What's the matter
with you all?'

'Keep your voice down,' cautioned Russell.

'Why should I? She's my daughter. I'd rather like an
explanation of this frozen silence on what is – in normal
families – considered to be an occasion for rejoicing.'

Russell draped an arm round Allan's shoulders and
led him a few feet away from Julie and Melissa. 'The fact
of the matter is, old chap, Alice was adopted.'

'Adopted?' In stunned disbelief Allan turned and studied his daughter. Her hair was now curling gently, each
curl a deep buttercup yellow, and her violet eyes glowed
just as Alice's glowed, catching the attention of everyone who saw her.

'But that's impossible! I mean, look at her! She's the
spitting image of Alice. Remember those photos, well
you can't mistake the resemblance.'

'Of course I remember. We all remember Alice.'

'There must be some mistake. It isn't possible for

something like this to happen by chance. The odds must be millions to one against it. Someone's lied, covered up a family indiscretion or something, but she can't have been unrelated. She can't have been.'

'Well, she was. Her birth certificate gave the names of her real parents. There was no cover-up, no family secret. My aunt was barren and they adopted Alice; end of story.'

'Then how do you explain Melissa?'

'That's what we're all wondering, Allan. How *does* one explain Melissa?'

The two men turned and watched Julie with her daughter. All at once the child became aware of their regard and turned her face towards them. Her eyes widened and her lips curved upwards in a slow, fascinating smile.

Russell removed his arm from Allan's shoulders, gave a muffled gasp and ran stumbling from the room. Father and daughter surveyed each other solemnly and then, for the first time since Melissa's birth, Alice slowly materialised beside the child.

She was wearing a check gingham dress, her gold curls short like Melissa's, and on her lips the same secret smile. Slowly, tenderly, Alice stretched out a hand to the baby who twisted round towards her, her face strangely expressionless.

For a brief moment Allan remained rooted to the spot, then instinct took over and he dived across the room and scooped his daughter up in his arms, snatching her out of Alice's reach before her fingers had time to touch the child.

With a scream of rage Melissa's hands shot out and she raked her nails down his face, missing his eyes by inches. Then she began to wail and Julie grabbed her back.

'Are you mad? You'll frighten her to death grabbing hold of her like that. What's the matter?'

68

He didn't answer. There was no acceptable answer to give.

'Are you drunk?' she continued incredulously.

'No,' he said slowly, 'but I wish to God I were.'

After that the party broke up rather quickly. The guests left, sensing the abrupt cessation of festivity. Eventually only the immediate family remained.

'I'm going to change Melissa's nappy,' announced Julie, and slowly took the child up the stairs. After a moment's hesitation Russell followed her. Allan wanted to go too, but Mr Pask cornered him with queries about his forthcoming promotion board and all he could do was sit with half his mind on the conversation and the other half wondering what Julie must think of him.

Upstairs Russell stood in Julie's old bedroom doorway and watched his niece as she wriggled around trying to roll off the bed. 'How long have you known?' he asked quietly.

'Known what?' Julie sounded genuinely puzzled.

'About Melissa.'

'What about Melissa?'

'Don't be so stupid!' he snapped, glancing behind him to make sure that no one had followed them. 'She's Alice's double.'

'So?'

'How did it happen?'

'Pure chance. A mixture of genes, a fluke. It's meaningless.'

Russell studied the back of her head, the defiant set of her shoulders and he wanted to shake her, to shout his suspicions aloud, but he didn't dare. There were some things that he was probably better off not knowing. Once voiced, spoken and heard, there was no going back. He didn't know if he was yet strong enough to cope with the truth.

'You're lying,' he said tonelessly. 'I hope you know what you're doing.'

'I'm changing a soaking nappy. I think we'd better go home once I've finished. Would you ask Allan to pack up the baby things in the basket?'

'I don't like Allan very much, but for the first time today I began to pity him.'

Julie turned, pulling Melissa onto her lap so that she was looking straight at her uncle. 'There's no need to pity Allan, I'm quite sure . . .' She stopped. '*Almost* sure,' she corrected herself, 'that he doesn't know anything.'

'You mean he hasn't ever mentioned Alice to you?'

'I must get Melissa home.'

'In other words he has. What did he say?'

'I rather think that our married life is a private matter, Russell, although I appreciate your concern.'

Russell put out a hand and touched his niece tenderly on the cheek. She smiled in apparent innocence, but he wasn't deceived.

'Julie, do you ever feel that you can't carry on? Do you have days when you wonder if it wouldn't be better to end it all?'

'No,' she retorted briskly. 'That's the last thing I'd ever do. I'm determined not to be beaten. I get depressed and yes, to be honest, sometimes Melissa frightens me, but I'll never give in, *never*.'

'You're much stronger than I am.'

Her face softened and she moved closer to her brother until they were almost touching. 'You must learn to be strong. You're destroying yourself. Alice is dead but you're alive. It's the one thing she can never change; an advantage she can never take away from us. Use it Russell, otherwise everything that happened was pointless.'

'Perhaps it was.'

'No,' she said vehemently. 'It was necessary. Never doubt that.'

'But the advantage you talk about so convincingly, are you sure we've still got it?' and his eyes moved over Melissa.

'Stop it, Russell!' She was talking quietly now, trying to calm him. 'If you start thinking along those lines, well . . .'

'They'll lock me up again? Is that what you mean?'

'They never locked you up. You had a breakdown, it happens to one person out of every ten. You were a voluntary patient at a mental hospital, not committed against your will and locked away at night. Stop being self-pitying.'

'You haven't said anything about Melissa I notice.'

'There is nothing to say about her,' she said slowly and precisely. 'She is an ordinary, if highly attractive, baby girl.'

'But, Julie, you must . . .' She put a hand over his mouth. 'Don't say it; don't even consider it. Concentrate on being strong. You have to be strong.'

All the time they had been speaking Melissa's eyes moved from one to the other, her gaze alert. Now, as Russell slumped against the doorpost shaking his head she gave a shriek of laughter and clapped her hands together.

'You *must* be afraid of her!' he said in a trembling voice. 'You're not stupid, think what this could mean!'

'Afraid of a baby! Really, Russ! Darling, Russell finds tiny babies frightening.' Allan's arrival hadn't been noticed by his brother-in-law who now gave a sheepish grin and shrugged. 'I think the responsibility would frighten me the most,' he confided, all his fears and doubts concealed beneath his normal, casual air of laziness.

'Never mind that! Are we going home tonight or not?'

'Just coming,' responded Julie and watched her husband walk away downstairs.

'I'm sure he knows something,' murmured Russell. 'He's far more moody these days.'

'That's probably marriage! It changes everyone, as you'll discover one day.'

'Don't be ridiculous. I'll never marry; you should know that.'

'Nonsense! Look, come round and see me next week. Any morning will be all right. I'm usually there: cooking; cleaning; mothering or staring out at my new neighbours. You will come?'

'I'll come.'

Julie nodded with satisfaction. It was tiring carrying Russell along, but as the years passed she'd learnt how his mind worked and discovered the best ways of keeping him within the accepted boundaries of normality. It was only since her marriage that he'd begun to regress, and that could be remedied by more frequent contact between them.

Twenty minutes later Julie, Allan and Melissa arrived back home. With the baby asleep in her carrycot the two adults sank down into armchairs and closed their eyes.

'Champagne doesn't really agree with me any more,' murmured Julie. 'I always get a sick headache after drinking it.'

'I should think it's your lunatic family that's given you a headache. What a commotion over Melissa's eyes! It's as plain as a pikestaff that Alice *was* a blood relation, albeit only half a one. Probably an indiscretion by your uncle. It's a harmless enough deception, and the only logical explanation.'

Julie didn't answer.

'Don't you agree?'

'As a matter of fact, no. I knew Alice. I saw her birth certificate and I listened while my uncle and aunt worried themselves sick over so-called bad blood coming out.'

'Then how does one explain Melissa?'

Julie hesitated. 'I've given it a lot of thought,' she said slowly, 'and I think that if anyone can explain Melissa it's probably you.'

He gave a nervous laugh. 'Well, she is what she is because of us. You and me. The result of our lovemaking, that's certainly true!'

'That's right. She's the result of one night of lovemaking. A night I don't even remember. Probably the most one-sided conception within a marriage that it's possible to get. Only you know the truth about that night. Perhaps there's an explanation that occurs to you if you give your memory a small jog?'

She was watching him closely and saw his expression change. The colour drained from his normally fresh-complexioned face and a look of startled horror filled his eyes.

Yes, thought Julie, fear touching her, he did know something. She had reasoned that he must, and here was confirmation. Closing her eyes she tried to hide her rising terror.

'I'm going to have a nap. We've both drunk too much and we're not thinking clearly. After all, Alice wasn't the first person in the world to have violet eyes, it's very likely a flaw in the actual pigmentation, or something revoltingly prosaic like that,' she stated firmly.

Allan watched her put her head back on the chair and remembered with hideous clarity the way in which Alice had instrumented that night of sex – it couldn't justifiably be called love.

He recalled her pleasure; the voracious excitement in her eyes, and that final, distant sigh of ecstasy.

All at once he became aware of watching eyes; experienced the sensation of an invisible presence that had thankfully been absent for so long. He turned to check that Melissa was still sleeping and saw with panic the faint outline of Alice bending over the child, dangling a small fluffy bear in front of her eyes with a peculiar expression of triumph on her face.

Abruptly, sensing Allan's attention, she let the bear fall onto the cover of the carrycot. Now she was wearing an apricot-coloured cotton two-piece with capped sleeves and a deep V-shaped neck. The skirt fell just below her knees and her feet were bare, but the toenails were covered with matching apricot varnish.

Her feet scarcely skimmed the ground as she floated over to him and sat down on his lap, her fingers immediately loosening his tie and undoing his shirt buttons.

Despite the automatic and instantaneous longing her appearance had aroused he pushed her hands away angrily, but she only gave a gurgle of laughter that was chillingly echoed from the direction of the carrycot.

'What is it?' she whispered. 'Aren't you pleased to see me? Surely you've missed me?'

'Go away,' he murmured, terrified that Julie would wake. 'Haven't you caused enough trouble?'

She pouted. 'I haven't done anything wrong. Besides, they deserve to suffer. They made me suffer.'

'You *are* Alice, aren't you?'

'Of course! It certainly took you a long time to find out. I expected you to be more inquisitive right from the start, but you weren't. Anyone would think you were used to spectres from the past turning up in your bedroom! Or perhaps you were, and I'm not the first?'

'Of course you're the first; and hopefully the last too. I didn't know where to start finding out about you, and as you refused to talk about yourself I thought the task pretty hopeless. Still, I found out in the end.'

'Naturally; it was time for you to know.'

'But it's the Pasks who are your relations; why come to me?'

'Because of what happened.'

'What did happen, Alice?'

She shrugged. 'Nothing dramatic, but they all hated me. All those stuffy cousins, aunts, uncles, grandparents and aged distant relations; none of them liked me. Now it's nice to be able to influence their lives, even if only by having an affair with a cousin's husband. I get so bored you see; think of this as a minor diversion for me,' and she smiled winningly at him.

'I don't believe you. There's more to it than that.'

'Like what?'

'I don't know, that's what's annoying me; but I'm sure you're leading up to something. I don't want Julie hurt. She's my wife and . . .'

'I know, you love her, cherish her and will stick by her in sickness and in health until death you do part and all that crap!'

'Just as long as you know.'

'I know everything that goes on in your mind, Allan. Sometimes it isn't the same as the words that come out of your mouth either!'

'Oh push off, you're nothing but a troublemaker. Incidentally, was Russell in love with you?'

'Why should you think that?' she queried, her fingers playing a tune on his chest. 'Has he said as much?'

'Get *off* me. No, he hasn't, but I'm sure I'm right.'

'You're very sweet,' she laughed, taking his right hand and placing it inside her cotton top so that it closed automatically round one firm, thrusting breast. 'But incredibly naive! Never mind, I rather like it. It's a pleasant change.'

Swiftly he removed his hand. 'You make me sound like a country yokel. If I'm so stupid – or naive as you politely term it – why choose to spend all your time with

75

me? What do you get out of it?'

For once Alice looked genuinely astonished. 'I don't! I've never said that I wanted to spend *all* my time with you.'

'Of course you have. You said that once I married Julie we'd be together for ever, or something like that.' She put her head to one side, thought for a moment and then nodded. 'Oh yes, I remember. I suppose it's because you're reliable. I know you won't go round trying to convince people that I exist, nor will you try to get me exorcised or anything ridiculous like that! It's tiring living as I do, and I don't want any opposition. It's exhausting if I'm fighting people all the time. Actually I really like you too.'

'If it's so exhausting why keep returning? Can't you leave? Are you trapped in some way?'

'Trapped? No; I can do what I like. One day, when I've finished, then I'll go and perhaps I won't come back ever again. I haven't really decided. Would that make you sad?'

'No!' screamed a voice in his head, but with her supple body pressed to his and her hands wandering all over him, while his sexually disinterested wife slept opposite, unaware of what was happening, it did make him sad.

He was stimulated by the excitement; the sense of danger; the illicit quality of their meetings. Like forbidden fruit the final frantic coupling was all the sweeter for these things. Logically he knew that he ought to be able to tell her that he longed for her to leave, but at that moment, with every sensation imaginable causing his body to tremble with anticipation he had to say, yes; and having done so despised himself.

'What do you mean "when you've finished"?' he murmured, catching his breath as her fingers wandered lower down his body.

'It doesn't matter; it's unimportant to you. You and I

76

are only concerned with pleasure.'

With a muffled groan he made a pathetic attempt to curb her hand from its relentless quest. 'You mustn't hurt Melissa,' he muttered urgently. 'If any harm ever came to Melissa I'd . . .'

Her fingers stopped through sheer shock and she stared at him in wide-eyed amazement. 'Hurt Melissa? You really are incredible! Why, I care for Melissa as if she were my own daughter!' and with a deep gurgle of laughter she finally forced a climax from him.

As she did so Melissa's waving hands caught hold of the elastic string across the carrycot, and all the tiny bells chimed out as though in celebration, but it was impossible to see what Alice made of such irony for she was rapidly de-materialising. Even before she had removed herself from her lover's body her form was fainter than he had ever seen it and her eyes were frightened, as though the speed of her departure had caught her by surprise.

Chapter 6

After that evening, months passed without Allan seeing Alice again. At first he was pleased; relieved by the absence of a girl whom he was now beginning to fear, but as week followed Alice-less week he started to long for just a glimpse of her. One opportunity to caress her silken flesh; and gradually, but insiduously, he became morose and irritable.

His promotion had duly been achieved with the result that he now worked longer hours and travelled more. He didn't mind. Julie still hadn't returned to her old, cheerful self and home was far less appealing these days. Her pills made her sleepy, but failed to lift her spirits.

At night she would often cry out in her sleep, then wake in fear and collapse weeping into his arms. As she claimed that she couldn't recall these dreams there was little that he could do except hold her, much as he would hold Melissa. This was – in any case – all that Julie wanted from him most of the time, and he waited with decreasing patience for things to right themselves. It made Alice's absence all the more frustrating.

By the time Melissa's first birthday arrived she was walking unsteadily, and had a limited but clear vocabulary, consisting mainly of 'Daddy', 'Mummy', 'drink' and 'no'. She was truly an exceptionally beautiful child.

Her curls were now an even deeper gold, and the violet eyes were made more distinctive by long, dark lashes contrasting sharply with her fair hair.

Only Julie was unimpressed by her daughter's looks. She discouraged Allan from taking too many photos of her, expressing the fear that she would grow up vain and self-centred. On the rare occasions when he did take a snap the child would always move, and every one of them showed Melissa as an indistinct blur due to her constant activity.

In an attempt to force herself out of her depression Julie had joined the local young wives group, and also took Melissa to a mother and toddler club once a week. With so many social friends it was decided that there should be a small birthday party to celebrate the occasion.

Julie's mother baked a cake in the shape of a teddy bear, covered it with pink icing and piped Melissa's name on it in white. There were crisps, tiny sandwiches and paper bowls of jelly. Melissa seemed highly delighted with it all.

Allan was reading the paper when Julie brought Melissa down into the living-room wearing her new party dress.

'There you are! Doesn't she look nice?' It was the first time Allan had heard such a note of pride in her voice and he looked up.

For a moment he couldn't believe his eyes; then he leapt to his feet with a muffled exclamation. His daughter looked like an inanimate replica of Alice as she sat primly on one of the armchairs, hands folded in her lap. She was wearing a cream cotton dress with a lace collar, patterned bodice and calf-length skirt. She stared ahead of her without any expression on her features and the resemblance was so uncanny that he wondered if he was having a nightmare.

'Don't you like it?' asked Julie, a look of curiosity on her face. 'We both fell in love with it at first sight.'

'It's far too grown-up for her. Where did you get it?'

'At a small shop in town. I think she looks sweet.'

'But you've made her look . . .'

'Yes?' Her eyes were keen, almost challenging.

'Like a doll,' he finished lamely.

Julie laughed. 'Don't be silly. There won't be anything doll-like about her once the other children arrive.'

'I'll get my camera; this is the first time she's ever sat so still.'

Julie glanced at Melissa and back to Allan. 'There isn't time. I think I heard a car outside.'

Allan looked out of the window. 'There's no one there.' He turned back, and found that his wife had scooped Melissa out of the chair and up onto her hip.

'What did you do that for?'

'She doesn't like having her picture taken, do you, Melissa?'

Melissa shook her head, staring at her father. 'Rubbish!' he retorted. 'She doesn't even know when I'm taking it. She's far too young to be camera-shy.'

There was a ring at the door. 'Well, it's too late now. Come along, Melissa, let's open the front door.'

For the next twenty minutes an almost endless stream of mothers and children arrived, and most of the babies began crying or grizzling within the first ten minutes. They quietened down over the food, and Allan noticed with pride that despite the noise and excitement Melissa remained calm, indeed almost oblivious of her surroundings.

It was only on closer inspection that one could see how her eyes travelled from one child to the next in a peculiarly assessing way.

As soon as the food was gone the children started to

play and fight while the mothers talked. The only observer was Allan, and he was intrigued to discover that even at the age of one year, Melissa paid scant attention to the other girls. It was the boys she mixed with. She would smile coquettishly, giving one a piece of broken biscuit as a present while pushing away another who was less to her liking.

By four-thirty the first of the children were dressed in their outdoor clothes, and their mothers all chatted and laughed vivaciously with Julie as they departed. Allan hadn't seen his wife so animated for months. She exchanged small jokes with everyone and exuded an air of interest and pleasure that delighted him.

However, as soon as the last visitor had gone she reverted to withdrawn disinterest, and Allan tried to remember how she had looked in the days before Melissa. He could vividly recall her smile; her soft, laughing eyes, and also the sheen of her auburn hair: hair that she now neglected, letting it grow untidily long. He resolved to speak to their doctor himself before their marriage deteriorated beyond repair.

Sighing at the sight of the biscuits trampled into the carpet and the strawberry jelly beneath the table Julie wearily set about righting the damage, unaware of her husband's scrutiny.

Allan picked up Melissa, putting her on his knee. She wriggled impatiently for a few seconds then sighed, much as her mother had sighed, and remained passively where he had put her.

'Who's a lucky girl then, Melissa? Did you like your presents?' She didn't answer, he would have been astounded if she had, and yet he could have sworn that her eyes were glinting with contempt. It was an unsettling expression to see on a small child's face.

She pointed to the floor. 'That's right; Mummy's picking up all the spilt food. It isn't every little girl who gets a party on her first birthday. It's given poor Mummy a lot of work.'

'I wish you wouldn't talk to her as though she was half-witted,' protested Julie. 'When she points to the floor it means she wants to get down. She isn't emphasising my humble role of servant.'

'She doesn't want to get down. You like Daddy's lap, don't you, darling?' Melissa looked at him and pointed to the floor again. Allan hugged her tightly. 'You're growing up too fast, Melissa. Give Daddy a love!' He bent his head to kiss her, and without a flicker of expression she spat straight into his face. With a shocked cry of dismay he pushed her off his lap.

Julie turned round and watched Melissa scampering away on all fours. 'What's the matter?'

'She spat at me.'

'It's a phase she's going through. Ignore it; I do.'

'But she deliberately spat at me!'

'I heard you the first time. You should have put her down when she asked.'

'She can't go through life spitting when people don't do as she wants.'

'I expect she'll change her method of showing disapproval as she gets older! Don't be so serious about everything. She's only a baby. Why don't you go and get me a sponge and some clean water for this carpet?'

'Does she spit at you?'

'Allan! Please, get me some water!'

With his normal image of Melissa as a dainty child with perfect manners in temporary disarray, he did as she asked. He scarcely noticed the arrival of Alice until she handed him the bucket from beneath the sink, and then he took a quick step back.

She was wearing an identical dress to Melissa's, but on her the high neck-line and lace collar looked spectacularly alluring because of the stark contrast with her normally scanty clothing.

His heart began to pound, and he stared hungrily at her. He heard Julie calling impatiently from the other room but all he could do was stand and gaze.

'It's all right,' she said huskily. 'I'm not going away again. I'll come and see you tomorrow afternoon.'

'We're at the in-laws tomorrow.'

'Say that you're ill. You do *want* to see me, don't you?'

'Of course I do! I've been getting frantic. I thought you'd left me for good.'

'Oh never for good, Allan! You'd better hurry with that water.' He took the bucket out of the sink but kept his eyes fixed on Alice. 'You're wearing the same clothes as Melissa,' he whispered.

'I know. I didn't want to stand out!' and she gave her familiar tinkle of laughter.

Back in the living-room he nearly slopped the water his hands were trembling so much, but Julie was too busy to notice. Melissa was surprisingly quiet, slumped on the floor with her head on her chest and her eyes closed. Allan wondered if she was ill, but then she suddenly lifted her head, straightened her back and busied herself with wrapping paper.

He gave a slight cough. 'My throat's a bit sore. I hope I'm not getting flu.'

'So do I; we're taking Melissa to my parents tomorrow, and they've turned it into a party for relations.'

'If I'm not well you can always take Melissa on your own.'

'Yes, I can, but I'd rather you came. They see so little of you.'

'I can't help being ill. Besides, Russell redresses the balance. He nearly lives here these days. It's about time he got himself a job.'

'Don't start on Russell, Allan. I'm far too tired.'

'I was only saying . . .'

'Shut up!' she shouted. 'Can't you see that I'm exhausted.'

He went over and put his arms round her, quite expecting a rebuff, but for once she seemed grateful for the contact and leant her head silently on his shoulder. She then allowed him to bath Melissa and put her to bed, a job that she rarely relinquished. When he came down, after tucking his daughter tightly in her bed, Julie was lying on the sofa, her eyes closed, with dark shadows beneath them.

He knelt beside her. 'I love you,' he murmured. She opened her eyes and they were full of tears.

'I don't deserve your love, Allan.'

'That's foolish. You're going through a bad patch; it will pass.'

'I'm so tired all the time.'

'Perhaps you've got flu too.'

'I wish it were that simple.'

'What do you mean?'

'I'm pregnant again.'

He stared at her. 'But . . . we've hardly . . .'

'I know. I couldn't believe it either.'

'Perhaps you're wrong. It could be your pills, or . . .'

'I'm afraid the doctor confirmed it last Monday.'

'Why on earth didn't you tell me straight away?'

'I didn't think you'd be pleased.'

'Of course I am, at least for myself and Melissa. I'm sorry for you having another child before you're well, but it will do Melissa good to have a brother or sister.'

'Will it? I'm not sure. Do you think you could spend more time at home for a while?'

'Darling, I can't promise that. You know what it's like . . .'

'It's all right,' she said, trying to check the tears sliding down her face. 'I'll manage. I must follow people's usual advice to Russell and pull myself together.'

They sat quietly together for the rest of the evening. In bed that night Allan found himself longing for a son. A son who was open and more demonstrative than Melissa. There were times – only brief moments as yet – when he felt a sense of disappointment in his detached little daughter. Some days, the only indisputable point in her favour was her beauty. He didn't mind if their next child was less attractive as long as it was loving and outgoing.

By next morning, Julie was fully recovered, and even managed some sympathy for Allan. 'Take a couple of aspirin and go to bed for the afternoon,' she instructed as she collected Melissa and set off for her parents. 'You might shake it off if you take it easy today.'

He felt guilty at deceiving her when she herself wasn't well, but his craving for Alice was too great for him to sacrifice the afternoon. 'I intend to,' he replied with complete honesty.

'I'll be back about six-thirty. If you want anything to eat I'll see to it then.'

She kissed him on the forehead and left the house, Melissa lolling over her shoulder and waving rather limply, as though exhausted herself.

As soon as they'd gone he took the stairs two at a time and ran into the bedroom. To his relief Alice was already standing at the window with her back towards him. She was completely naked, and when she turned to face him all thoughts of his family vanished; only Alice was reality.

Two hours later he was exhausted, completely sated, and had perspiration running down his face. Alice giggled.

'What's happened to all your stamina? Don't tell me it's old age!'

'I'm out of practise. I haven't seen you for eight months.'

85

'You're not entirely out of practise. After all, Julie's pregnant again!'

Propping himself up on one elbow he stared down at her exquisite features. 'How do you know that?'

'I know everything. You're pleased I take it?'

'Naturally. It will do Melissa good.'

'You make it sound like a large helping of spinach! Why will it do her good?'

'She's too self-centred. It's time she learnt to share things.'

'Melissa won't ever share things unless she wants to. I know. I was young once, and I remember my mother getting pregnant. It would have been her own child as well, not adopted like me. I hated the thought of sharing. Luckily the baby was stillborn.'

'You must have been older than Melissa! You'd scarcely remember anything from the age of one!'

'When you're dead,' said Alice coldly, 'you can remember everything.'

'Well, this baby won't be stillborn and Melissa will adapt. All children do.'

'She's your daughter,' remarked Alice, 'but don't say I didn't warn you.'

He didn't want to talk about pregnancies, nor even about Melissa. They only had another hour, and the sight of her small, swollen breasts and slender, tanned thighs aroused him despite his exhaustion. He laid a hand on Alice's tiny waist and lowered his mouth to her breasts.

She remained still for a few seconds and then pushed his head away. 'You're being clumsy!' she said angrily. 'I'm not edible you know. That's the trouble with men, they're so insensitive.'

'You weren't complaining earlier,' he said furiously.

'Well, I am now. I think it's time I was going.'

Allan reached out and grabbed her left wrist. 'Before

you disappear, how long will it be before you're back?' She shrugged. 'Alice, I'm obsessed by you. The days when I don't see you seem pointless. Do you realise the effect you're having on me?'

She smiled. 'Of course I do! Don't worry, I'll be back tomorrow. You're going to Birmingham aren't you. I'll come too.'

'But Alice I'll be working. What will you do all day?'

'You mean we won't have *any* time together?'

'No, I can't possibly . . .'

'I don't call that much of an obsession.' She sounded sulky.

Allan frowned. 'What do you want of me?' he asked slowly. 'I'm apparently clumsy in bed, and I don't delude myself that my obsession is reciprocated, so why *do* you keep returning? Has it got something to do with your death?'

'Naturally. If I wasn't dead I couldn't be a ghost!'

'It's more than that. I'm not stupid. You must have . . .'

'I'll see you soon,' she said abruptly and vanished. Only the dent on Julie's pillow showed that she had ever really been there.

Twenty minutes later, Julie and Melissa arrived home. Allan said that he felt better; Julie reported that the party had been a dismal failure, with her father constantly picking on Russell and her mother trying to act as peacemaker all the time.

'I wish I'd stayed with you,' she said, and kissed him on the forehead. Her affection made him feel horribly guilty. 'Melissa was no help either,' she continued. 'I couldn't even wake her for tea. Some birthday celebration!'

'I'll get up, Julie. I can eat some supper off a tray after Melissa's in bed.'

'Liss,' said Melissa from the doorway and both adults turned their heads.

'There's a clever girl!' said Julie brightly. 'Isn't she clever, Allan?'

'What did she mean?' He was acutely aware of the lingering scent from Alice.

'She was saying her name, of course! What else could it be?'

'Sorry! I wasn't thinking. Well done, Melissa.' His daughter hesitated, and then advanced into the room until she was standing by Julie's side of the bed. She tried to scramble onto it, but its height prevented her and she stamped her foot in temper.

Julie picked her up and placed her next to Allan. For a fleeting second her violet eyes watched him, their expression shuttered, and then she laid her head exactly where Alice's had been and curled up into a ball. 'Liss,' she repeated, and promptly fell asleep.

It was horrible looking down at her, seeing the innocent child's head lying where the far from innocent woman's had lain only half an hour earlier. He looked at the golden curls, the small mouth and the tiny bones and his stomach heaved. It was unbelievable and unnatural but she resembled Alice so greatly that he knew his body was starting to respond as though she were Julie's long-dead cousin instead of an exhausted one-year-old.

Hastily he got out of the bed and pulled his dressing gown tightly round him, hiding all physical signs of his arousal.

He and Julie tiptoed from the room, leaving her for a few moments while Julie prepared her bath. As they closed the door behind them her eyes, apparently closed in slumber, snapped open and she put one tiny hand on the pillow next to hers. Slowly, languidly, she smiled. Her lips parted and curved up at the corner. With a gentle sigh she wriggled deeper into the bed and there she stayed; a perfect, miniature replica of Alice.

Chapter 7

Julie sighed and put a hand to her aching back. It was a blazing hot June day and she was feeling tired, irritable, frustrated and fearful. All of these emotions were familiar to her, but normally they came singly, not all at once like a tribe of unwelcome relatives descending on an unsuspecting household.

In the middle of the lawn, Melissa was sitting playing with her dolls. She rarely glanced towards her mother, indeed Allan would have been amazed at the lack of contact between the pair, yet they were both comfortable and familiar with the situation. It was only when there were strangers present and they both had to pretend that they were a normal mother and daughter, that the difficulties arose.

The next child was due in August, but already Julie was larger than by the end of her first pregnancy, and in any case this was different. She felt apprehensive and unprepared. While she was carrying Melissa she had scarcely spared a thought for the future, feeling certain that everything would go right and she would bear a healthy child. This time it could all be very different.

She sighed again and tried to get comfortable in the high-backed garden chair Allan had bought for her at the start of the summer. At the thought of her husband a

deep wave of despair swept over her. How gullible she'd
been to think that falling in love and marrying would
change anything. As it turned out she'd made life far
worse for herself, and being unable to tell Allan the truth
she had to suffer his disappointment and incomprehen-
sion as well as her own heartbreak as their marriage –
embarked upon with such love and so many hopes –
floundered in the encroaching darkness from her past.

She did everything she could to help them both,
pushing every intrusive thought resolutely away, aware
that looking forward was a dangerous occupation which
simply increased her despair until she feared for her
sanity. But she was made of stronger mettle than
Russell, and so far had kept her terrors within reasonable bounds.

Lost in her thoughts, she jumped as a tiny hand
touched her on the knee. These swift, silent movements
of Melissa's had lost their power to surprise her, as had
the adult expressions that flitted across the child's face
whenever she was alone with her mother. Now the
familiar violet eyes looked into Julie's brown ones with a
look of mingled excitement and expectation that was
chillingly recognisable.

'What is it, Melissa?'

'Bell,' stated the little girl clearly, and she pointed
towards the house.

'There's someone at the door?' Melissa nodded.
'Someone important?' Again the nod. Reluctantly Julie
went slowly into the house. She found her next-door-
neighbour standing in the porch, and since it was quite
common for her to call round she wondered why Melissa
had seemed so excited.

'Peter's back!' Alison declared triumphantly. 'He's
decided to give it another try. I had to come and tell you.
I hope you weren't sleeping?'

'No, simply lazing in the garden. Oh, Alison, I am

pleased! When did this happen?'

'He rang me last weekend. We went out for a meal and talked properly. He's bringing his things back tonight. This time we're both going to work a lot harder at the relationship. I think he was surprised how lonely life was in a bedsit. You were right telling me to hang on and wait when I was all for rushing off to the solicitor. I can't thank you enough.'

'Thank me this time next year,' cautioned Julie, but softened the remark with a smile as she went into the kitchen to make tea. Behind her, hidden in the shadows cast by the window blind, Melissa stood listening.

The past six months had been difficult ones for Alison. Peter, her husband, was a salesman in knitwear and travelled a great deal. These enforced absences from home were made worse by the fact that he was, even to the most dispassionate eyes, devastatingly attractive while Alison was merely pretty in a fresh-faced way. She also made her adoration of Peter far too obvious.

From what she had told Julie during numerous, uninvited confidences, Peter started having affairs within months of their marriage but Alison kept her eyes closed and pretended not to know. The move to their present house had been intended as a new start for them both and Peter had promised that his philandering days were over. However, within weeks Alison knew by the telltale lipstick marks on his handkerchiefs that nothing had changed.

She would still have put up with it. She regarded marriage to Peter as a triumph, an almost impossible achievement, and whatever he did she wasn't going to show her family and friends that their doubts and warnings about the marriage had been right.

On the rare occasions that Julie met Peter she could tell that although he played the devoted husband with exemplary care he slightly despised Alison; and with a magnetism so great that even she could feel it she knew that her neighbour was doomed to an early divorce or a life of self-sacrifice.

Surprisingly, Peter suddenly took it into his head to leave Alison, saying that he was being unfair to her, that she should forget him and start life again with someone more suited to life as a suburban husband.

It astonished her further to discover that Peter was living alone and not – as she had suspected – with another woman. Accordingly, when asked, she told Alison exactly what she knew Alison wanted to hear; that she should wait and not make any hasty decision.

The small domestic drama intrigued Julie because of its very lack of originality. This was life as many people knew it, and she greatly enjoyed participating, albeit in the role of spectator. It was possible, when involved in Alison's troubles, to pretend – however briefly – that her own life was normal too. Unfortunately it increased the pain of the ever-widening rift between Allan and herself.

'He says he can't think what came over him,' Alison chattered on while Julie took the tea things into the garden, Melissa trotting along beside her. 'He really missed me. You wouldn't believe the things he said. It was quite touching to find out how much he depends on me. We're going to have a party next month. It's my birthday, which is a good excuse, and . . .'

'Here's your cup,' interrupted Julie, 'and why do you need an excuse for a party? You could call it a wife-warming!' Melissa, standing beside her mother, gave a soft laugh. Julie quickly frowned at her.

Alison looked very hurt. 'It isn't something to joke about, Julie. This is my life we're discussing and . . .'

Julie listened sympathetically. People had always confided in her, and as good listeners were rare she perfected the art in order to prevent people from invading her own privacy. Her life could never be brought out into the open and dissected, it had to remain locked inside her like a living nightmare; there would never be the relief of shared fears for her. It was the only way.

'You will come, won't you?' concluded Alison. 'Remember, if it wasn't for you I'd have started divorce proceedings already.'

'Of course we'll come, providing junior here doesn't put in an early appearance.'

At that moment Julie caught Melissa's eye and noted the malicious gleam of pleasure. She knew that compassion was an unknown emotion to the small girl, and always would be. Quickly she turned her wandering attention back to Alison.

'. . . but that's always been so good, and I suppose – in the end – that's why we both want to try again. I mean, sex *is* important, isn't it?'

'Yes, but there are other things in marriage!'

'They're all so boring! Just imagine, if it wasn't for your sex life could you and Allan put up with all the hassle of a toddler? Or the day to day tedium of housework? Don't you think that it's only through sex that you really come together?'

For once Julie was speechless. She hadn't anticipated such a personal question, and she knew that Melissa was waiting with unholy pleasure for her answer.

'I hadn't really . . .' she began, then stopped, highly relieved, as Peter strolled casually in through the back gate and wandered across the grass towards them. Melissa drew in her breath sharply, moving closer to her mother's chair.

'No key!' he explained with a wry grin. 'Hello, Julie. How's it going?' His eyes strayed to her stomach.

'Much as it usually does! It's nice to see you home again.'

'I'm surprised you noticed my absence!' The words were spoken lightly, but there was a look in his brown eyes that Julie recognised.

'Of course I noticed. I missed the squeal of tyres when you did your spectacular early morning spin out of the drive; the crashing of gears when you were in a particularly bad mood. These small touches make a difference!'

'So if I'd been a better driver you wouldn't have noticed?'

'I didn't say that!'

'Neither did you.'

Alison looked anxiously from Peter to Julie. Her husband's voice had that lightly teasing note she knew only too well, but surely Julie – seven months pregnant – couldn't be a target for his roving eye? On the other hand their neighbour was highly attractive, and Peter always went out of his way to speak to her. Standing up she linked her arm through his possessively.

'Come along, darling. We'd better leave Julie and Melissa in peace. Allan will be home soon.'

'He keeps more regular hours now, does he?' His enquiry was apparently innocent, yet Julie had the feeling that he knew the difficulties her marriage was encountering.

'No, but that isn't his fault. Irregular hours are part of the job.'

'If I were your husband nothing would keep me late at work!'

Julie smiled. 'I bet you say that to every woman under seventy!'

'Certainly not. Under sixty perhaps, but never seventy. One has to draw the line somewhere!'

'I'm glad to hear it!' she laughed.

'Darling!' Alison gave an impatient tug on his sleeve and he glanced down at her. 'All right, I'm coming. See you, Julie.'

'Bye-bye,' called Melissa, then laughed when he jumped.

'She gave me a fright. I'd forgotten how silent she can be. Goodbye, beautiful.'

Julie watched them go, admiring Peter's broad shoulders and aggressively masculine aura. She could well understand why women fell for him. Melissa too watched the couple's departure. When they were out of sight she looked up at Julie, her eyes glowing.

'Yes,' whispered Julie softly. 'I bet you loved that. A compliment from a handsome man, however practised in the art of philandering, must boost your ego no end! Well, you're unlucky, he's a trifle too old for you. Why, if I weren't pregnant I might, just might, fancy him myself!'

She was laughing, but stopped abruptly as Melissa's hand shot out and she scratched her mother's face from temple to cheek and then ran off.

Shaken, Julie mopped off the beads of blood with a tissue. In the distance Melissa turned her head, but it was impossible to see the expression on her face because of the sun shining directly into Julie's eyes.

The movement of the upstairs bedroom curtains in Alison's house suddenly caught her attention. Slowly Julie stood up and began to tidy the garden. She didn't want to sit outside staring at drawn curtains while Alison and Peter celebrated the first of what would undoubtedly be many reunions.

She didn't mind for herself. At the moment, heavy with the child and increasingly disturbed by personal fears, sex was of little interest; but she didn't want to see the expression of vicarious pleasure that would undoubtedly light up Melissa's face once she realised what was happening.

As she took hold of her daughter's hand to lead her indoors she met the expected resistance. Melissa sat firmly on her rug and refused to move.

'Come on,' said Julie coaxingly. 'It's teatime.'

'No!'

'Come along. I'm not leaving you out here.'

'Melissa play.'

'No! You are *not* staying. Come indoors at once.'

'NO!' screamed Melissa, her eyes darting furiously from Julie's scratched face to Alison's closed curtains. There was no point in smacking her, that never seemed to cause any pain.

'Very well,' she sighed, and left the child alone. She knew that it was senseless to battle against her. In the end, Melissa always got what she wanted.

With an aching head she started to prepare a mixed salad, but was suddenly surprised by the sound of a car in the driveway. She looked out, hoping that Allan had managed to be early for once, however it was Russell.

'You shouldn't be back again,' she chided him affectionately as he kissed her cheek. 'You were here all the morning.'

'Can't a chap visit his own sister when he wants to? Besides, it's hell at home. Father's on about my lack of ambition. His latest expression is: "No spine; that's the trouble with you boy, no spine"! I wish I'd a fiver for every time he's trotted that out this week.'

Julie giggled. 'Poor Father; he's always been the same. If you've come to see Melissa she's in the garden.'

'What's she doing?'

'Alison's husband's returned. They're upstairs celebrating.'

'In that case she might not want to come with me. I had intended to take her to the learning pool for the early evening session. I thought she'd probably be good at swimming, all things considered.'

Julie ignored the latter part of the sentence. 'Isn't she rather young to be good?'

'They start the second they're born these days! She'll do well.'

'She hasn't any arm-bands.'

'I'm sure she won't need arm-bands with me around to hold her.'

Julie's hand froze in mid-air, poised over the egg-slicer. She tried to keep her breathing steady as she glanced at Russell. His expression was nonchalant, he might have been suggesting tea on the lawn, but he wasn't; they both knew that very well.

'No, thank you, Russell. Allan can teach her.'

'Don't you think . . .?'

'I said, *no*.'

For a moment he tried to outstare her, but finally dropped his eyes and kicked aimlessly at the pedal bin. 'Suit yourself. You might be sorry one day.'

'I doubt it. Excuse me, please, you're standing in front of the fridge.' Russell watched as she moved briskly round the room, deftly cutting the radishes into tiny-petalled flowers.

The silence was an awkward one. 'How's number two coming along?' he asked at last.

'All right. No problems so far.'

'What do you want, boy or girl?'

'I really don't mind. A boy would be nice, but I've got a feeling it's another girl.'

'At least it isn't likely to bear much resemblance to . . .'

'Who?' Her voice was sharp with a mixture of fright and anger.

'Melissa, of course. Who else?'

'Why shouldn't she look like Melissa?'

'Well . . .'

'As far as I'm concerned she might look exactly like Melissa, and that's the way we have to play it for the rest of our lives. Melissa isn't special. She's a normal little girl who happens to be highly attractive. There's nothing else unusual about her. Do you understand me?'

'Oh yes, very well; crystal clear in fact. See no evil, speak no evil, and all that rubbish.'

'Russell!'

'Don't sound so indignant. You might be fooling yourself but you don't fool me, not for one second. I'd better get off before your husband arrives home and adds his voice to Father's concerning my life of leisure. I honestly don't know why you married him. Tell me, is he as boring in bed as out of it?'

Julie flushed, then looked beseechingly at her brother. 'Russell, please! He's my husband and I love him. I hate it when you snipe at him. If you keep on, all you'll succeed in doing is alienating *me*. I think you should go home: I'm beginning to feel a lot of sympathy for Father.'

She had never sounded so cool towards him before; stunned he tried to undo some of the damage. 'Sorry! You know me, speak first and think after. You're right, wifely loyalty should have priority.'

'It isn't blind loyalty. I love him. Is that clear now? *I love Allan.*'

'O.K. I believe you.'

'I hope so, for both our sakes. Would you call Melissa in before you leave? It's time for her tea.'

'Doubtless she's worked up quite an appetite out there.' he retorted.

'What's that supposed to mean?'

'Really, Julie! Must I spell it out for you? You're not that unintelligent, surely!' She gave him a quick nervous glance, then turned away. He wanted to shake some sense into her, but instead pushed past and slammed out of the house.

Julie covered her face with her hands, feeling hot tears sliding down her cheeks. She waited until she felt composed again before calling Melissa. This time she came in without protest.

The curtains next door were no longer drawn and doors could be heard opening and closing, the celebration was plainly over. As Melissa came indoors she smiled sweetly, and if her colour was a little high then Julie reasoned that it was most likely because she had been sitting in the hot sun.

As it turned out Julie only just managed Alison's party. All that day she had experienced twinges of pain in her back, but with four weeks to go before the baby was due she decided that she'd pulled a muscle lifting Melissa and ignored them.

It was quite a good party, and Allan plainly enjoyed it. He liked Peter, blaming Alison for her husband's faults, saying that she was the epitomy of a clinging vine wife while Peter was a man's man and needed some freedom. Julie hadn't agreed but didn't say so. They had enough problems of their own without quarrelling about their neighbours.

Finally the pain in her back got so bad that she sat down in an armchair and tried to take deep, steady breaths. It was Peter who came over to her, his expression concerned.

'You all right?'

'I'm not sure. I've got shocking backache. Would you mind if we left early? I really don't feel too good.'

'You don't look it; I'll fetch Allan. Incidentally, has anyone ever told you that you've got the most fascinating mouth?'

'Yes, lots of men; they were all sales reps too. Is it part of the training course?'

He smiled. 'I think you could be quite an interesting person to know, Julie Firmager. I look forward to seeing you more once you're safely back home again. You're not like other women.'

'Go on, say it,' she joked as she eased herself up from the chair. 'I'm more like a brother!'

'Nothing was further from my mind!'

'You've got an excellent line in chat, Peter, but it's somewhat wasted on a woman in labour!'

Just then an irritable Allan arrived and he continued grumbling during their drive to the hospital. He seemed to regard this early labour as a deliberate ploy inflicted on him in order to ruin his first party for months.

'Look,' cried Julie in exasperation, 'if the party's so marvellous then go back to it. All I ask is that you deliver me, plus baby, safely to the hospital. I can manage the rest on my own.'

'There's no need to take that attitude!' he muttered, and once again Julie wished that she could halt the decline in their marriage. This second child's birth was in such sharp contrast to their mutual joy during Melissa's arrival it was painful to face exactly how badly it had deteriorated.

As though to underline the point Allan chose to wait outside the delivery room for the birth. Seven hours later his second daughter weighed in at 8lbs. 4ozs., and they named her Isabelle, after Allan's mother.

The same ward sister was on duty as when Melissa was born, and she chatted to Allan while the doctor stitched Julie up. 'No problems this time!' she said cheerfully.

'What *did* go wrong with Melissa's birth? We never really knew.'

'It was rather strange. The labour had progressed perfectly until the final stages and then the baby's heartbeat vanished. We couldn't pick it up at all, and when she finally arrived and gave a lusty yell we were highly relieved I can tell you.'

'So why did it happen?'

'She must have been lying awkwardly I suppose. Luckily there wasn't any such worry this time.'

Isabelle bore no resemblance to her sister. She was bright red, wrinkled and with minute wisps of dark hair.

100

Her eyes were screwed tightly shut and she made little grunting sounds, like a small animal he thought with a fleeting feeling of distaste which took him by surprise.

After five days mother and child were to be allowed home following the routine inspection by the paediatrician.

He arrived late and Allan was already waiting in the ward with Julie. At first his examination appeared perfunctory, but all at once his attitude changed. He drew the curtains round the bed and his tests became more extensive. Julie and Allan exchanged apprehensive glances.

'What's wrong?' asked Allan as Isabelle was finally wrapped up in her shawl. 'Is something the matter?'

'It's difficult to tell, but some of her reactions are a little slow. We'll arrange for you to bring her back next week to see the consultant. It may be nothing, but I'd like him to see her. Apart from that she's fine, absolutely A.1.'

Two weeks later a weeping Julie, with Isabelle in her arms, stumbled from the consultant's room and made her way down the corridor, Allan's arm around her shoulders. Isabelle was brain damaged. It wasn't known how extensively or why, but it seemed likely that when the forthcoming battery of tests were completed they would be left with the knowledge that her capacity for learning was virtually nil.

Six months later, after endless hospital visits and countless examinations Julie and Allan were told that Isabelle was mentally retarded. Only time would tell the degree of severity, but none of the prognoses were encouraging.

Julie took the blow badly, laid all the blame on herself and took to her bed with a nervous collapse. While Allan looked after her and tried to cheer both her and the grandparents, Isabelle would lie for hours without crying, and he was grateful to her. It was the only positive advantage of her condition but it helped him over the first few hectic weeks.

When he was occupied with his wife, Melissa would tiptoe over to her sister's cot, look inside at the bland, placid face and then, very slowly, she would smile with deep satisfaction before moving away.

She never touched the child; she simply stared, and drew immense secret pleasure from watching her whether she was asleep or awake. It was – in any case – very difficult to tell the difference with Isabelle.

Chapter 8

'This has to stop,' said Dr Sharpe as he made his second
visit of the week to Julie. 'It's nearly Christmas. You've
got a husband and two small daughters remember. Stop
thinking about yourself and consider them for a change.
If you're not up by this time next week, then I'm putting
you in hospital.'

'Is that a threat?' Julie queried lethargically, staring
out of the bedroom window.

'You were a nurse, if you think of it as a threat that's
rather an indictment of our hospitals!'

'I think of it as a threat!'

'That sounds more like the old Julie. Come along, my
dear; this really isn't like you.'

'I know. Perhaps it's a judgement on me for slightly
despising Russell when he gives in. Now I know better.'

'Julie, Isabelle isn't severely handicapped. She'll
never go to an ordinary school, but with remedial
teaching she'll master the basic things like speech and
hygiene in due course.'

'She's simple,' stated Julie. 'I can see that for myself.
Those vacant eyes, that unnatural passiveness. There
isn't a flicker of intelligence there, and there never will
be.'

Dr Sharpe made his voice even brisker. 'Remember,

she'll never know the doubts and fears that assail the rest of us. She'll also be a very affectionate and cheerful child. You know for yourself that retarded children thrive on love. Try and think of it like that.'

Julie turned her head. 'Or you think of it like this: she'll always need looking after; she'll never grow up and marry, leaving us free to carry on our lives in middle-age. Then, when we die, she'll be put in a home and become a burden on the state until the day *she* dies. That will be it; one life, pointless and expensive from the cradle to the grave. Still, that's what the National Health is all about if I remember correctly.'

He snapped his bag shut. 'I expect to see you up next week. Get back to your family; they need you.'

She watched him leave and let out a deep breath. She should have known that it would come to an end, there was no way that Dr Sharpe would allow her to remain in peace, her thoughts wandering back to happier days; days when she hadn't known, and life had been happy and the future full of promise.

As for Isabelle, well probably it was her fault, but that particular burden didn't lie as heavily on her as people supposed. It was tiresome and unfortunate, but she had always known the risk factor. No, that wasn't why she'd taken to her bed. She'd taken to her bed in order to try to make sense of the rest of her life, but without any success. She – like Russell – would simply have to wait and see.

Allan opened the bedroom door and walked tentatively in. 'Dr Sharpe said you were improving. Is that right?'

'Yes,' she said wearily, and saw the pleasure in his eyes. 'I'll come downstairs this evening and we can watch television, if there's anything decent on.'

'We could always play backgammon,' he said eagerly. She forced a smile. He had coped marvellously with both the girls while she had been lingering in bed, and his concern touched her.

'I'd like that. Why don't you send Melissa in to me, I expect her hair could do with a good brushing.'

Melissa didn't tiptoe into the room, she marched in aggressively. 'My hair doesn't need brushing. I did it. I am nearly two now.'

Julie looked at the child and listened to the sharp clear voice. 'You know, I think you should be more careful,' she said casually. 'If anyone else hears you talking like that you'll be sent to school early. Somehow I don't think that would suit your purpose at all.'

'Mummy brush hair?' Melissa piped in a childish treble. 'Pretty ribbon for Liss.'

'I think that's even worse. Get the hairbrush off the dressing-table, please.'

Slowly and carefully Julie brushed the soft, curling hair and admired the deep-gold colour with the ash-blonde strands that ran like a thread through each curl. 'There you are, beautifully groomed as always. I'm getting up tonight. My rest period is over; it's back to reality.'

'Russell's taking me . . .'

All at once Allan burst into the room. 'Is that Melissa talking?' he asked, but his eyes barely lingered on his daughter, instead they roamed the room, searching for someone else.

Julie watched, and her previous suspicion turned slowly to certainty. Russell had told her of Allan's overwhelming interest in Alice's death, and she realised that in some way Alice had managed to ensnare another victim. She pitied her husband, but it increased her own personal fear as she wondered at the reason behind this new manoeuvre.

Coupled with the constant presence of Melissa it gave Julie a mounting sense of isolation; almost as though she were a prisoner in her own home. If Alice now controlled Allan to any great extent then the danger, whether personal or otherwise, must be high. She wished with all her heart that she knew in what direction her dead cousin intended to strike out.

'Yes,' she said gently. 'Why? Who did it sound like?'

'I . . . That is . . . It sounded too mature for Melissa.'

'Uncle Russell take me swimming,' chanted Melissa, and it was lucky for Allan that he missed the look of scorching derision in the child's eyes.

'Fine. Better come along and have tea now.'

'I don't want her going swimming with Russell,' Julie said quickly. 'He isn't reliable. If he meets a leggy brunette he's quite capable of going off and leaving Melissa alone in the learning pool. Why don't you take her when I get up?'

'But Russell's already taken her three times while you've been ill.'

It was definitely time to get up realised Julie. 'Has he? Well, I'd rather he didn't in future. You'd like to go with her wouldn't you?'

'Sure, if you'll be all right with Isabelle.'

'According to the good doctor, Isabelle will never give us any trouble.'

'She's certainly well-behaved at the moment. All right, then, I'll do that.' He scooped Melissa up in his arms and carried her away, leaving Julie to ponder yet again over the problem of Russell.

Later, alone in the house except for Isabelle, she wandered aimlessly from room to room. Allan and Melissa had only left five minutes before and yet the house didn't feel comfortable. It was almost as though someone were watching her. Paranoia now she thought with a grin, and picked up Isabelle as a diversion.

'Poor little thing,' she whispered. 'At least you'll never know. You'll never be able to blame me. What will become of you, I wonder? How bad is your condition? If only we could look into the future, Isabelle. Would you like that?'

Isabelle crooned and spluttered. 'Yes? Well, I'm not sure I want to. The past is enough for me. Oh, Isabelle, how did I ever let it begin? If only I could turn the clock back, start again, but I can't, can I? No, you're right; no one can. Besides, what would I alter? How can I tell where it really all began?'

The room grew darker, only the single wall light casting any brightness, but Julie sat motionless, a sleeping Isabelle lying on her lap, and she slipped away into her memories, trying to recapture the bitter-sweet pleasure of what she would always consider the final summer of her childhood.

'For God's sake what are you sitting in the dark for? Are you ill?' shouted Allan, crashing into the room and switching on the main light. Julie jumped in surprise and Isabelle began to scream with fright.

'You idiot!' said Julie crossly. 'She was just dozing off. Do you have to charge in like an elephant crashing through the jungle?'

Melissa giggled. 'Nellyphant!'

'I'm sorry,' he said more quietly, 'but I was afraid of what you might have . . . you frightened me.'

'I see. Actually I was quite simply half-asleep. How did the swimming go?'

'It's the most extraordinary thing, and I can't imagine why your brother's kept it a secret, but Melissa swims like a fish.'

'A fish in arm-bands?'

'No, a normal fish.'

'Ah! With gills and fins!'

'You're certainly in good form! Yes, Melissa's completely at home in the water. I felt quite superfluous.'

107

'Well done, Melissa. It's time for bed now.'

He stared at his wife. 'Is that all you've got to say? Doesn't it make you feel proud? It did me.' Melissa smirked at her mother from the safety of Allan's arms.

Julie shook her head. 'I didn't do the swimming,' she said levelly, 'Melissa did. I hate parents who bask in their children's reflected glory. Anyway, loads of children can swim at two. Don't encourage her to get conceited.'

'I don't understand you,' he said slowly, taking Melissa's hand and leading her off to the kitchen for supper.

No Julie reflected silently and sadly, fortunately you don't.

Later, over supper, Allan apologised for snapping. 'I don't know what's come over me lately, Julie. I'm sorry I'm so ratty all the time. It isn't much fun for you.'

'I'm the one at fault. You've been marvellous. Does Isabelle worry you?' Allan looked blank. 'Obviously not! Another woman, then?'

Colour flooded his face. 'Of course not!' he blustered. 'What a stupid thing to say.'

'Is it? In that case I give up. There's only the change of life left!' They both laughed and the tension eased. Each of them silently wished that they could always be like this together, and each of them for different reasons, knew how unlikely it was that their wish would come true.

Allan, who now longed obsessively for Alice every day and night, sought to bring her name into the conversation. Even to speak of her made her seem nearer, more a part of his life.

'It's probably a good thing that Melissa can already swim,' he remarked nonchalently. 'At least she won't suffer Alice's fate.'

'Alice could swim, but it didn't save her.'

He swallowed hard. 'Julie, would you tell me about

the way she died? I know that she was man-mad and hurt your feelings badly, but all the mystery about her has me intrigued.'

He did not deceive his wife. She understood very well how badly he wanted to talk about Alice because she had seen it all before. Nothing was Allan's fault – indeed she was ashamed to realise that it was only because he had married her that he had ever become involved – and she wanted to help him as much as she could. Her feeling of pity was tinged with sorrow since Alice had never, to Julie's knowledge, let her victims escape completely unscathed.

'There's no mystery, Allan. Russell and I only saw her a couple of times a year and I can't honestly say that she chased *every* man around. On the whole she confined it to her cousins' boyfriends during the holidays. It was probably more enjoyable for her that way.'

'How many girl cousins did she have?'

'There were six of us. Six girls and Alice. Four are my father's nieces, one is my mother's and I make up the six. I'm younger than the rest, which is doubtless why I was the least affected. I wasn't planning to marry anyone when I was fifteen!'

'You mean she broke up really serious relationships?'

'That last summer Karen was engaged to Steve. He was a thoroughly nice person and devoted to her. By the time their stay at Penzance was over so was the engagement.'

'Because of Alice?'

'That's what Karen said. Alice denied it and Steve insisted that she had nothing to do with his decision, but Karen had seen them in the cove. She knew. We all knew.'

'Did Alice keep in touch with Steve?'

'She died before the holiday ended, but if she'd lived I don't suppose for one moment that she would have contacted him. Once she proved her power over people they immediately became redundant.'

'Was Russell infatuated by her as well?'

Julie shifted in her chair. 'You'd better ask him that. He might have been, for a time.'

'He had his breakdown because she died, didn't he?'

'Yes.'

'Well, there you are then. It speaks for itself.'

'Perhaps.'

'I don't see that there can be any doubt. I notice you still haven't told me *how* Alice drowned.'

'Because no one really knows. One afternoon she simply didn't come home from her swim. She was finally washed up on the beach a couple of miles along the coast twelve days later. My uncle had to go and identify her. I imagine it was pretty horrible for him; there are a lot of rocks everywhere you see.'

Allan shivered. He could picture Alice so clearly. Her small, flawless features, her dainty hands and immaculate clothes. He didn't want to think of her battered by the tide, her beauty destroyed by one moment's inattention or over-confidence.

'And she was a good swimmer?'

'I've already told you that! Yes, she was good. She swam for her school and went in for area galas.'

'But she still managed to drown.'

'As usual Alice thought that she knew best. She went in when the red flag was flying. It was a very windy day, that's why none of us had gone with her.'

'She must have been terrified. What a horrible few seconds they would have been before she actually died.'

'Minutes more likely. She was a strong enough swimmer to put up quite a fight. Must we talk about this any more? It isn't a very pleasant conversation for a Sunday evening.'

Allan stood up. 'Sorry! You're quite right. It's just

that you all seemed so mysterious about her death it made me extra inquisitive.'

Julie decided to try and warn him. She felt that it was her duty; if he didn't listen it wasn't her fault. She would have done her best.

'There isn't any mystery; the reason we don't talk about her is because secretly we're pleased. Not that she died so horribly, no one could be pleased about that, but pleased that she's gone. You can't imagine what she was like and I'm not going to try and explain, but the one thing that frightened us all was the way she could manipulate people. She had the knack of getting them to do whatever she wanted, and do it willingly, even if it went against their conscience. I don't know how she did it, but if ever there was a girl with power in her eyes it was my cousin Alice.'

And she had it still, thought Allan, going into the kitchen to make coffee. Even dead she had the ability to manipulate him. Slowly she was estranging him from his wife and daughters. He knew it was madness, but these days only time spent with Alice was reality; it was everyday life that was the dream, and a time-wasting one at that.

He was beginning to resent the presence of other human beings because they meant that he and Alice were unable to communicate properly. Even if she materialised he had to sit silently and wait in frustration to be alone with her.

Yet it was still Julie that he loved, he knew that, and the knowledge only served to increase his guilt and despair. Unreasonably he felt a surge of hatred sweep over him as she entered the kitchen. His wife, the mother of his children, innocent and trusting, but for one brief moment he could have struck her simply because she wasn't Alice.

Seeing the expression on his face Julie halted. I'm

111

going mad, thought Allan, completely mad, and he tried to smile. He never knew that to Julie it looked like a ghastly grimace, a demonic warning of forthcoming horror.

'What is it? she stammered. 'Why are you looking at me like that?'

He could tell that she was frightened. 'Like what?'

'I don't know, almost as though you hated me.'

'Darling Julie, you really must be far from well still! I smiled, that's all.'

'It didn't look like a smile.'

'Then I must practise more! Come on, coffee's made. What were we talking about?'

'Alice.'

'Yes, of course. You blame her for Russell's breakdown, don't you? That's really why you're so against her.' Before Julie could reply Alice appeared, standing close behind her cousin's chair. Allan kept his gaze resolutely on Julie.

'No, I don't think Alice was completely to blame. There must have been some inherent weakness in him. After all, the rest of her cousins survived without too much trouble.'

Swiftly Alice turned her head and her eyes glinted with hatred. 'For some of us,' continued Julie, oblivious of the glacial stare, 'it was almost a relief. No more games within games; no more summers dominated by Alice. Yes, from what I can remember the rest of us were relieved.' Her voice was emotionless, as though the death had caused scarcely a ripple in most of the teenager's lives. Allan knew otherwise. She was too casual, too controlled.

'Russell said that you had a crush on someone that last summer. He called it a bad case of puppy-love.'

Julie's face went blank. 'I can't remember anyone special.'

'There must have been someone. He said that Alice stole the boy away.'

'If there *had* been a boy,' stated Julie flatly, 'then Alice would undoubtedly have stolen him away; but there wasn't.' Alice poked out the tip of her tiny, pink tongue at Julie's back and pulled a grotesque face. Allan laughed.

'It wasn't funny for the people involved at the time,' Julie said crossly.

'I know, it's just that . . .'

'I don't want to talk about her any more,' cried Julie, and she ran upstairs.

For a moment Allan and Alice stared at each other and then he almost fell upon her, his hands tearing at her clothes in his haste. He was fortunate that he didn't see the expression of distaste on her face before she pulled him to the floor and slid his trousers and pants down his legs.

She then bent her head and let her tongue play lightly over the entire length of his shaft before lowering her velvet mouth over the top as she applied gentle suction with her lips. Allan tingled from head to toe, the pleasure was exquisite but he knew that he couldn't control himself much longer. He looked down at her golden curls and buried his fingers in them as he felt his climax approaching.

When it was over he groaned and turned away from her. He realised that he must be mad to make love on the kitchen floor when Julie could walk in at any moment.

'What is it?' asked Alice petulantly. 'Wasn't it good?'

'Yes, of course, but what's the point? You're dead aren't you? What sort of a relationship can we have? You're a ghost, or possibly a figment of my imagination. I must be mad to get so intense about you.'

She put out a hand and her fingers stroked the top of his left leg lightly. 'I'm not a figment of your imagin-

113

ation, and we can have a wonderful relationship. I thought you understood. There's a special bond between us. Surely you don't want to throw that away?'

As she talked her fingers were moving deftly over him. He felt her nails lightly scratch his testicles. 'Alice, don't! Julie's here, remember?' She took no notice but began to croon gently to herself as her fingers continued their dancing progress. Just for once he pushed her away, re-arranging his clothing.

'Bugger off!' he cursed. 'You think I'll always wait for you and welcome you whatever the circumstances, but you're wrong. I'm not your slave. Just go away. Go away before you ruin my marriage completely.'

Making a strange angry, rattling sound in her throat Alice went. Surprised, but feeling altogether better Allan mounted the stairs and joined his sleeping wife. For the first time ever he felt that perhaps he was beginning to take charge of the situation, and the feeling was a pleasant one.

Allan most definitely did not understand Alice.

Chapter 9

Although Melissa's birthday and the Christmas holiday were properly celebrated in the Firmager household, Julie's recent illness made it easy to keep everything in a low key. They only invited the two sets of grandparents to visit, and since Allan's parents had become increasingly cool towards him and his family – a fact that distressed and bewildered Julie – only the Pasks spent any length of time in the house.

This was fortunate because Allan's ever-increasing guilt was making him silent and withdrawn, and nothing that Julie said or did changed things. The Pasks, used to Russell's spasmodic withdrawals from social life, accepted the situation without undue comment. Mrs Pask merely said that she herself always found Christmas, with its enforced gaiety, a trifle depressing.

By the time Allan returned to work Julie appeared fully recovered, and neither one of them admitted their sense of relief that the holiday period was over. The less they saw of each other the easier it was to hold on to the illusion that all was well in the marriage.

'I'll try not to be late home,' he promised, kissing her goodbye. 'Remember, if you can't cope ring me up. They're very understanding at work.'

'I'll be fine. Say goodbye to Daddy, Melissa.'

'Bye,' called Melissa, waving a hand indifferently in the air. He smiled and blew her a kiss.

'Be a good girl for Mummy, darling.'

'Don't forget Isabelle,' Julie reminded him, and he dutifully bent over the six-month-old as she sat in her high chair staring vacantly round the room, ignoring the rusk clutched in her plump, weak fingers.

As he left Melissa slipped quietly away, leaving her mother and Isabelle alone. Once in her room she stood in front of the long mirror inside her wardrobe door and studied herself. Then she closed her eyes in concentration.

At first nothing happened, then, almost imperceptibly, her flesh began to swell until she was bloated beyond belief. Just when it looked as though she must burst open like a sausage cooked too rapidly she opened her eyes again.

The ghastly image before her was obviously a familiar sight for she showed no fear. Indeed she moved her swollen lips in a small smile and then pressed her face close to the glass.

Now her eyes began to swell, forcing the lids back until they disappeared, and continuing to grow before finally, with a hideous popping sound, the eyeballs sprang out of their sockets and vanished.

Immediately, from out of the dark holes, shimmers of silver light appeared. They swirled around the child's form, shaping and re-shaping themselves time and again. There was one final, gigantic upheaval of the silver mist and then, at last, Alice herself stood before the glass and at her feet lay a soft boneless mass that had previously been Melissa.

The eyelids were mercifully closed, hiding the worst physical evidence of the true horror of the metamorphisis, and with one glance down at the floor Alice smiled, then glided out of the bedroom and purposefully down the stairs.

116

Julie was so engrossed in watching Isabelle, trying to assess exactly how slow she was in her ability to co-ordinate her movements, that she wasn't at first aware of what was happening. It was the perfume that alerted her. Her heart seemed to leap into her throat and her stomach lurched. Slowly, very slowly, she turned her head and there – for the first time since her marriage – was Alice.

Allan would scarcely have recognised her. She was wearing jeans and a shabby short-sleeved denim jacket. Her hair was scraped back off her face and tied at the back with a dark blue ribbon. She looked young and innocent, a long way removed from the sensual siren he always saw.

'You're back, then.' Julie hoped that she sounded suitably casual. 'I didn't expect to see you again after I married Allan.'

'Don't sound so disappointed. I thought you'd be pleased. You are pleased, aren't you, Julie?'

'Not very. My life's quite complicated enough at the moment without you adding to it.'

'But we've been companions for so long now. I couldn't just let us drift apart. That wasn't what you wanted, was it?'

'It wasn't why I married if that's what you mean. I married because I love Allan, not because of anything to do with you.'

'That's nice. The trouble is I'm not sure I believe you. You may think you love Allan, but that's quite different. You don't look pleased to see me.'

'Frankly, I'm not. I'm a typical housewife with two small children, one small house, one obsessed and distracted husband and a continual guilty conscience that never lets me rest.'

Alice smiled; it was the carefree, open smile of a schoolgirl. 'You deserve to have a guilty conscience. If it

117

weren't for you . . .'

'Don't go over all that again,' said Julie wearily. 'I'm not in the mood. Incidentally, I take it that I'm right in assuming you're visiting Allan?'

Alice giggled. 'Of course I am! He's quite sweet, and far more sophisticated sexually since I took him over. I quite enjoy our times together now. Mind you, I don't see him so often now.'

'Why not?'

'It's become difficult,' said Alice evasively. 'I get more tired and it's tricky to arrange.'

'Good. What do you want, Alice?'

'How unkind you are! Why should I want anything? I'm here to see you, that's all. I wanted to see you again, properly that is. It's been a long time.'

'Well, Alice, I'm sorry but I don't want to see you. I've got to take Isabelle to the clinic; Melissa to her toddler group; and then I've promised Alison that she can come round for the afternoon, as her husband has apparently started straying again. Quite a busy suburban day as you can tell.'

'Can't I come with you? Except to the toddlers; I'll give that a miss.'

'No. All I want is for you to go away and leave me alone.'

Alice's eyes darkened. 'You're being unkind,' she said sweetly, but Julie was too busy clearing the table to heed the warning contained in the words.

'I'm not, I'm just being practical. Come back tomorrow. I might have more time, then,' she added hastily, belatedly realising that she had probably made a tactical error.

'Julie!' called Alice coaxingly and Julie looked up. Her cousin was loosening her ribbon and letting her hair fall round her face. As the tendrils escaped so they began to change colour, turning from sun-bleached gold to a dark, medium brown.

118

At the same time her face was altering. At first it was so subtle that it was virtually indetectable, a slight blurring of the fine features, a lack of colour in the cheeks. Julie frowned, her attention caught.

Alice's violet eyes gleamed out from behind the rapidly tangling mane of hair. Then, horribly, her face began to puff up, almost as though someone was blowing air into her.

The skin tone changed from white to a horrible shade of green, and the mouth fell open revealing small, green particles on the previously sparkling, pearly teeth.

Rooted to the spot, Julie watched in growing terror as Alice's face literally fell apart before her eyes. The rotting skin flaked away from the bones and hung in tatters. The eyes disappeared until there were only empty sockets, sockets from which small creatures began to emerge, slipping and sliding as they crossed the front of the rotting skull.

The mouth gaped wider, revealing a swollen tongue, blackened and distorted, and even as the hair began to disappear, turning into thin, damp clumps that clung to Alice's skull, so the kitchen was invaded by the most ghastly stench of rotting flesh and escaping gas.

Julie began to scream, trying to edge away from this hideous travesty of her cousin, a travesty made all the more terrifying by the fact that the rotting skull was still set on the top of an ivory white neck above the small, perfectly formed body clad in the jeans and shirt.

Remorselessly the walking death's head followed Julie, who tried to run screaming from the room; tried, but her limbs were heavy with terror and all at once Alice stood between Julie and the door and the black, gaping hole that had once been a mouth opened even wider and a gurgle of water-clogged laughter bubbled up and echoed round the room.

'NO!' screamed Julie. 'Get away! We didn't mean it.

We didn't know. Don't touch me! GET AWAY! No! Please, no more.' She was sobbing frantically, but the hideous creature merely choked with renewed laughter and slowly the room turned dark as Julie sank unconscious to the kitchen floor.

She didn't know how long she had been lying there, but when she tentatively opened her eyes the kitchen was back to normal. There was no trace of Alice. No lingering smell of putrification; not even a hint of the sandalwood perfume that had heralded her arrival. There was only Isabelle, vacant-eyed with her nose running, and Melissa.

Julie got slowly to her feet, her eyes darting nervously in every direction in case the dreadful spectre was lurking in a corner, but with sunlight streaming through the window by the sink and Melissa's blonde hair gleaming brightly as she bent over some crayoning it was difficult to believe that anything had really happened.

'Mummy sleeping?' queried Melissa, not even turning her head but behaving as though she was quite used to Julie taking a brief nap on the kitchen floor. Julie ignored her. She moved to clean Isabelle up and her foot slipped on something beneath her.

She skidded towards the pine table and just managed to stop herself from falling. Lifting her right foot she checked the sole of her red, fluffy mule and there, sticking tenaciously, was a thin strand of dark seaweed. With a scream she threw the slipper across the room and ran to the telephone, dialling the number with fingers that trembled so much it took her three attempts to get it right.

'Mother? It's Julie. Is Russell there?'

'Julie, darling! How are you? Is Melissa behaving herself? If not we're always . . .'

'I want Russell!' she shouted. 'Get him for me!'

'Really, darling, I don't think you should take that

attitude. You know how unstable your brother is. If you need assistance your father and I . . .'

'Get me Russell!' Julie was sobbing now, her breath coming in short, sharp gasps and her teeth beginning to chatter despite valiant attempts to keep her jaw clenched.

'He's in bed, Julie. He's sleeping a lot at the moment. It's the new pills. Your father doesn't understand, but I do. He's too highly-strung, poor boy. The doctor says . . .'

'For God's sake get him for me!' screamed Julie. There was a stunned silence the other end of the line, and then the sound of muted footsteps followed by a dimly heard knocking and far-off voices. Finally, there was the loud slamming of a door, and she knew that at last Russell was on his way.

'What is it?' his voice was sharp with anxiety.

'I've just seen . . . That is, I know now . . . Russell, it was awful. I had no idea. She looked so . . . Russell, you've got to help. She's never done that to me before, why now? It wasn't my fault. I didn't . . .'

Her sentences were broken up by her tears, and the more she tried to talk the greater her loss of control became. In the end, she simply stood there, one foot bare, shaking from top to toe and clinging desperately to reality.

'Stay where you are. I'll be over in ten minutes. Where's Melissa?'

'*Melissa*? Russell I'm talking about . . .'

'Where is she?'

'In the kitchen.'

'Leave her there until I arrive; and Julie, don't give in. I've done that, and believe me it's hell.'

'I had no idea,' she repeated pathetically, but the line was dead and now she could only wait.

After a few moments Melissa peered out into the hall. 'Me go play school?'

'Not this morning, I don't feel well. You'll have to amuse yourself.'

'Play school. Liss play school!' and she stamped one small, leather-sandalled foot.

'Go away. Go and do some more crayoning.'

'Liss give Mummy a love?' she suggested winningly, her head to one side.

Julie closed her eyes. 'No, thank you.'

'Liss loves Mummy,' the child persisted. 'Mummy love Liss?'

'No, I do not,' whispered Julie. 'At this moment I don't love you one tiny bit, and please stop calling yourself Liss. You're Melissa, and you can say that perfectly well when you wish.'

Melissa shrugged and retreated to the kitchen. Once there she proceeded to torment Isabelle by rubbing her round face in rusk crumbs mixed with milk. Isabelle gave one or two whimpers, but Melissa knew that her mother wouldn't even hear and continued gleefully with her game.

Julie remained at the bottom of the stairs with her arms clasped round her knees, watching the glass panel in the top of the front door and willing Russell to arrive swiftly. He came far more quickly than she had hoped, and immediately pulled her tightly to him. She sobbed and gabbled incoherently, her entire body trembling with terror.

When the sobbing began to ease he led her into the living-room, then poured her a generous measure of brandy from Allan's drinks cabinet.

'I shouldn't' she protested weakly. 'I'm on pills.'

'It won't kill you this once. I'm going into the kitchen, you stay here.'

In the kitchen, Melissa was still busy with Isabelle. She was now decorating the small face with coloured hundreds and thousands. Isabelle had stopped

122

whimpering and sat immobile, passively accepting the discomfort.

'Let her alone you wretched girl,' Russell snapped. Melissa jumped in surprise. He fetched a damp cloth and carefully cleaned Isabelle's face and hands. A smile flickered on the loose mouth and he fought down his instinctive distaste for the baby, picked her up, then carried her into the living-room where he placed her in the safety of the playpen.

Melissa waited in silence. When he came back she was sitting on the table kicking her legs aimlessly against one of its legs, but her eyes were alert, cautious. 'Play school?' she suggested hopefully.

Without a word Russell finished dressing his niece and drove her to the church hall where the group met. He explained that Julie was ill and the sympathetic supervisor handed him a large envelope. 'This is Melissa's photo, the children all had one taken. I'm afraid it's not very good, but if Julie should want a copy ask her to let me know; and do give her my best wishes.'

He nodded and smiled, and the woman thought how attractive and pleasant he was, but in reality he heard nothing. Her words were simply a collection of sounds, and as soon as the sounds stopped he got into the car and sped back to Julie.

'Right then, we've got nearly two hours. Tell me all about it, and tell me slowly.'

She did. She spared him nothing. His eyes reflected no surprise, merely deep understanding. When Julie finished she lifted her eyes to meet his. 'Is that what you see? Is that how she *always* looks to you?' He nodded. Julie stared. 'I don't know how you keep sane. If I thought that she was going to do it again I'd . . .'

'She won't. It sounds as though it was only because you didn't have any time for her. You know how Alice always had to come first. She won't want to terrify you again; in fact, she's probably regretting it now. As you say, it wasn't your fault.'

'It was. I was what the police would call an accessory.'

'You happened to be there and saw it all. There was nothing you could do. It's different for me. She'll never show herself to me in any other guise; I know that now.'

'If we could go back,' said Julie softly, 'and begin the day again, would you behave differently?'

'Knowing then what I know now?'

'Yes.'

He hesitated. 'I suppose so, but that's because I'm such a coward. As you rightly said, Alice deserved to die. Nothing can change that fact.'

'Except that she hasn't.'

'No. I wonder why that is? What happened to enable her to come back like this? How does she do it?'

'And why?' asked Julie. 'Will it go on for ever, all our lives, as a punishment?'

Russell stood up and touched his sister lightly on the shoulder. 'No, I don't think so. I rather think that at present she's got a very strong motive for coming back, a mission if you like. Once it's completed she'll go away.'

'Then let's help her. I'd do anything to prevent another scene like . . . I don't think I could stand . . .' She began to cry again.

'Julie, it isn't possible. If Alice wants what I think she does we've got to fight her. She mustn't win.'

'I can't think of any price too high if it would keep Alice away for ever.'

'I can. No, Julie, she has to be beaten. Don't worry, I'm working on a few ideas.'

'What about Melissa?'

Russell's eyes went blank as though he were afraid of showing too much emotion. Julie felt cold again and resolved to keep Melissa close. After all, she was her own flesh and blood.

'Talking of Melissa,' he went on, 'that chatterbox of a supervisor gave me her photo, but she says it isn't very good.'

Julie took the envelope and pulled out a large print. It was obviously Melissa, there was no mistaking the golden curls and violet eyes, but the entire picture was out of focus. Only her eyes were sharp; they smouldered from the mist like cat's eyes in the dark. After a few moments careful study she replaced it in the envelope. 'No, it isn't any good.'

'Let me look.'

'She's difficult to photograph; she always moves at the vital moment.'

Russell gave her a scathing look. 'Is that what you tell Allan? Is that how you explained the failure of the christening pictures? The blur that's Melissa on every family snap? Why don't you admit it? Melissa's . . .'

'She isn't. She isn't, do you hear me? SHE IS NOT!'

Russell could see how frantic fear was making his sister and immediately regretted the comment. 'Sorry, I'm probably being over-sensitive. I always am when it comes to anything concerning Alice. Isabelle doesn't look too bad, all things considered.'

Julie was grateful for the change of subject. 'I know. In fact people who don't know think she's wonderfully placid and say that she's exactly like me. Not really a compliment!'

'She could have been much worse.'

'I know that! If only life wasn't so complicated, Russell. Sometimes I feel as though my head will burst when I go over and over things in my mind. I've decided now that if I could go back I *would* change things. I'd change them all.' She sounded almost defiant.

'All?'

'Yes,' she said firmly, 'all.'

There was a long silence. 'I don't think you mean

125

that.' His voice was gentle. 'Alice has upset you. Naturally you're seeing things out of proportion.'

Julie's smile was bitter. 'You men are all the same! It doesn't matter anyway; we can't go back. We have to go on.'

'You're still not well,' he reminded her. 'Things will look better once you've got over the shock. She won't do it again, I promise.'

'How can you promise any such thing? No one ever knew how Alice's mind worked, you least of all.'

Russell rose to his feet. 'I'm not going to get caught up in an argument. Let's have coffee and then I'll collect Melissa. How about a trip out this afternoon? We could go to the park. Melissa loves the swings.'

Julie pictured her daughter on one of them, with Russell pushing her. Slowly at first, but then more fiercely, higher and higher until . . . It was all there on his face, she had always been able to read him like a book.

'I can't,' she responded, trying to sound genuinely regretful. 'Alison's coming round to weep on my shoulder.'

'Haven't you enough problems of your own?'

'Alison takes my mind off them! Besides, she fascinates me; I'd like to understand her better. Another time perhaps.'

'What?'

'The Park. We'll go another time, when I'm feeling better.'

'Sure. I'll put the kettle on.'

Julie insisted that they all collected Melissa, then handed back the photo and agreed that yes it was a pity the child had moved but there was always next year.

She seemed to have recovered her composure well. However, when Russell got ready to leave she clung tightly to him. 'She really won't come back, will she? You are sure? I'll go mad if she does.'

126

'I did try and tell you what it was like,' he reminded her.

'I know, but somehow . . . well, it's beyond description, isn't it? My imagination wasn't capable of picturing what you endured. Russell, suppose she keeps returning?'

He smoothed her hair off her forehead. 'I'm positive she won't. Try not to think about it any more.' With one final embrace he left her alone, except for two small children, and returned to the false sense of security engendered by the solitude of his bedroom.

They had only just finished their lunch when Alison arrived with sweets for Melissa and white chocolate for Isabelle. Melissa promptly favoured her with a beaming smile and a display of baby-talk that sickened Julie to the core. Alison, however, was enchanted which gave Julie time to clean Isabelle's face and put her down for her afternoon sleep. That was one great advantage with Isabelle, she would sleep all day if she was given the chance.

Melissa finally settled herself with crayons and wooden puzzles so Julie decided to stay in the kitchen rather than risk disturbing her. No sooner had she and Alison sat down than Melissa lifted her head. 'What's that smell?' she demanded.

'Smell? I can't smell anything. Can you, Alison?'

'No.'

'It's a pong!' giggled Melissa.

Julie felt the flesh on the top of her arms prickle. 'A nice pong?' she queried.

'Yes; like perfume' and with a glowing smile Melissa lowered her head to her drawing. Julie quickly put their mugs of tea on a tray and moved into the living-room.

She didn't want to wait until the smell reached her. Melissa's warning, genuine or not, was enough. Alison was there as an antidote to Alice, and her visit wouldn't help in the least if Julie was constantly aware of Alice listening and laughing at tales of suburban drama, full of strife and adultery. Sex had always amused Alice.

After Alison had imparted her two momentous discoveries; the first being that she was pregnant and the second – predictably – that Peter was having another affair, Julie sighed. 'Quite honestly, I don't know what to suggest. You've got to weigh up what you've got with what you stand to lose, and if you plump for what you've got then you'll just have to stop thinking about this affair and look to the future. Perhaps being a father will make him face up to his responsibilities,' she added, more in hope than expectation.

Alison nodded. 'That's absolutely right. Why is it that you can always see things so clearly? After all, I won't be pregnant for ever and I couldn't bear to lose him. I'd never find such a fantastic lover again.'

'There you are then, that's the answer. Another coffee?'

'Super!'

Out in the kitchen Melissa was still drawing. She flicked her eyes towards her mother. 'Super,' she drawled, and crouched over her drawing.

'You've been listening at keyholes again, haven't you? What are you hiding there.'

'Nothing.'

Julie thought quickly. 'Do you want some orange juice?' Melissa nodded, scrambling off the chair. She was then able to cast a swift glance at the paper, and saw a square shape with two stick figures tangled up on the top. It was meaningless, Melissa had told the truth. She poured out orange juice and put in a long, plastic squiggly straw; Melissa loved to watch the liquid making its way along the curling, transparent plastic. Taking the mug carefully in her hands the child wandered out of the kitchen and up the stairs.

As Julie leant across the work top to unplug the boiling kettle she felt her arm brush against something wet and cold. With a scream of fright she closed her eyes in terror. After a few seconds she gingerly opened them. There was nothing there, only a small pool of water showed that she hadn't imagined the sensation.

Her hands began to shake and she slopped half the contents of the kettle onto the work surface. The terrible smell was beginning to overwhelm her, and she had a job not to retch.

'Want any help?' called Alison.

'It's all right. I've spilt some water; I won't be a minute.'

'Fine. I'll keep Isabelle amused.'

'Not a difficult task!' said Alice in bell-like tones as she materialised on the chair Melissa had vacated. She was tanned this time, and her hair hung loose. Her bright red and green kaftan brought back many memories, and for a brief moment Julie forgot that her cousin was dead and took a step towards her. Then she remembered and hastily backed off.

'I said, not a difficult task.'

'I heard you. I don't think it's very funny to mock Isabelle's handicap.'

'Poor Isabelle. If only she knew *why* she was retarded. I'd like to tell her. I've actually tried, but she's too stupid to understand.'

'At six months she probably is!'

'She'll be equally stupid after six years. How can you put up with that pathetic, whining neighbour in the other room? She drives me up the wall.'

'Don't listen then,' hissed Julie. 'Now go away, I'm busy.'

'Careful,' cautioned Alice lightly. 'Remember this morning.'

Julie swallowed hard and tried to stop the trembling of

her limbs. 'That was very unkind of you,' she said tearfully. 'Why did you do it?'

Alice shrugged. 'I was annoyed. You made me very cross.'

'It wasn't my fault, you know,' continued Julie, looking fearfully to the doorway lest Alison appear. 'I didn't do anything.'

'Sometimes that's just as bad as participating. Anyway, that's not why I did it. I just wanted to hold your attention for a little longer.'

Julie tried to sound pleasant. 'Look, Alice, I'd like to talk to you, there are loads of things I need to say, but right now isn't the time.'

'I understand that. The trouble is, I can't come and go as I please any more; not since Melissa. Now that she's older, it's more . . . difficult.'

'Why?'

'She needs more energy, sometimes . . . It doesn't matter. Forget it.'

'I don't know what you're on about. Alice, why won't you leave Russell alone? Hasn't he been punished enough? He's . . .'

'They say it's the first sign,' said Alison cheerfully, striding into the room.

'What is?' queried Julie while Alice shimmered briefly and then vanished.

'Talking to yourself! Why, here's Melissa again. Where have you been, beautiful?'

'Having a pooh. My tummy ached.'

Julie frowned. 'Thank you, Melissa; spare us the details, please. Are you staying out here?'

'Yes. Drink all gone.'

'I'll make you another.'

That done they returned to the living-room, and for the next hour Julie listened to Alison's life story. She was very frank about it all. How Peter was her only lover, and the scathing comments he'd made about her lack of experience the first time they made love. She also stressed how much she'd improved, rather as though she were playing a game of tennis Julie thought, and how his eventual approval was sealed with a marriage proposal.

'I'm sure he does love me,' she concluded. 'I know my trust fund when I reach thirty will make us well off, but I honestly don't think Peter's interested in money. It isn't as though I were going to inherit millions.'

How blind she was reflected Julie. It was perfectly obvious Peter liked fast cars, high-powered living and sophisticated women, yet Alison plainly believed that it was her personality which had captured him. One thing was very clear; the longer Alison talked the less attractive a person her husband became, despite his wife's intentions to the contrary.

'. . . and I *always* have an orgasm,' concluded Alison. 'He's very good like that. So many women complain that their husbands don't think of them, but he does. That's something to be grateful for, isn't it?'

Suddenly Isabelle – much to her mother's relief – started to whimper. This quickly changed to the loud bellow which meant a dirty nappy.

'I'll have to see to Isabelle,' said Julie standing up. 'She gets very sore.'

'That's OK. It's time I went anyway. I feel much better for our talk. Friends are important aren't they?' Julie nodded, wondering to herself if they were more or less important than the regular orgasm.

'Thanks for listening and being so helpful. Incidentally, if you ever want a break don't forget that I'll be happy to look after Isabelle.'

'I'll probably take you up on the offer some time. Come on, Isabelle, let's get you clean again.' Isabelle stared blankly at her mother and dribbled. It was wrong to feel repulsed, but Julie was only human, and the day had been an exceptionally bad one.

Immediately Alison had gone, Melissa entered the living-room, switching on the television and settling down to watch children's programmes. For a brief time the house was peaceful.

Chapter 10

True to his word Allan got home from work early, for which Julie was extremely grateful. The ghastly episode in the morning had drained her, and throughout the rest of the day she felt as though she were trying to wade through treacle: every smile, every action, required maximum physical and mental effort.

He took over completely. Melissa, who always behaved better for Allan, ate her tea, listened to a story and even kissed Isabelle goodnight without pulling one of the grotesque faces that physical contact with her little sister usually generated.

At seven o'clock, as Allan was cooking an omelette, the telephone rang, since it was at a crucial point in the cooking he quickly passed the receiver to Julie. 'It's Russell. Don't be long, omelettes go all leathery if they're not eaten straight away.'

'Julie?' Russell sounded extremely agitated. 'How are you now? Did she come back?'

'Fine thank you,' she said cheerfully, aware of Allan's close proximity. 'Alison came round this afternoon, which helped pass the time.'

'Did you see her again?'

'As a matter of fact, yes. She looked very attractive. I think you'd like her.'

'I take it Allan's near?'

'That's right.'

'She came to me just now.' His voice was high, and she could sense his fear over the phone. 'She looked even worse than usual. Julie, what are we going to do?'

'Thanks. I've got to go, Allan's omelette will be ruined. Why not come round and see me tomorrow afternoon? Melissa would like that too.'

'I'll see you then . . . Julie, I wish you still lived here.'

'Bye for now, Russ.' She stood frowning for a moment before fixing a cheerful smile onto her face and turning her attention to the food.

'It's time he got a job,' was Allan's only comment. Julie was grateful for his lack of curiosity. 'What did you and Alison talk about all the afternoon? Peter I suppose,' he continued.

'Some of the time, but also children. She's pregnant.'

'I can't imagine Peter as a father! I saw him the other lunchtime. He had a stunning brunette with him, and they weren't just good friends either.'

'Alison loves him,' said Julie quietly. 'Loving people can be very hurtful, but sometimes the pleasure outweighs the pain.'

'You sound as though you speak from experience.'

'Not personal experience. I was thinking of Russell.'

Allan pushed his empty coffee cup to one side and gave her a curious glance. 'He was deeply in love?'

'Yes.'

'With Alice I assume!' His laugh was bitter.

'Why do you assume that?'

'It strikes me that every man who met your cousin fell in love with her.'

'Perhaps not every one, but most did, yes.'

'So he *was* in love with her? Despite all the denials!'

'That's really his business, isn't it? If he wants you to know then presumably he'll tell you – one day.'

134

'I don't know why he's so secretive. There's no law against cousins marrying even if they're blood relations; but Alice wasn't a blood relation, she was adopted.'

'You're absolutely right. Now, if you don't mind, I think I'll go on up. It's been a tiring day.'

Allan jumped to his feet. 'Of course. I've been forgetting how weak you still are. If you're asleep before I join you I promise I'll keep very quiet.'

From the look in his eyes and the eagerness with which he hustled her off to their room she guessed that he was hoping for a visit from Alice. Perhaps he would be lucky.

She gave him a gentle kiss and left him waiting in the living-room. Waiting for Alice who might not bother to come. It was all very, very sad.

Julie fell asleep quickly. She wasn't sure how much time had passed when she awoke, but her head was muzzy and she had trouble forcing her leaden eyelids open. She made the effort because Melissa – who generally never gave any trouble at night – was whimpering.

In the small, brightly coloured bedroom illuminated by a nightlight, Melissa was lying on her back in bed. She was staring at the ceiling, apparently awake but unaware of the whimpering sounds issuing from her mouth. She didn't turn to look at her mother.

'What's the matter?' asked Julie sleepily. 'Have you had a bad dream?'

There was no answer, however the whimpering stopped. 'Melissa, what's wrong?' Her daughter didn't move a muscle, it was almost as though she were in a trance.

Feeling worried Julie bent over the little girl and put a hand to her forehead, only to withdraw it with a startled gasp. The child's skin was icy cold and felt brittle, as though all the moisture had been drained from it.

'Melissa!' With shaking hands she scooped her off the bed, and then cried out as the small, blonde head lolled hideously on the slender neck, like that of a newborn baby.

Every muscle in her body was limp, as though turned to jelly, and when Julie turned towards the light switch in order to study Melissa better one of the little girl's arms fell from her mother's grasp and flopped feebly back to Melissa's side.

With the main light finally on it was possible to see the extent of Melissa's plight. Her face was a waxen yellow, and her eyes closed. She lay in her mother's arms, an ice-cold, seemingly random collection of muscles and soft bones which flopped and swung in grotesque patterns as she was moved by a now terrified Julie.

She tried to lay the child neatly on top of her bed before fetching Allan, but despite her care it proved impossible, and her daughter resembled nothing more than a large, badly-made rag doll.

Carefully Julie decided to lift one eyelid in order to see how deeply unconscious Melissa was. Gently, very gently, she rolled it back, then stared in mind-numbing horror at the dark, empty socket that was revealed.

Terrified she jumped back from the bed, her hand to her mouth, unable to believe what her brain was telling her. Summoning every ounce of courage she forced herself to return to the child and lift the other eyelid. This time she began to scream, running along the landing to the top of the stairs as she did so.

When Allan didn't immediately respond she gave way to hysterics, and by the time he finally emerged from the living-room, looking flushed and dishevelled, she was half-crying, half-laughing like a woman out of her mind.

He took the stairs two at a time. 'Julie! What on earth's happening?' he shouted clasping her in his arms. She leant against him, and smelt the scent of sandalwood on his clothes. Knowing at once that his night's vigil had not been in vain, rage began to take over from the hysteria; pure, primitive, rage.

'It's Melissa!' she cried, repulsed by the thought of what had been happening downstairs while their child lay mutilated and senseless in her bedroom.

'What about Melissa?'

'It's unbelievable. She's all floppy . . . Her skin's . . . I can't explain, it's so revolting. She's like a . . . a . . . and her eyes. *She hasn't any eyes*!'

Allan frowned. 'No eyes? Darling, you've had a nightmare. Obviously you overdid things today.'

'I DID NOT! Come and see her; come on.' She tugged impatiently at his arm, infuriated by his frequent backward glances. No doubt he was hoping that Alice would wait she thought, and virtually pushed him into Melissa's room.

Their daughter lay exactly as she'd been left. Her arms were bent at peculiar angles, almost as though she were boneless, and her head was no longer the perfect shape that they knew but more like a soft, round ball.

Her eyelids were both open, and now it was Allan who began to moan at the sight of the dark, empty sockets where normally there were her beautiful violet eyes. He shook his head in disbelief, then forced himself forward and put out a hand to touch his daughter's face.

His weight caused the mattress to move, and immediately the head rolled round so that the sockets were directly in line with Allan's own eyes. He leapt away, withdrawing his hand in horror.

'For Christ's sake, what's happened?'

Julie's teeth were chattering with shock and her words half-choked by tears. 'I don't know. I've never seen . . . Feel her. She's completely cold. She's dead, she must be dead.'

'But her eyes! What's happened to her eyes?'

'I don't know!' screamed Julie. 'I don't understand anything. Touch her. Go on, touch her.'

He reached out again and lightly brushed one small, plump hand. It was so cold that he gave an exclamation of shock and pulled his own hand away quickly. Quickly, but not quickly enough, for there was a small, red, burn mark on his middle finger, as though he had been handling ice cubes. He tried to moisten his dry lips.

'You're a nurse; have you ever seen anything like . . .?'

Julie shook her head from side to side, still staring at this boneless, sightless, collection of matter that had once been Melissa. 'No,' she whispered, 'I've never seen anything like it before.'

For a moment they stared at each other across the shapeless mass on the bed. As they moved closer together, seeking comfort in the face of such horror, there was the sound of the front door slamming followed by a cold current of air coming up the stairs and dispersing on the landing, leaving condensation running down the wall next to the stairs, collecting in a small pool at the base of the banister rail.

They jumped, instinctively turning their heads towards the sound. Allan went outside the room, saw the wet wall and felt the last of the cool air.

He himself was frozen to the bone by now, but due to fright, not unexplained currents of air. His teeth chattered and his back ached with tension. Whilst he tried to work out what was happening, Julie gave a loud scream and he rushed back to her side, prepared for almost anything.

Almost anything, but not the sight which greeted him. Melissa was slowly beginning to move; her limbs straightening, her bloated features regaining their delicate outline, and her waxen skin gradually returning to its normal, peaches and cream complexion.

She moaned once or twice and her eyelids snapped shut. Julie and Allan backed away, hands linked for

138

protection. The lids were only closed briefly and then abruptly opened revealing Melissa's normal, wide-set, violet eyes.

The adults glanced at each other as their daughter straightened her legs, sat up and stared at them in surprise.

'Is it morning? Liss cold.'

Allan felt tears of joy running down his face as he took his beloved child in his arms and held her now warm, supple body close to his. 'No, darling, it isn't morning. We heard you crying and came to see what was wrong. I expect it was a bad dream. Come on, let's get you under the covers and warm again.'

Melissa dimpled and smiled and meekly let him fuss over her and tuck her tightly in before kissing her for the fifth time. She looked behind her father and her eyes met Julie's. Julie's were cool, almost detached, because although still in shock she was no longer terrified, for now she thought that she understood.

'Mummy kiss!' commanded Melissa. Reluctantly Julie advanced towards the bed, but it was difficult to get past Allan. 'Let Mummy kiss Liss,' commanded her daughter, quickly regaining her position as a two-and-a-half year old despot. Her father shifted slightly and Julie planted a quick kiss on Melissa's cheek.

'Go back to sleep now,' she murmured. 'Uncle Russ is coming to see you tomorrow afternoon, so you need your beauty sleep.'

'Uncle Russ,' she mumbled contentedly, and closing her eyes fell into a deep and normal sleep. They watched her for five more minutes before daring to leave the room. Once on the landing, Allan released a sigh of relief.

'My God! I thought we'd lost her. What was it do you suppose? Some form of hysteria?'

'Hysteria? What about her eyes?'

'I meant *our* hysteria. We must have panicked, over-dramatised things. Children's bones are very supple, it's easy for them to take up positions an adult would find impossible.'

'Really, Allan!' She could scarcely believe her ears.

'I'm right; I know I am. It was a trick of the light, that's all. The best thing we can do is forget about it before we let our imaginations run away with us.'

He was talking quickly, desperately trying to stop Julie from saying anything he didn't want to hear. She knew that, and realised with dismay that she was slowly beginning to despise him for his increasing weakness and blunt refusal to face facts.

Looking at the damp wall she ran her fingers along the banister rail, causing small drops of water to drip onto the stair carpet.

'Are you sure it wasn't a mutual nightmare?' she asked caustically.

'Of course not. Don't be silly! We're both over-tired and . . .'

'Silly!' Julie glared at him, all patience gone. 'You are being incredibly obtuse, Allan. Do you honestly expect me to believe you? Tell me, is this nasty charade being stage-managed by a mutual acquaintance of ours? I think I have the right to know.'

'I've no idea what you're talking about.'

'Really? What time is it?'

Allan looked puzzled. 'Three o'clock.'

'Three o'clock! What happened? Did you decide to sleep on the settee?' Her voice was deceptively gentle.

'No. I was reading and . . .'

'What book?'

'The . . . that blue one with a busty blonde on the cover.'

'And I take it you were deeply engrossed?'

'I'm afraid so. I knew you wouldn't want a bedside light on, which is why I stayed downstairs.'

140

'It might interest you to know that Russell took that book back to the library for me yesterday. Now, if you've nothing to add I'm going to bed.'

He dropped his eyes to the floor and watched her walk away, knowing with certainty that his behaviour tonight had driven a wedge between them that nothing would ever remove.

Julie couldn't sleep. She lay awake, turning the events of the evening over and over in her mind. The only logical conclusion went so far beyond what even Julie had suspected that she tried every other possible solution to explain Melissa's condition. None of them were acceptable, and finally the unbelievable had to be believed.

Accepting it was difficult enough, living with it was even worse. She tossed around in the bed, trying to work out how she would treat Melissa from now on; no satisfactory answer came to mind.

If Allan had been free, instead of bewitched by Alice, then he might have helped her, but that was definitely out of the question. After his feeble attempts to explain away the horror of the evening she knew that she was alone.

Until Alice got what she wanted she wouldn't go, Russell had already made that plain. Since he also felt that Alice must be thwarted a bargain had to be discounted.

In fact, when she finally fell asleep at five a.m., she still had no idea how she would cope from now on. All she knew was that Allan mustn't be blamed. However she felt inside about his liaison with Alice's temporal body she wouldn't let him know. Too many innocent people had suffered from Alice's machinations when she was alive. Allan wasn't going to become a victim now that she was dead. Julie would stand by him, feign ignorance, and pray that eventually Alice would be banished and her husband would once again be free to return her love.

Fortunately, next morning they scarcely had a moment alone together. Melissa poured her cereal over the tablecloth, and Isabelle decided to keep her mouth permanently open so that all her food simply spilled straight out. Whether it was deliberate naughtiness or another symptom of her lack of intelligence Julie didn't know, but she was grateful for the fact that it kept her too busy for conversation.

Allan was equally anxious not to discuss the previous night. He left for work twenty minutes early and wouldn't meet Julie's eyes as he gave her the briefest of kisses on the cheek. Even when Melissa clung round his neck and planted a full, if somewhat sticky, kiss on him he didn't respond. In fact he grabbed a piece of kitchen roll and wiped off the cereal with an expression of distaste.

Julie didn't think it was her imagination that made her see distinct signs of apprehension on her husband's face when he was near Melissa.

As the front door closed behind him Melissa jumped down from the table.

'Uncle Russ come soon?' she piped.

'After lunch. You're going to toddler group today. Wendy is fetching you and bringing you home again.' She knew that her voice sounded different, curt and harsh.

'Why?' Melissa's eyes were suspicious.

'Because I still need plenty of rest.'

'Does your head hurt?'

'No.'

'Your throat?'

'No! Just leave me in peace, please.' Melissa chuckled and went to wash her hands in the bathroom.

Wendy was prompt. As soon as Melissa had gone, Isabelle went to sleep in her cot, so that Julie had time to do some hoovering and cleaning before lunch. She was

142

surprised at how much it exhausted her. The doctor wasn't completely right she thought. She *was* physically weak, and even if the cause was mental, it still had to be coped with.

Chapter 11

At three o'clock Russell arrived. By then Melissa had nearly driven her mother mad with her incessant whining for 'Uncle Russ,' but when he came she scarcely deigned to notice him after the initial kiss and hug. She simply took the small bag of sweets that he'd brought her and ran upstairs, presumably to play with her toys.

'You look very tired,' he commented, settling down comfortably in Allan's chair.

'I had a . . . disturbed, I suppose you'd call it, night.'

'Isabelle?'

'No, Melissa. I'll tell you all about it, but please don't say anything until I get to the end. All right?' He nodded and Julie began her tale. Most of the time she was talking he kept his head down, staring at his knees and listening intently. Only the incessant swinging of his left foot betrayed his agitation. When Julie finally finished he lifted his head.

'Hadn't you guessed? Didn't you know that it had to be something like that?' he asked quietly.

'No! I realised that Alice and Melissa were connected in some way, but more along the lines of Melissa being used as a transmitter or something similar.'

'Have you ever seen Melissa and Alice in the same room at the same time?'

144

'No, but . . .'

'And why did you imagine I warned you to stay away from her after Alice showed you her specialised line in horror?'

'I didn't think. I was so frightened I simply did everything you said without questioning it. All I wanted was your presence. I suppose I dimly imagined that Melissa herself might look – well, frightening in some way. I never imagined that she isn't really . . . hasn't got . . .'

'Substance?'

Julie nodded.

'Well, I knew. Or perhaps I shouldn't say knew, but I thought it probable. Melissa is so much like Alice on her baby days. You remember that revoltingly childish manner she would adopt when trying to wheedle something out of her father. I loathed her winsome, piping voice, although it was certainly effective with him. That's all Melissa is. One facet of Alice's countless personalities. She isn't real, Julie. I'm quite sure of that. I don't believe that Melissa is truly alive.'

'But that's ridiculous! I gave birth to her. I carried her round inside me for nine months. She's no spirit from whatever world Alice inhabits, she's flesh and blood. If she falls and cuts herself she bleeds. She's real enough, Russell. That's why I won't let you take her out on your own. I've always thought that you might . . .'

'I used to think about it, but then I realised there was no point. Melissa is the least harmful thing Alice has done to our family since she died; and since I'm sure I know why she's put her here, and feel positive I can prevent her from succeeding, I'm slightly more tolerant than in the early days.'

'Tell me,' urged Julie, her eyes dark and shadowed with fear. 'Tell me what Alice wants.'

'I can't.'

'Why?'

'It's something I'd rather keep to myself. You've got enough to cope with as it is.'

'I have a right to know,' she said, her voice rising. 'After all, Melissa does live in my house, and is to all intents and purposes my daughter. I need to know.'

Russell smiled reassuringly. 'No, Julie, you don't need to know. Trust me; but never, ever lower your guard when Melissa's around.'

Julie sighed and lay back in her chair. 'Do you remember all our summers with Alice well, Russell? I do. They're clearer in my mind than things that came later, after Alice died.'

'Are they? Naturally I can remember them well, but I can remember the years after, too. The summers were just as hot, and we enjoyed ourselves as much as when she'd been alive. Well, for a couple of years, until my nerves let me down for the second time. I've been on so many pills since then that my memory isn't what it used to be.'

'If you're always seeing what I saw yesterday, I'm not surprised. Russ, if Alice doesn't get whatever it is she's after, what will happen? Will she remain with us for the rest of our lives? Is that why we've got Melissa, as a perpetual reminder? I don't think I can stand the strain of wondering and waiting. Isn't there any way of banishing her?'

Russell frowned. 'I'm looking into it. I use the public library a lot; in fact they probably think I'm thoroughly weird judging by the books I request!

'The trouble is that although there are a lot of well-documented visitations from the dead, both benign and malignant, I can't find any incident when positive actions by the living have changed things. Occasionally moving house or calling in a priest seems to have worked; but we know that moving house doesn't trouble Alice, and I don't really think we can call in a priest. He'd need to know too much.'

'Alice thought the church was ridiculous. Filthy rich and preying on superstitious fears she used to say.'

'She didn't say that the fears weren't always groundless by any chance?' asked Russell.

'I don't suppose she knew. After all, none of us understands about dying, souls or after-life, do we? We make up our own minds and either hope we're going to get a bonus by living on in a kind of spiritual paradise, or else accept just one life and cram in every experience possible to our three score years and ten.'

'Mmmm. Why was Alice here last night? It was careless of her considering that you were alone upstairs, near enough to Melissa to hear her whimpers.'

'She was here for Allan. I smelt the scent of sandalwood on him when he ran up to look at Melissa. She could have been here for hours, in fact she probably was – Melissa was icy cold.'

Russell leant closer to his sister. 'You thought that Allan was the answer didn't you? Well, obviously he isn't. If anything he's assisting Alice, not diverting her. Your marriage hasn't helped us one iota.'

'It has! Things are quite different now that I'm away from the house.'

'Let's be honest; Allan isn't helping to keep Alice at bay.'

'No, but he has made me extremely happy.'

'You're happy at the moment are you?'

'Of course not! But that isn't Allan's fault.'

'I think it is.' Russell's eyes glittered. 'I've always hated him; such a smug, self-satisfied man, and quite unforgivably plebian. I'd like to get rid of him. He's committing adultery with Alice, you do realise that?'

Julie moistened her lips. It was at times like this that her nurse's training proved useful. She simply had to treat her brother as she would a mentally disturbed patient; divert him and bring him back to reality.

147

'I don't think adultery with a dead soul would be grounds for divorce, Russell! It *isn't* his fault, we both know that. Besides, I love him. I've loved him from the moment we met, and I'd never want any other husband.'

'I wish I knew why.'

'I can't explain. It was such an instantaneous attraction, and it hasn't diminished. I love Allan. You have to accept that, even if I can't tell you why because I don't know myself. So, no more talk about getting rid of him, all right?'

The excited gleam in his eyes had gone, to be replaced by a dull acceptance. 'I suppose so. It was just . . . Well, it's like everything else. After the first time it becomes easier.'

'Easier yes, but not addictive. That could lead you into a lot of trouble, Russell; trouble you don't deserve.'

As they had talked so the winter evening had been drawing in, and realising that the room was in virtual darkness Julie switched on one of the wall lights.

It was only then that she saw Melissa sitting silently on the leather pouffe, her arms round her knees and her head bent down, revealing the vulnerable white skin on the nape of her neck. Julie tentatively put out a hand and stroked the child's flesh.

'How long have you been here?'

'Me just come now. Play school time.'

'Is it? Turn the television on then, I'm going to make both Uncle Russ and myself a mug of tea. Would you like a drink?'

'Pretend beer, please.'

Julie walked away to pour out the dandelion and burdock that represented beer. Behind her, she heard the television and Play School's familiar signature tune.

With a smile she plugged in the kettle.

As her programme got under way Melissa turned to her uncle. 'You're pathetic,' she spat at him, and there was nothing childish about her voice now, 'a pathetic, useless excuse for a man. You think you're clever, but you're not. Just a little more time, a few extra visits, and you'll be finished. Locked away for life, a gibbering lunatic. How does that appeal to you?'

'You bitch,' he whispered. 'God, I hate you. Do you honestly think that you can frighten me more than you've done already? You've been playing the same hand for too long, little Alice. I'm stronger these days. Much, much stronger.'

Melissa stared for a moment, then gave a small sigh and slumped to the floor. In her place was Alice: Alice as she'd been on that last day; tanned, dressed only in a microscopic bikini, and laughing at him.

She began jeering, just as she'd jeered that terrible afternoon. He shrank back as she advanced, feeling the awful damp coldness that surrounded her. She stopped in front of him and held out her hands. Hypnotised by her eyes he reached out and grasped them, letting her pull him gently from the chair.

This was new, different. This time Alice was beautiful, not damaged and broken, but golden and perfect, just as he remembered her.

'Don't be afraid,' she whispered, 'come with me.'

All at once he was standing where they had last stood together, their bare feet clinging onto the sharp slate-grey rock. She laughed over her shoulder as he took those familiar few steps up to her, then it changed.

The sea grew rough, the waves began to break over their rock; huge, white-crested waves that threatened to pull them both into the water. He tried to move, but now Alice had his hand firmly imprisoned in an unbelievably strong grip, and she pushed him remorselessly towards the swelling sea.

He spluttered and gasped, then glanced at the almost green water and saw the largest wave imaginable

149

heading for their rock. He tried to escape, but couldn't. Alice held him securely and when the wall of water crashed over their heads she gave him a push in the small of his back and then skipped away so that he found himself gasping and choking as sea water filled his nose, mouth and eyes.

He tried to breathe, but it was impossible. The water was now sucking him down, down into freezing oblivion. To his terror-filled mind it seemed that there could be nothing worse, but he was wrong. Even as he tried to stop struggling and hasten his end the current slammed him back against the rock upon which he had been standing.

He crashed face down onto the sharp, bone-shattering slate and felt his nose crunch and his teeth shatter. Not only felt it happen, but even tasted the warm salt stickiness of his blood as, for a brief moment, the water subsided and he moaned feebly, aware of countless broken bones yet still hoping for a miracle, anything that could prevent the sea from taking him again.

His water-filled lungs and the force with which he had struck the rock made breathing virtually impossible, however he did manage one brief, pain-filled gasp before the deathly cold wall of water returned and sucked him away; down into the rock-strewn depths where he knew he was most surely going to die. There was one final flash of pain as though his chest was about to burst, and then nothing but the overwhelmingly bone-chilling cold.

'Here we are,' said Julie cheerfully. 'Your beer's in the glass, Melissa. Take it off the tray.' Melissa slowly got up from the floor and carefully took it. Then, as usual, she returned to the flickering images on the screen in front of her.

'Here's the tea, Russ. I took a while because Isa-belle . . .' She stopped abruptly and stared at her brother.

He was huddled against the back of Allan's chair with his legs pulled up off the floor but spread out over the winged arms, much as a child of seven or eight might sit.

His eyes were fixed on something far away in the distance. They were dark and fear-filled, and as she approached she noticed how the tendons of his neck stood out like whipcord while he laboured frantically for breath. One hand was groping for his throat in an attempt to ease some obstruction, but every short, rasping breath sounded like that of a man choking to death.

'Russ! Russell, what's the matter?' He didn't answer. 'It's me, Julie. You're safe, Russell. You're quite safe.' She touched his rigid shoulder, there was no response. He continued to gasp until there was a brief respite followed by one shocking, piercing scream and then he fell ominously silent.

For a dreadful moment she thought that he was dead, but his pulse – though weak – was there and his eyes did not have the blankness of death. He was alive physically. However, his mind had retreated beyond her reach. Reluctantly she left him in order to telephone their doctor. He knew all about Russell, and would do everything that was necessary.

Half an hour later her brother had gone. Carried out on a stretcher, the look of horror still in his eyes but completely mute. She watched him go and was filled with apprehension. She needed Russell, needed him all the time. It was obvious that this wasn't going to be a short stay in the private hospital where her parents had finally agreed to him going during his first breakdown. This time he was going to be gone for weeks, possibly months, and without him she was horribly and terrifyingly alone.

The doctor had left before Russell, anxious to speak to the parents. He knew that Mr Pask in particular regarded his son's illness as a somewhat unmanly and anti-social disease that could be cured by a hard day's work with firm discipline. He would probably recommend the reinstatement of national service, he usually did. Even so, his grief and bewilderment would be genuine, and Mrs Pask doted on her son. There were times when the doctor hated his job.

As the ambulance drew away, Julie sat down by the kitchen table and burst into tears. She wondered what on earth had happened while she was out of the room. What new nightmare had Russell been forced to endure this time? He had been showing signs of strength lately, but plainly they were misleading; either that or Alice was determined to break him for ever.

Abruptly Julie went into the living-room, turning the television off and standing between the set and her daughter. Melissa gave a scream of annoyance.

'What happened?' demanded Julie. 'What did you do to him?'

'Uncle Russ poorly, doctor come.'

'Stop that bloody childish way of talking. What did you do? WHAT DID YOU DO?' As she spoke she began to shake the child by the shoulders, getting a savage delight from Melissa's inability to free herself. She watched the golden head shaking to and fro and increased the power of her hold, yelling the same question over and over.

'Julie! What in god's name's going on here? Let her go. You'll kill her if you're not careful. Get away from her at once!' Allan's voice broke the spell. Automatically she released her hold and stepped back, watching as Melissa sped sobbing into her father's arms, where she was petted and soothed as she hiccuped her way back to coherent speech.

'Mummy cross. Mummy bad to Liss.'

Scarlet with fury and with his lips tightly closed to hold

152

back his words, Allan carried Melissa carefully from the room. He didn't see her glance back over his shoulder to smile maliciously at her mother who stood silently in the living-room with tears rolling down her cheeks.

Julie didn't know whether she was crying for Russell or for herself, but she most definitely wasn't crying for Melissa.

She remained in the living-room for a long time. Allan took charge of both children and gave them tea, then their baths and Melissa's bedtime story, and all the while Julie sat, thinking.

When Allan finally joined her he was carrying a cup of coffee for himself, but nothing for his wife. She didn't notice the petty snub amidst the ever-growing terror infiltrating her life.

'Well?' His tone was belligerent.

'Well, what?'

'Don't you think that you owe me an explanation? I come home early from work to find you throttling the life out of our oldest daughter and you never say a word, not even an apology. She was terrified; she clung to me like a baby all the evening.'

'Yes; I expect she did. Alice clung when she wanted to be childish.'

'But we're not talking about Alice, are we?' We're talking about Melissa.'

Julie stared directly into his eyes. 'They're the same person: you know that.'

'The same person? Don't be ridiculous! I'm beginning to wonder if mental instability runs in your family. First Russell, now you.'

'You've heard about Russell?'

'That's why I came home early. Your mother rang me at work. Why didn't you do that?'

'You and Russell are scarcely close. I didn't consider it

important enough to bother you at work; you're always so busy there.'

'He's been admitted to The Manor, I gather. What happened?'

'I don't know. I was in the kitchen making a drink. Only Melissa was there.'

'You mean that she saw him have this . . . this fit or whatever? She had to watch that, then you turn on her and try to kill her? You *are* insane. I'm not surprised about Russell, he's always been peculiar, but you of all people. Steady, competent, Julie; the perfect nurse and eternal shoulder upon which to lean!'

Julie remained silent.

'Come on, I'm still waiting. Why were you assaulting Melissa?'

'Because she knew what had happened and wouldn't tell me.'

'Are you surprised? At two years of age she's probably not up to coping with men freaking out before her eyes. You should have been comforting not punishing her.'

'Allan, Melissa isn't a normal two-year old. You know that. She isn't any age; she's a part of Alice.'

Allan's colour heightened and his voice was tight with fury. 'A part of Alice? You really have gone round the twist. Alice is dead, remember?'

'Yes, Allan, I remember. But do you? When she visits; makes love to you; whispers her promises in your ear, do you remember *then* that she's dead? Or is it only later, when she's gone, that you realise? I've often wondered. Perhaps you could enlighten me?'

There was a long, long, silence. Allan took a sip of his coffee and his cup rattled against the saucer. Dumbfounded he leant back in his chair and closed his eyes.

Julie waited. The silence was almost a tangible thing, enfolding them both, isolating them from reality.

At last he lifted his head. 'You know!' he said softly, his voice shaking with shock.

'That's right, I know.'

'But how?'

'Because I recognised the signs. You no longer want to touch me; you drift through your days irritable and distracted unless Alice has deigned to visit you, in which case you exist in a state of euphoria until she keeps you waiting again. When that happens it's back to the beginning. I've seen it all before remember, when Alice was alive.'

'Then you believe in ghosts, spirits or whatever? Have you ever seen her yourself?'

'I believe in the unquiet dead,' said Julie softly, ignoring his second question.

Allan bowed his head. 'I must apologise, even if you do understand what's happening. I simply can't re-kindle my love for you, Julie, and God knows I've tried hard enough. You see, Alice is, I don't know . . . the epitomy of erotic love I suppose, and when she stays away I get . . .'

'Desperate?'

'Precisely! She's an obsession, and an obsession it's impossible to lessen. Unfortunately I can't even surfeit myself of her so that my appetite sickens and dies as the bard said. The more I see her, the more I possess her, the greater my need.

'I disgust myself, but I can't change the situation. Isn't it possible to tire of Alice?'

Julie heard the note of fear in his voice, a note that had once been familiar to her. It was how Alice had affected all her men, and listening to Allan's words and watching his haggard features she hated Alice more than ever. 'No,' she said pityingly, 'no one ever tired of Alice. Only Alice was allowed to end relationships, and it was impossible to know how long each one would last.'

'Then *she* may tire of *me*?' All at once there was a gleam of hope in his eyes.

'She may, but I doubt it. After all, there can't be many men who are able to see her materialisations. You have to be special – or so I'm told – and obviously you're special. More sensitive, with an open mind concerning life after death. I'm surprised, but plainly it's a gift that you possess.'

He rubbed his knuckles against his chin. 'I don't think it's a gift I want any more. To tell you the truth, Julie, Alice is beginning to terrify me.'

'Yet you protect Melissa! Even after last night, when you must have realised that as Alice uses up all her energy to become, however fleetingly, a facsimile of a flesh and blood woman so Melissa ceases to exist. Her physical form remains, but that's all. An empty husk is what we saw last night. Once Alice left Melissa revived. You know I'm right, but still you protect the child. Why?'

There were tears in his eyes. 'Because Alice told me to. If I don't she'll never come to me again, and I can't live without her. I simply can't, Julie. I'm sorry, but it's the truth. Besides, I still think of Melissa as my daughter.'

'I'm sorry too; it seems there's nothing to be done. One question: do you love me at all any more?'

'Yes! Yes, of course I do. Not in the same way as I love Alice; I mean not in the same physical sense, more as a brother loves his sister. I imagine that I feel the same way about you as Russell does. I know it isn't a lot, and I'm truly sorry, but it is something.'

'I wish I could be grateful, unfortunately I can't. Not when I remember how we started out.' Her voice broke.

'Do *you* still love *me*?' he queried.

'Yes, unhappily I do. I'll try and get over it though.' She fought desperately to keep her grief under control.

'Please don't! You're a very desirable woman. If I can only get rid of Alice . . .'

'You won't, Allan. You're another of her victims. From now on there's no point in me loving you because you're lost. You're no longer the person I met and married. All your emotions are focused on Alice. If I can learn not to love you then perhaps, but only perhaps, I'll be able to survive on the few crumbs of kindness she allows you to let fall in my direction.'

'But . . .'

'And it's all my fault, darling, that's what makes it doubly hard. If you hadn't met me then your life would have been normal. You could have had a wife and children and been content, but because you fell in love with me you're lost.'

'I'm not lost. I admit at the moment she . . .'

'You're doomed, Allan. I only wish that I knew why. If I understood what Alice wanted I'd be able to counter-attack, but I don't.'

'She loves me, it's as simple as that.' To his horror he heard a note of pride in his voice.

'If only it were,' she said sadly.

'Why try to complicate things?'

'Because Alice was always devious. I've no doubt you satisfy some kind of need in her, but ultimately she's after more. Russell knows, however he won't tell.

'I've loved you so much, Allan, and I envisaged such a wonderful life for us. We were happy, briefly, weren't we? You didn't meet Alice before me? No, you couldn't have done.'

He swallowed a hard lump in his throat. Tears were spilling down Julie's face, and more than anything he wanted to comfort her. His guilt over Alice bore down on him like a weight. 'No, I didn't meet her until . . . well, after we were married.' It scarcely seemed tactful to say it was the night before their wedding, or to men-

157

tion his occasional glimpses of her on the fringe of groups during their courting days.

'And we *were* happy?'

'Yes! What's more, we will be again.'

She shook her head. 'No, we won't; not now that Alice has you.'

It was true, and finally he accepted this. 'It's all such a terrible waste,' he cried. 'We're like puppets waiting for Alice to pull our strings.'

To his shame he felt tears wet on his cheeks as well.

'I'm sorry, I'm being feeble. I suppose it's the shock of finding out that you know when I've been terrified of discovery for so long. The whole situation's grotesque.'

'There's nothing grotesque about us, Allan. It's Melissa who's grotesque.'

'I know that!' He continued to cry. 'I do realise she's not a normal human being, but she isn't grotesque. She's too beautiful to be grotesque. Besides, I'm her father.'

'And I'm her mother,' she reminded him.

'Are you? The night it happened, the night she was conceived, I didn't think I was making love to you. I thought that you were Alice. She came to me, she was lying with me, arousing me, exciting me; it was Alice all the time, never you.'

Julie blinked. The words were painful, but she was grateful for his honesty. 'Is that true? I sometimes wondered. Nevertheless, I carried her and I gave birth to her. It still doesn't prevent me from accepting that she's grotesque.'

'Stop it! I mustn't think like you. Alice will be angry. I'm meant to protect Melissa. Alice likes having Melissa in the house.'

Julie's brain registered this first tangible clue as to what Alice was doing, and the realisation that she might be close to discovering the motive for everything was exciting but terrifying.

158

'I think we'd better go to bed,' she said reluctantly. 'There's nothing more to be accomplished from sitting here talking about it. We've just got to make the best of things. Perhaps it would be a good idea if I put Isabelle into Melissa's bedroom and you had the spare. After all, we don't have much sexual contact these days, do we?'

'I like sleeping with you,' he protested. 'Please, Julie, I'd rather stay in our room.' She gave a strained smile.

'It was for your sake, Allan. I don't want you to feel obliged to fulfil the husband's role in bed.'

'You do enjoy our lovemaking when it occurs, don't you?'

Julie hesitated. 'It's very pleasant, but in all honesty, Allan, I can't say it lifts me to heights of ecstasy. That isn't your fault; I've always been the same.'

In the silence that followed she went up to bed, leaving Allan behind to recover his composure. He still wept; he wept because he was lost, frightened and possessed, yet there was no one to whom he could turn for help. All he could do was wait and see if Julie was right.

Interlude

Melissa was bored with playing in her own garden. After a quick glance at the house to check that her mother wasn't looking she slipped through a small gap in the fence and stood for the first time at the top of Alison and Peter's lawn.

Silently she crossed the turf and came to a halt next to Peter, who was wondering if he should have cut back the enormous pear tree in the autumn. Melissa coughed and he looked down in surprise.

'Hello, beautiful! How did you get here?'

'Through the fence. What's that?'

'A spray.'

'What's a spray?'

'It's for killing pests.'

'What's a pest?'

'You are!'

Melissa didn't laugh. Her eyes travelled all over him, and he was startled by the look of calculation on her face. It was identical to the one most women used when they first realised that he was available. He found it remarkable that it came so naturally to even the youngest female.

'Do I pass?' he joked, bending down to her level. Melissa patted his face with one tiny hand. 'Nice man!' she crowed. 'Pretty man.'

'Ladies are pretty, men are handsome.'

'Lift Liss?' She stretched out her arms. He wasn't very keen, but in view of his own impending fatherhood decided to play along with her. He sat on the grass and gestured for her to sit next to him. Instead she perched on his legs and rubbed her hands up and down his jeans.

Peter understood that she merely liked the feel of the material, but he felt strangely uncomfortable and trapped her hands in his. 'Come on, Melissa, let's play pat-a-cake,' She frowned. 'Don't you know it?'

'No.'

'I'll show you.'

For the next ten minutes they practised and Melissa quickly grasped the mechanics of the game. Soon she was giggling with pleasure, then rolled around on the ground as Peter started to tickle her waist and stomach.

Just when he was becoming worried about over-exciting her she slipped beyond his reach and stood up. The sun was behind her, shining directly into Peter's eyes, and it took him a while to realise that with slow, sensuous movements she was peeling off her wool dress and cotton underwear until finally she was naked before him.

'Liss pretty?'

He was terrified in case Alison or Julie should look out of an upstairs window and misinterpret the scene.

'Very pretty. You'd better put your clothes back on. You'll catch a cold, and in any case young ladies aren't meant to take their clothes off in front of gentlemen.'

As he spoke the sun went behind a small white cloud and he caught a glimpse of wanton amusement in her large, violet eyes. She smiled demurely. 'Bullshit!'

'What!'

'Liss sit?'

I'm going mad, he thought. 'Sure, you sit, only put your clothes on first, OK?'

'No. Liss happy. Liss wants to stay like this for ever.'

'You'll get pneumonia.'

She stamped a small foot. 'Nearly three. Me want to stay nearly three.'

'Oh, I see! Well, you may have a point, but there are compensations for growing older, as I have no doubt you will quickly discover. Probably very early on too!'

'Liss was happy then.'

'Not was, is. Melissa is happy now.'

'Ass-hole.'

Peter blinked. 'I beg your pardon?'

'Plank hole in fence. Me find plank hole.'

He put a hand to his head which was beginning to ache. Why did he keep hearing her incorrectly? Were all little girls budding Lolitas, or was Melissa unusual? He was more certain than ever now that he wanted a son. This small girl was virtually gaol-bait at two years of age. He made his voice firm.

'Melissa, put on your clothes or I shall have to call your Mummy to come and get you.'

'Shan't.'

He stood up. 'Right, I'll call her.'

'I'll tell.'

At the sound of the words he swung round. She wasn't smiling, her face was perfectly blank; blank, but not innocent.

'Tell what?'

'That you touched me.'

For a moment they stared at each other. 'You're sick,' Peter said incredulously. 'You're sick in the head. I've never laid a finger on you.'

'No, Liss *three*, not six.'

He looked down at the small, stunningly beautiful child and sensed a core of corrupt decadence deep within her. Something dark and dangerous that would almost certainly remain hidden from most people all her life.

He'd known a lot of women, and prided himself on being able to pick out and avoid the dangerous ones. He hoped that young men in the future would sense the depravity lurking beneath the glittering surface of Melissa.

'Go home,' he said curtly. 'Go home and don't come back.' For a moment it seemed that she was going to start screaming, but something in his eyes, or some sixth sense of her own, told her that this would be unwise. She glared at him, the hatred naked on every feature of her elfin face, and then finally she slipped the dress over her head.

165

Peter kept his gaze averted from her body until she was covered up again, and when he turned back to her he knew at once that from now on she was an enemy. The hairs on the back of his scalp prickled.

'Peter like Mummy?' she enquired. He was outraged. This tiny child, not yet three years old, had tricked and embarrassed him more in half an hour than any woman ever before. His fury made him indiscreet.

'Yes, as a matter of fact I do.'

Melissa smiled. 'Liss go now. Ta-ta Uncle Peter.'

He watched her walk daintily away and felt immense relief. It was ridiculous, but for a brief time she had actually frightened him. This relief was – although he had no way of knowing it – horribly misplaced.

By the end of the day he had mentally re-written the entire scene, the truth being too incredible for belief. Then, being Peter, having re-written it he promptly forgot the real version of the episode.

Melissa, being Melissa, did not.

Chapter 12

It was March the 21st, officially the first day of spring, but the weather was damp and cold making it difficult to believe winter was really over.

Julie looked helplessly at the leaking washing machine, then surveyed a pile of soiled nappies in the sink. Why did it have to be like this? she wondered. Why couldn't the magic and enthusiasm of their early love have lasted a little longer? Of course she was as much to blame for the atmosphere in the house as Allan. The secret that haunted her every waking moment was exhausting, clouding her judgement and making her irritable and tense. Coupled with which, since she knew about Allan and Alice, it was hardly surprising if she felt depressed and unloved.

In addition there was Russell to worry over. He had been in the mental hospital two months now, but still wasn't allowed visitors. She wrote to him every week; long, chatty letters full of domestic trivia, containing nothing that could cause alarm or hinder his recovery. She hoped that he read them, at least then she was not entirely alone.

This particular morning Melissa was at the toddler group and Isabelle fast asleep upstairs. There were no recent signs of progress in her younger child. After mastering how to sit and how to grasp things, albeit somewhat feebly, she had stopped learning. She was in most respects like a tiny infant, and her cheerful smiles were meaningless.

Frequently Julie found Isabelle smiling to herself despite a dirty nappy, or food smeared round her face and neck where Melissa had been playing 'mothers' with her moving, breathing, much-abused doll.

After their one long, revealing discussion that January evening, Julie and Allan hadn't mentioned Alice again. She had no doubt that he still saw her, but she never smelt sandalwood perfume about him, and for a time he attempted to resume making love to his wife. He never, succeeded, but since Julie had no desire to share her husband with Alice she felt only relief when he finally ceased trying.

On a sudden impulse she grabbed her fur-lined jacket and popped next door to see Alison. At least Alison, although large and still feeling nauseous, would chatter about normal womanly things. For a brief time Julie could forget all about her dead cousin, and the golden-haired daughter who dogged her footsteps whenever possible.

She was thoroughly taken aback when Peter answered the door. He was wearing tan slacks and a chocolate-brown sweater. With a tingle of excitement she realised afresh how handsome he was, and unconsciously her eyes began to sparkle. Colour tinged her cheeks, and she ran a hand through her tousled auburn hair. Peter was quick to notice the signs and he too felt a flicker of excitement. Julie, with her lively nature that could suddenly change to a still, quiet secrecy, had always fascinated him. He also found auburn hair highly attractive.

'I came to see Alison,' she said at last. 'Is she in?'

He smiled warmly. 'Sorry, not today. She's gone to

visit an old schoolfriend. A friend from schooldays that is, not an elderly crone who went to the same school!'

'I did understand! It's all right, it wasn't anything urgent. I simply felt bored.'

'That makes two of us. I'm on holiday, supposedly decorating the bedroom ready for our offspring, but somehow I can't get very interested. Why don't you come in for a coffee? Alison wouldn't mind.'

Julie hesitated. She was very tempted. It was a long time since she had seen admiration in a man's eyes. 'Not today, thanks. I'd like to, but I've left Isabelle alone at home.'

'That wasn't going to stop you staying with Alison!'

She blushed. 'I tell you what. If you're really fed up, come round to me. We can have coffee, and then you might find yourself eager to get on with it.'

'The decorating?'

'Yes, the decorating!'

'Thanks. I'll be round in five minutes.' Once again he smiled his heart-turning smile and Julie hurried back home. She was acting completely out of character, but for once she didn't care.

Peter was normal, attractive, and free of complexes or inner tensions. It would be nice to flirt with an uncomplicated man again. She was feeling increasingly isolated with two children inside the same four walls month after endless winter month, plus a husband who was no longer a husband. Worst of all she was constantly alone with her fear. Peter was the perfect antidote.

When he arrived she led him to the kitchen. He eyed it appreciatively. 'This is nice. Does Allan enjoy decorating?'

'Not really; it was done before we moved in. My father paid for it. He bought us the house as well.'

'Lucky you!'

'Yes, lucky me.'

Peter raised his eyebrows. 'You don't sound as though you mean that.'

'Don't I? Oh well, it's one of those bad days we all get. I'm feeling sorry for myself. The trapped little-woman syndrome!'

He looked surprised. 'I always think of you as perpetually cheerful. A kind of local agony aunt for Alison!'

'You make me sound very dull! Besides, Alison doesn't need an agony aunt.'

'Of course she does. I'm sure you've heard all her tales about my philandering; my unreliability; my susceptibility to a pretty face and good legs!'

'She loves you very much. Even if she does sometimes mention things like that she's very loyal. I think *you're* extremely lucky.' He gave her his very warmest smile.

'I am. A faithful and worshipping wife and the prospect of a lot of money. What more can a man ask for?'

'Precisely.'

'Well, I'll tell you, aunt Julie; it's a small thing called excitement! I suppose it's the equivalent to salt in cooking; without it everything's flat and tasteless.'

Julie laughed. 'That's a very good line! Almost as good as the one about only Alison being fit to bear your children!'

He grinned. 'She told you that, did she? Well, it went down splendidly with her, and now she's about to do that very thing.'

'While you continue your affairs because she's unwell, shapeless and rather tiresome with her complaining. You really have got a nerve. Don't you feel in the least guilty?'

'Guilt is a waste of time and energy. You only live once, so live well. Alison doesn't mind that much; in her heart she's proud to think that other women chase after her husband. It shows what a good catch she made.'

'Alison is afraid to face up to the enormity of her

170

mistake, that's all!' She was enjoying the verbal sparring.

'You're quite wrong. My dalliances with other women turn Alison on. She likes to hear the details. Whispered descriptions of how they perform; it's quite normal, second-hand voyeurism!'

Julie put down her mug and smiled. It was impossible to resist him. He was obviously without conscience, but so supremely confident of his personal attraction that nothing and no one could dent his good-naturedly high opinion of himself. He was his own man, and whatever you thought of his morals he was at least honest. Honest, and more important to her, normal.

'It wouldn't suit me,' she said firmly.

'You'd turn Allan out if he strayed?'

She thought of Alice, and all that his obsession with Alice involved. 'No,' she said slowly, 'but that's because our relationship isn't as intense as yours and Alison's. I wouldn't like him moving swiftly from one affair to the next, and I most certainly wouldn't want to hear about the other women.'

'I don't suppose you need to worry. He looks thoroughly reliable to me.'

'You sound as though you mean boring.'

'I wouldn't know about that. He might be the most fantastic husband on earth. Sometimes appearances are very deceiving. Still, I don't think he can be, otherwise you'd sound more positive about him. If you ever get too bored you can always let me know.'

Julie looked at him. He was smiling, but he put out his right hand and covered hers where it was resting on the breakfast bar. 'I mean it. I find you a very stimulating challenge.'

'Why a challenge?'

'I don't really know. There's something different about you; and before you ask that isn't one of my

171

standard lines.'

'I'm very ordinary indeed,' she said firmly, wondering how she could lie so convincingly.

'Fine. Well then, I'd better make a start on that bedroom as it doesn't look as though there's more than coffee on offer here this morning! I enjoyed our chat, and don't forget what I said.'

'I shall most definitely forget what you said! You get off home and think about Alison and the forthcoming responsibilities of parenthood!'

Immediately he remembered Melissa. He thought briefly of mentioning the scene, but then changed his mind. He wanted Julie, and worrying her about her daughter wasn't going to advance his cause. She'd probably think he was a paedophiliac who'd created the entire situation himself.

'I'm leaving! Try and think of something exciting you want to do, and then do it. You look in need of some excitement, and when you're old and infirm you'll look back on these years and wish you hadn't wasted them.'

'At least you won't suffer that agony!'

'I doubt if I'll even get old and infirm; some irate husband will probably catch up with me first! Don't forget now, I'm only next door.'

She stood up. 'I've got to admire your cheek! I'll come to the front door with you, Melissa's due back any minute.'

At the sound of the name he hesitated, then bent down and brushed his lips against Julie's forehead. 'Thanks again for the chat. I feel like a new man! You were right; I can hear Melissa tripping daintily up the path. See you.'

As he walked out so Melissa walked in, and neither of them looked at the other.

'Did you have a nice time?' Julie enquired, helping her daughter undo her duffle coat.

172

'Yes. What was he doing here?'

'Having a cup of coffee and telling me about Alison's baby. Did you do any drawings today?'

Silently Melissa handed over a sheet of black paper, then dragged off her outdoor shoes and walked upstairs to look at Isabelle.

Julie studied the paper. The drawing had been done in chalks, and the black surface was covered in blue and turquoise swirls and one large dark-grey lump.

She studied it from all angles, gave a rueful smile and put it on the kitchen table. She would ask Melissa what it was meant to be when she came down.

All at once the phone rang. She was astounded to hear Allan's mother on the line. His parents had seen less and less of the couple since the birth of the children. Julie frequently quizzed Allan about the reason for their lack of interest, especially considering Allan was their only child, but he was as puzzled as his wife.

She also sensed that whereas at first they had liked her this had changed, and their original warm acceptance had turned to a cool, remote politeness.

'We thought we'd like to drop in on you this afternoon,' the older woman said briskly. 'We were going to play golf but the course is flooded and it seems a pity to waste the spare time.'

'I'd love to see you. About two? That's fine. Thank you for phoning.' With a frown she replaced the receiver: the words had been right, but beneath them there was definitely this repressed chill. She wished that she knew what was wrong. She didn't need any additional problems in her life, Alice was quite sufficient.

Melissa got hopelessly over-excited when she heard they were coming. She insisted on wearing pink dungarees and a bright yellow jersey, then spent ages in front of her mother's mirror brushing and re-brushing

173

her blonde curls. 'Pretty,' she crooned as Julie pushed
her aside. 'Liss pretty?'

'Devastating; now I'd like to see what I can do to
improve myself.'

'Nuffing!' giggled Melissa and ran down to the living-
room where she pressed her nose to the window.

She too knew that her grandparents didn't care for
either her or her mother, but unlike Julie she knew why
and hugged the pleasurable secret tightly inside her. It
was all so exciting. She found it hard to bide her time
waiting for the conclusion to everything, but there
wasn't such a very long time to go now.

'Grandma and Grandpa's here!' she shouted as their
car drew up, then ran to open the front door. Julie
reached over her head and released the catch. Her
mother-in-law had a smile on her face that failed to reach
her eyes, and didn't attempt to greet Julie with a kiss,
instead she ran a hand through Melissa's curls.

'Me brushed them!' she shouted. 'Now all spoilt!'

'Don't be silly,' admonished Julie, holding her face up
to her father-in-law. He mumbled something and
extended a hand, which she in turn ignored. 'Come into
the living-room,' she said stiffly. 'Isabelle's in her
playpen.'

'Sweets?' asked Melissa beguilingly as her grand-
father bent and kissed her, smiling reluctantly when she
widened her glorious eyes at him and then lowered her
thick lashes.

'Sorry, we forgot,' he murmured, missing Melissa's
look of fury as he walked away.

'Isabelle's grown a lot,' Julie pointed out as Mrs
Firmager approached the playpen.

'Yes. She isn't a bit like our Allan though, is she?
Come to that neither's Melissa.' She made it sound like
an accusation rather than a comment.

Julie looked at blank-eyed, white-faced, slack-lipped

Isabelle and turned to the other woman. 'Do you think she looks like me, then?'

'Just a little, my dear. If she were more alert she'd be very like you.'

'And Melissa?'

She glanced at her oldest grandchild. 'No, Melissa isn't like you. We can't imagine who she looks like, can we, George?'

Her husband murmured something non-committal and busied himself with his pipe.

'Liss went playgroup today,' said Melissa, tugging at her grandmother's expensive cashmere skirt.

'That's nice, dear.'

'Mummy had man in. Nice man stay with Mummy.'

The older couple exchanged a brief, complicit glance. 'Who was that, Julie?' she asked, and Julie cursed herself for blushing like a schoolgirl when there was nothing to blush about, unless thoughts were a crime.

'Peter from next door. Alison – his wife – is a good friend of mine. She's away for a few days so I promised to keep him supplied with coffee and tea while he decorated the smallest bedroom. Their first baby's due soon.' She wondered if she'd over-elaborated but Mrs Firmager had plainly lost interest and started to look round the room.

Her eyes came to rest on a small framed photograph of Russell. 'How is your brother, Julie? Any better.'

'A little, but it will take time; breakdowns do. It isn't like healing a fractured leg you know.' She knew that she sounded sharp, but she hated their faintly patronising air of superiority, as though mental illness was something suffered only by the already feeble-minded.

'Of course being a nurse you'd know more about these things than I do, but I'm afraid that in our day people were told to pull themselves together. An absorbing job might have helped him.'

'I doubt it.' Despite herself Julie was becoming increasingly annoyed.

'A congenital flaw you think? Well, it makes sense,' and the older woman's eyes went straight to Isabelle.

Not trusting herself to speak Julie went into the kitchen to put on the kettle. When she returned with the tray of cups she found Melissa dancing round with her arms extended, her steps graceful and not in the least child-like. Mr and Mrs Firmager were watching her in surprise, but Julie had known another girl who had danced equally gracefully and her hands began to shake.

'Does she go to classes, Julie? She looks very accomplished.'

'Not yet; she's still too young.'

'Where did she learn to dance so well?'

'Not here I'm afraid! She's a fairly graceful child. Dancing will probably come naturally to her, foxtrot and all!'

'No one dances properly any more,' said Mr Firmager gloomily. 'All this leaping about to flashing lights and blaring noise. I can't understand where the pleasure lies.'

'At least it doesn't involve classes, which makes it easier for everyone to join in. I can remember how the boys who grew up with me all hated dancing classes and left as soon as they could.'

'Allan went,' stated his mother with pleasure.

'Well, I'm afraid you wasted your money. He's got two left feet!'

Her mother-in-law ignored the remark. 'Speaking of Allan, his father and I are rather worried about him.'

Here it comes, thought Julie, the reason for the visit: Allan. I should have guessed. 'Why's that?' she enquired politely.

'He's changed so much over the last two years. He used to be such a friendly, outgoing young man and he

176

took all his troubles in his stride. Now he looks permanently harassed and exhausted. We can't help worrying.'

Julie wondered what they'd say if she told them about Alice, and how exhausting Alice could be, then quickly lowered her eyes to conceal her expression. She could understand their fear.

'He's very busy at work,' she pointed out. 'Besides, it does make a difference when the children come along. The troubles aren't quite such "little" ones after that, and there are new responsibilities to be faced.'

Mrs Firmager drained her cup and stood up. She fixed Julie with a penetrating stare. 'Quite. Marriage itself entails a lot of responsibility. All those vows aren't just a formality, they're the very foundation for a lifelong partnership.'

'I agree.'

'We brought Allan up carefully, and instilled him with a good set of moral principles. Unfortunately not everyone has the same set of values.'

'I suppose not but . . .'

'We don't want to see him hurt,' put in George. 'He's devoted to you and the children, as you must be aware.'

'I really don't think . . .'

'We know *that*,' responded her mother-in-law coldly. 'What we're doing now is asking you to try and do so in the future. We would never disillusion him about you. In a way I feel guilty myself, but that's neither here nor there as far as you're concerned. We wanted you to realise that we know what's happening and we'd like it to stop. I'm sure you understand me.'

'No! I'm sorry, but I've no idea what you're talking about. If you could elaborate a little?'

'Certainly not! We've said what we came to say and that's the end of it. You must realise why we don't spend a lot of time with the children; we do try to make an

177

effort for Allan's sake, but it isn't easy. We're disappoin
ted in you, Julie, very hurt and disappointed. Come
along, George, I think we should leave now.'

Julie rushed into the hall after them. 'Please, I don'
understand! What have I done wrong?'

'Very well, I'll spell it out for you. We know you're no
a faithful wife. Now, it's said. I shan't mention it again
Just remember, we know.'

'That's ridiculous!' Julie burst out. 'I'm not the one
. . . I've always tried . . .'

'Not, it would appear, hard enough. Good afternoon
Julie.' With one final glacial stare she walked out of the
house, and she never entered it again.

Back in the living-room Melissa sat cross-legged on
the floor watching as Isabelle tried to put a hand through
the mesh of the playpen. 'Dumb!' she exclaimed poking
out a tongue at her sister who laughed, then promptly
wobbled and fell from a sitting position onto her back
She lay there, arms and legs waving in the air.

'Isabelle playing beetles!' Melissa told her mother as
she entered the room. Julie didn't even glance at the
playpen. 'Don't be silly,' she responded automatically as
she sat down, her mind still dwelling on the extraordinary behaviour of her in-laws.

While she sat thinking Melissa trotted away, then
returned bearing her drawing from the morning. She
thrust it onto her mother's lap. 'Liss's drawing.'

Julie nodded. 'I know. I saw it.'

'Nice drawing.'

'Yes.'

'Pretty drawing!' she persisted, picking it up and
thrusting it under her mother's nose. 'Look!'

'I have looked. What's it meant to be?'

'Seaside.'

'Really? What's that grey thing?'

'Rock. A big rock.'

178

She took the picture from Melissa and studied it more carefully. Of course, she should have known at once. It was all there. The bluey/turquoise hues of the Cornish sea that day, the grey slate rock that had been an attraction to them all, and was the reason why they had chosen that particular cove for their own special place that year.

As she studied the chalky scribbles so they became more real; she could almost smell the sea, and hear the sound of the breakers as they began their slow but steady advance towards the rock.

Up in the sky Melissa had drawn a round orange blob, and now Julie could feel its heat and pictured Alice in her vivid red and green bikini stretched out, her arms and legs positioned so that she resembled drawings of pagan sacrifices. It was not a far-fetched theory; she had been pagan, but not a sacrifice, not an intentional sacrifice.

The salt spray almost seemed to blow off the sheet of paper. Julie moistened her dry lips and tasted the tang of the sea on them. She flung the paper away from her and watched it float in the air and then fall to the carpet where it landed face up. Now it was once again a childish scribble, a toddler's attempt to recreate a seaside. A seaside that she had never seen.

Quietly the child retrieved her drawing and ran away to her room with it, her eyes alive with excitement and her mouth upturned in her own special smile.

When Allan returned that evening Julie told him about his parents' visit, and merely remarked that they hadn't been very easy to entertain. She didn't want to tell him what had been said until she had worked out what it meant herself.

At first she had automatically thought of Alice; but it was impossible to imagine Mrs Firmager ever seeing a ghost, and Alice wasn't likely to bother with such a petty piece of malice. Alice liked big dramas, not trivial squabbles.

'That was nice. I told you they like you. They're not the gushing kind, that's all. Unlike your parents they've left me to get on with my own life. They don't interfere.'

'You've never thought that might be due to indifference?'

'I've considered it. Certainly they didn't plan any children, and I must have got in their way at times, but perhaps it's better than having a family like yours with the parents unwilling to let go. Look at the way they pander to Russell. He might have benefited from some healthy indifference. Visiting them's never easy either. It's like seeing a psychologist. Your mother's so intense about every remark.'

'That's quite untrue, she's simply interested in us all. She likes to know we're happy. She's always been the same.'

'It didn't work out that way, did it?' Allan sounded almost spiteful.

'Why not?'

'Russell's mad, and you're just another discontented housewife. I wonder what will become of little Jill?'

'Allan! Whatever's wrong? Why the bad mood?'

'I'm not in a bad mood. If I don't come home chattering nineteen to the dozen I'm in a bad mood these days. What do you want? A live D.J. to entertain you in the evenings? If so tape one and play him non-stop as soon as I get a little dull.'

'I don't know what's got into you but you're becoming quite impossible to talk to.'

'How dreary for the little woman!'

Julie could have wept. He sat there, his face set in a frown, his tone peevish, and hurled insults at her family after she had endured an afternoon of his mother's cryptic insinuations. She wondered how much longer she could endure the strain of living with him.

'Never mind,' she sighed. 'I gather from your black

mood that Alice isn't around much these days.'

'She's broken her promise!' he shouted, jumping up from the table so fast that his chair toppled over behind him. 'She swore that after you and I were married she'd always be with me, but she isn't. She isn't! And when she does turn up nothing's the same. She laughs at me! Can you believe that?

'She instigated the affair. She sought *me* out; and now, when I see her she laughs. I swear to you if she were alive I could kill her with my own bare hands! That's what she's reduced me to, an impotent, would-be killer!'

All at once his anger left him and he began to sob. Julie watched for a moment, then slowly collected up their dirty plates.

'That was Alice's weakness,' she said softly. 'She never knew when to stop. She didn't realise that you can drive people too far, that even the most stolid, down-to-earth man has his breaking point. You'd do better to stand up to her.'

'I can't! You knew her, it isn't possible. Every moment we're together is too precious to waste in recriminations; besides, her laughter always comes after, never before.'

'After what?'

He hung his head. 'You must know.'

'Yes, unfortunately I do.'

'Do you know what I wish?'

'Tell me.'

'I wish I'd never set eyes on you, then none of this would have happened, would it?'

Julie blinked away her own tears. 'No,' she murmered. 'It's all my fault, but I didn't know it would happen. Believe me, if I'd had the faintest inkling of the damage our marriage would to to you I'd never . . .'

Just then the telephone rang, and with relief Julie went to answer it.

'Russell's coming home tomorrow, he's much better,' gushed her mother excitedly. 'The doctors are *very* pleased with him. He's on some new drug, but he doesn't behave as though he's heavily sedated. He looks really well. I knew you'd want to be told, darling.'

'That's fantastic news, Mother. I'll come over in the afternoon, shall I? The girls won't bother him, he's so used to them.'

'If you could he'd be delighted; he's very anxious to see you.'

'Good. I'll be with you around two o'clock. Bye for now.'

In the kitchen Allan had begun washing up. 'Barmy brother coming out is he?'

'Yes,' she said placidly, determined not to let him pick a quarrel.

'Will you be back here in time to cook the evening meal? Or is that too much to ask?'

Despite her good intentions her temper flared. 'Listen, Allan, I shall stay there as long as I like. If you can't cook yourself ask your precious Alice to help. She does everything else a wife's meant to do. I should however warn you that she was quite useless in the kitchen, in case you're considering it a viable prospect. Now I'm going to bed. I've had quite enough of your company for one evening.'

After she'd gone Allan rested his head on the breakfast bar and closed his eyes. A few moments later Melissa put a small hand on his knee. 'Daddy sad?'

He stared at her, trying to find Alice in the tiny, fragile face of his daughter, but he couldn't. Melissa was so innocent and guileless. He picked her up and sat her on his knee.

She wound her arms round his neck and kissed him on the mouth. He drew back; the kiss was over-intimate, almost adult. She looked hurt, and he felt terrible. He

182

was too Alice-obsessed even to respond normally to his daughter. To try and make it up he hugged her until she squealed with laughter.

'Liss pretty?' she asked, shaking her curls coquettishly. His sense of unease returned.

'Very pretty, but being a nice person is more important, Melissa.'

'Bullshit!'

'What?' He couldn't believe his ears. Her face was so child-like and pure he decided that he'd misheard.

'Boys kiss pretty girls,' Melissa continued.

'Do they kiss you at playschool?' he teased.

'Yes. Not very well, though.'

'What do you mean by "very well" may I ask?'

'This,' she whispered, and placing her lips on his, flicked her tongue into his mouth. He grabbed her shoulders and tried to hold her off but she wriggled on his knees and blew gently into his left ear.

She was changing shape beneath his hands, womanly curves pressed against his chest and one hand reached low to fondle and arouse him.

He resisted with all his strength, self-disgust fighting with his natural male reaction, but as he looked into her violet eyes, now darkened by excitement and passion, he finally accepted that this was no child, no daughter of his flesh, and the guilt faded. With a groan he sank back and let Melissa/Alice work her magic on him with lips and tongue until he climaxed with a spine-tingling shudder.

For a few moments he lay there exhausted and replete. Then he opened his eyes and saw his daughter standing by the chair, staring at him with tears in her eyes; eyes that no longer resembled Alice's.

'Daddy nasty,' she said in her child-like treble, and leaning over him spat the sticky white fluid over his trousers.

183

'Go away,' he groaned. 'Just go away and leave me alone.'

'No! Liss want cuddle.'

'I'm never cuddling you again, whoever you are.'

'Liss tell at playgroup.' Her eyes now began to sparkle with obvious pleasure at his shock and disbelief.

'But . . .'

'Cuddle.' She held up her arms. Numbly he reached forward and lifted her up. She sat perfectly still with her thumb in her mouth, the epitomy of a little girl who loved her father.

Suddenly it was too much. Allan pushed her violently off him and only just reached the sink before he began to retch. He was sick for a very long time, and when he had finished Melissa had gone.

Slowly he started to sponge the stain off his trousers. 'God help me,' he prayed silently. 'God help us all.'

Chapter 13

When Julie hurried into her parents' house the following afternoon she was horrified by the sight of Russell, especially after her mother's lyrical description of his appearance the previous evening.

He was scarcely recognisable. His face was thin; the cheeks hollow, the eyes sunken, red-rimmed and shadowed. They also burnt with an almost fanatical light that frightened his sister. He seemed tranquil enough, greeting his nieces with kisses and embracing Julie tightly, but his hands trembled constantly and his head kept twitching round in a nervous tick, as though searching for someone lurking close behind him.

'You look well,' lied Julie cheerfully. He gave her a cynical glance, making it clear he was under no illusions as to the state of his health.

Their mother twittered round them for what seemed an eternity before leading Melissa out into the kitchen to help arrange the biscuits on a plate. She also took Isabelle, carrying the heavy child on one hip. It gave Julie and Russell a moment alone together.

'I know I look ghastly,' he stated. 'Mother doesn't seem to notice, or rather she's determined *not* to notice, but I'm not retarded. I see my face every morning when I shave. I'm beginning to look like the consumptive hero of an old-fashioned novel.'

'Why? What's caused all this?'

'Alice, of course. Who else? Julie, I thought she'd already made my life unbearable, but believe me it was nothing, nothing at all, compared with what I've been through these past months. There were times when I feared I'd never retain my sanity. If there's a hell that's where I've been.'

'But why?' she whispered. 'Why now, after so long?'

'Because she realises that I know what she's doing. She doesn't feel safe with me on the loose, hence my enforced stay in the hospital. Unfortunately for Alice modern medicine and strong willpower have outwitted her, for a short time.'

'Tell me,' she urged him. 'If you know, and your danger is so great, then tell me. That way I'll be ready for her, because this involves me, doesn't it?'

He gave a strange laugh. 'Of course it does! Julie, you do remember everything don't you? Everything that happened on the day Alice died?'

'Yes.'

'Yet you never talk about it.'

'It's over. I don't want to discuss it ever again.'

'All right, I can understand that; but at least think about it. That way you'll be forewarned. I can't tell you, I suppose I'm too much of a coward, all I can do is be here on hand ready to act when she strikes.'

'Russell, I sometimes think . . .'

He never did hear what she thought because just then their mother came back with the children, and the telephone began to ring stridently in the hall.

Mrs Pask answered it and when she came back her pallor made the rouge on her cheeks stand out. 'It's Allan, Julie. He's calling from his parents' home. His mother collapsed and died half an hour ago. It was her heart the doctor says.'

186

Julie stared in disbelief. 'Is he still on the line?'

'Yes.'

'I'll speak to him. It doesn't seem possible, she was such an energetic person.' Stunned she left the room.

Allan sounded numb, but he dissuaded her from leaving the children with her mother and joining him. 'It's all right. I can handle everything, and besides my father doesn't seem to want . . .'

'Me?'

'Anyone, Julie. He's absolutely lost. It's such a shock. She was never ill in her life and now . . . She wasn't even old. I probably won't be home until about nine tonight.'

'I'm terribly sorry, Allan. I'll be home by four so you can reach me there if you need me. Give my love and sympathy to your father.'

'I must go now.'

She heard the click as he replaced the receiver, and was thankful that she'd kept quiet about his mother's accusations. At least she hadn't driven a wedge between the pair of them at the end. She had nothing to reproach herself with; and secretly – although she scarcely dared to admit it – she was relieved that the woman was dead.

Russell appeared exceptionally distressed by what had happened. 'Why did she die?' he demanded over-loudly, causing his mother to fidget nervously and glance at the bottle of tablets standing on the bookshelf.

'She had a heart attack, I suppose. It's not a bad way to go, but hard on the one who's left behind.'

'I don't like it. It's the beginning. It has to be.'

'Beginning?' asked his mother. 'What sort of beginning?'

Russell gave her a glance of such scorn that she physically flinched. 'Of the end naturally, what else? Everything that begins has to end. That's right, little sister, isn't it? You know that. You know . . .'

'Russell!' Her voice was like a whiplash.

All at once he stopped, and slowly sank back into his chair. 'It's true,' he mumbled as tears of weakness and frustration began to run down his face. 'It's true, Julie, I know it. This is the beginning, and I'm so damn weak I'll be useless. Christ, I wish I knew how it was going to happen!'

He thumped one thin, bony hand on the arm of his chair and then leant back exhausted, his lips moving silently.

'What's the matter with him?' Mrs Pask's voice was high with fright.

'He's been very ill and he's weak, that's all. Don't expect too much from him.'

'But they said he was better. I thought that once he was home with us he'd be completely well again. Why should Allan's mother's death upset him? It doesn't affect Russell.'

'Any death would upset him right now,' Julie lied smoothly. 'Give him one of his tablets, he'll soon settle down.'

He did, but it meant that Julie and her mother carried the burden of conversation, which was difficult with Russell staring straight ahead, apparently unaware of his surroundings but occasionally twisting his head round over his right shoulder with eyes that were enlarged by fear.

At three forty-five Julie decided to leave. The children had been good, but Melissa was starting to get restless and Isabelle needed a clean nappy. Russell watched her preparations for departure with haunted eyes. At the last moment she bent over and kissed him on the cheek.

'Take care, Russell. I'll be over tomorrow if I can, but it does rather depend on poor Allan's father and the endless red-tape of death. Try not to brood, Russ. Please, for my sake.'

He didn't answer. When she reached the living-room door she glanced back. He was staring at her with a look of

188

ill-concealed despair. 'It's happening too soon,' he said, regardless of his mother and the children. 'I'm not ready.'

'Russell, darling Russell, there's . . .'

To everyone's astonishment he burst abruptly into noisy weeping, his head in his hands, his back bent in a gesture of hopeless resignation. Julie's flesh pricked with fear but she summoned up a bright smile and hugged her mother tightly. 'Don't worry about him, Mother. It will take a long time, that's all.'

'But he's talking utter rubbish. He isn't making a word of sense. Shouldn't I call the doctor? He's getting worse at home, not better.'

'He wants to be at home, and that's what matters. Bear up! I'll call in some time tomorrow, whatever happens.' Her mother nodded, biting her bottom lip to hold back her own tears.

She was no longer young and had lived in troubled bewilderment for so many years that she felt far older than her biological age. With a sigh she watched Julie and the children drive away.

She was not a woman capable of great passions, but there had been many times when she had wished with an almost religious fervour that Alice had never been born. Everything had started to go wrong after Alice died.

She looked in on Russell, who now appeared to be sleeping, and then went into the kitchen. Being busy was the answer. It always had been, and so she bustled around and made a far more elaborate dessert than she had originally intended in order to keep her thoughts away from the demon-ridden young man in her living-room, and the terrible way in which he was gradually losing his tenuous grip on reality. At the back of her mind lurked the biggest fear of all; that one day he would enter the mental hospital and never come out.

It was after nine o'clock before Allan arrived home. He looked grey with fatigue and shock. Sitting him down in

189

the living-room Julie prepared a toasted sandwich and a large mug of hot, sweet tea. He ate and drank without any apparent awareness of his actions, and it was only after he'd finished that he spoke.

'Dad's taken it badly.'

'I'm not surprised. She always seemed very fit. Why doesn't he come and stay with us for a week or so until the funeral's over? He shouldn't be left on his own in the house.'

'I invited him; he wouldn't come.'

'Did he say why not?'

Allan fidgeted uncomfortably. 'He's not himself. He's developed some extraordinary theory that all isn't well between us. He says that he's never setting foot inside our house again.'

'That's nothing new. I didn't tell you, but when they called round yesterday your mother intimated the same thing. Mind you, I was the one they were blaming. I didn't mention Alice.'

'Alice?' He stared blankly at her. 'Why should you have done?'

'Because she's what's wrong with our marriage! I can't imagine how they could have known anything about her though.'

'They didn't.' You're right, it's you my father's blaming.'

'I see. Does he explain why?'

'For God's sake, Julie! His wife's just died. Do you honestly expect rational conversation from him right now?'

'Well, what did you say?'

'I said we were fine. He didn't believe me, but I kept repeating it.'

Julie frowned. 'When's the funeral?'

'Next Monday.'

'I'll ask Mother to have the girls. Is is morning or afternoon?'

Allan cleared his throat. 'Darling, I'm afraid he doesn't want you to attend.'

There was complete silence. In the distance a dog barked, then a train hooted as it approached the nearby level-crossing. Julie sat as still as a statue and waited for Allan to explain.

'I'm really sorry,' he said at last. 'I don't understand him, but as it's his own wife's funeral I can't very well insist that you come.'

'I'm *your* wife, and the mother of his grandchildren. People are going to think it extremely odd.'

'We'll say you're ill, or that Isabelle couldn't be left.'

'You may say it,' she said angrily, 'but don't expect me to back you up. I won't say anything unless I'm asked, in which case I shall tell the truth. It's a calculated insult, and I haven't any idea what I've done wrong. I don't think you realise how hurtful this is.'

Allan stood up. 'I'm sorry, truly sorry. I don't know what it's about either, however he's adamant. I'd like to argue, but quite honestly he isn't up to any kind of confrontation.

'I had to promise to spend Sunday night with him as well. He can't face sleeping alone in the house the night before the service.'

'Fine. Why not move in there permanently? Establish a private retreat for the times when your family get on your nerves? No! Why's that I wonder? Because you can't bear to be parted from us? Or because you know that Alice won't come to you there?' The bitter words tumbled out one after another.

Allan opened his mouth to reply. 'It's immaterial to me,' she continued angrily, 'so don't trouble to make yourself sound like a devoted family man in order to soothe my ruffled feathers. I've got more to worry about than some imaginary vendetta your parents cooked up.'

'Julie! My mother's dead.'

191

'That doesn't excuse her. I'm sorry she's died because she was comparatively young and it's a waste of life, but don't expect me to forgive her for that final afternoon of insults I suffered.'

'I had no idea . . .'

All at once the anger drained away from her. He looked so unhappy and exhausted that she instinctively moved towards him and put her arms round his chest in a gesture of comfort. For a moment he put his head on her shoulders and she could feel him trembling. 'I wish it had all been different,' he murmured. 'I'm sorry it's turned out so badly.'

'It's not our fault. Besides, it could be worse. At least we don't hate each other.'

'I think this is worse. We both know how good it could have been. I sometimes think that knowledge adds to Alice's pleasure.'

Secretly she agreed, but she told him not to be foolish, then sent him up to bed while she tidied round and laid breakfast for the next morning.

All the time she worked she kept remembering Russell; his gaunt, haunted face and fear-ridden appearance. It frightened her. Normally Russell didn't frighten her, but then normally his fears were for himself and this time she sensed that they were for her.

The next few days passed peacefully. Allan had time off work to arrange all the funeral details. Julie kept herself occupied with the daily routine of young wives' meetings, toddler group, afternoon visits to the park and the constant battle to keep Isabelle clean and presentable.

As Isabelle grew older her handicap was becoming more and more marked. The mouth was looser, the eyes lack-lustre. In the end she would probably have to go to a day centre for the handicapped thought Julie. Hopefully the specialists could assist her make a little further progress.

On the Sunday, Allan ate lunch with his family, then packed a dark suit and black tie before kissing them all goodbye.

'I'll ring you as soon as the last people have left,' he assured Julie, holding her close. 'Don't worry. If anyone asks I shall mention Isabelle, that's a sure way of stopping them in their tracks.'

All at once she didn't want him to go. She had a terrible premonition that something dreadful was going to happen, and that only by keeping him with her could it be avoided.

'Don't go, Allan. Stay with me, please. Stay here tonight and we'll both go together tomorrow. He can't throw me out in front of everyone. Please, Allan, if you ever did love me then don't go.' She was crying while she talked and Allan's face twisted in sympathy.

'Julie, don't make it worse. I feel terrible about this I really do. I'll soon be back with you all, but I can't let my father down at this late stage.'

With a resigned sigh Julie released him. Dark despair immediately engulfed her. 'I hope it isn't too draining,' she said automatically.

'I hope so, too. Kiss Daddy goodbye, Melissa.'

His daughter stared at him and shook her head.

'Come along, darling. I've got to stay at Grandpa's for the night so I can't kiss you at bedtime.'

'Don't care!'

'What's wrong with her?' asked Allan in surprise.

'I've no idea. Kiss Daddy, Melissa.'

'Shan't. Grandpa not like Liss.'

The adults exchanged glances. 'I suppose children pick these things up for themselves. She probably listened to you and my parents when they came round.'

'She didn't need to listen. She knows everything.'

Allan chewed his bottom lip, reminding himself that Julie was right and Melissa wasn't an ordinary child.

'Well, at least Isabelle will let me kiss her!'

'Isabelle would let a baboon kiss her!' shrieked Melissa with obvious delight at her malicious wit.

Allan quickly turned back to Julie and gave her one final embrace. They clung together with a desperation that neither of them understood. Finally they drew apart, unaware of Melissa's narrow-eyed scrutiny.

'Right, darling; now I really must go.' She nodded, too choked with tears to answer. They exchanged one final glance, a glance in which – for the first time in months – Allan showed love as well as care, and then he left. Julie's grief was as great as if he were never returning.

Melissa ran to the window and watched him leave, and her eyes were filled with knowledge. Slowly, silently, she continued to stare after him. Even when her mother called her she didn't move; she was lost in her own thoughts, and none of them were child-like ones.

Soon, very soon, her second childhood would vanish, and deep down inside her there was a treacherous desire to prevent this from happening, but common-sense prevailed and finally she went quietly to her mother. She had always known that this time would come.

By eight o'clock the children were in bed and Julie was watching television. Allan had rung earlier, confirming that his father was still the same, steadfast in his refusal to see Julie. 'I've put both our names on the wreath,' he whispered, and Julie had a vision of Mr Firmager senior tearing off the card and flinging it to the winds.

'Good,' she responded quietly, and then they said goodnight.

Allan returned to his morose, slightly frightening father, and for the first time he wished with all his might that he had brothers and sisters to help him cope with this tall, silent man. A man consumed by some secret knowledge, clearly imaginary, but nonetheless destructive for that.

Back home Julie watched in boredom as a policeman

194

chased a murder suspect over rooftops as easily as if they were running along the pavement. The sound of the doorbell was a shock, and she made certain that the chain was on the door before opening it. Outside, his collar turned up against the sleety rain that was falling, stood Peter.

Quickly she removed the chain and let him in. He gave her his usual charming smile. 'Sorry to disturb you but I thought you'd want to know. Alison's had to go into hospital, a threatened miscarriage.'

'Oh no! I am sorry.'

'They think she'll be all right if she rests. She isn't even allowed to watch television.'

'That wouldn't over-excite her if what I'm watching is anything to go by!'

'Where's Allan?'

'At his father's. The funeral's tomorrow.'

'Of course. Who's having the children for you?'

'No one. Isabelle's going through a difficult stage and . . .'

'Lucky you. Highly depressing things, funerals!'

Once they were comfortably settled in the living-room Julie poured them both large brandies and they chatted desultorily about their respective partners.

The brandy was potent, and Julie found herself unwittingly saying too much, revealing that she and Allan were no longer close.

Peter sat listening, his glass virtually untouched. He was an expert when it came to handling women, and at precisely the right moment he crossed the room and sat on the arm of Julie's chair. She didn't move or protest, so he put one hand on the nape of her neck and gently moved his fingers to and fro. She gave a small sigh and her shoulders relaxed slightly.

She was aware of what was happening, and she welcomed it. She yearned for some affection, a carefree moment in contrast to the normal demon-ridden days of her life with Allan, Russell and all the tension that accompanied them. For as long as she could remember she had been the strong one; always reliable, always sensible.

Suddenly she felt unable to cope. She resented the deceptions and concealed hurts that were her constant burden. Peter's visit was like a dream, offering a brief escape from the sense of encroaching darkness that was all around her since Allan's departure.

She had no illusions about Peter. He was a man who liked women and enjoyed a conquest, but at least he never tried to unload his troubles onto her. He was also highly experienced. Perhaps with him she would find love-making the earth-shattering experience so many women talked about. Even if she didn't she wanted the sheer comfort of another body close to hers. She needed someone to love her – physically love her – at least for one night. When he undid the zip at the back of her dress and slid it from her shoulders she made no protest, instead she turned towards him.

'Love me,' she whispered. 'Please, Peter, love me.'

He was certainly knowledgeable about women. His hands knew the precise places to touch; he was slow and gentle, there was no sense of urgency, none of Allan's barely concealed impatience when she took too long to become aroused.

Once or twice, as his fingers made delicate circular tracings over her flesh she could see a look of puzzlement in his eyes, but he made no comment beyond whispering to her to relax. 'There's all the time in the world,' he assured her. 'Let go; enjoy yourself.'

Slowly she began to unwind. It was pleasant and flattering to have a man devote so much time and trouble purely to giving her pleasure. She appreciated that, just as she appreciated his lack of questioning. He wasn't a man

196

who asked a woman what she wanted, or issued instructions as to what he expected, he simply let his hands and mouth travel over her body noting for himself what particular touch brought forth the strongest response.

Julie began to float. Her body was warm and her mind at peace. There wasn't going to be an earth-shattering climax after all, she accepted that even if Peter didn't yet, but she was at last free and happy. He whispered a question, she murmured consent and then felt him enter her.

He took her slowly, there was no heavy thrusting with this man, instead he was slow and gentle, filling her more completely than any man had done before, and all at once she felt the beginning of a deep inner tingling that promised more. Instinctively she moved against him, suddenly aware that perhaps it was possible, perhaps he was the one who would remove the secret fear of frigidity from her mind for ever.

Sensing what was happening he quickly slowed, changing his rhythm to hers in an attempt to help her. It was near now and she began to move her head from side to side, small moans coming from her mouth. She was almost there, and opened her eyes to try and see his face. She wanted to be looking at him as it happened.

It was a disastrous decision. Peter's face was shadowed, it was impossible to study his features, but behind him, looking over his shoulder and laughing with child-like glee was Alice. Alice wearing a turquoise-blue strapless silk dress, its bodice cut like the petals of a flower, her bronzed shoulders gleaming below the fall of golden hair.

Julie screamed and Peter, mistaking the sound, finally allowed himself his own climax before collapsing on top of her. She scarcely noticed his weight. She was hypnotised by the sight of Alice advancing towards them. Her small hands were clapping together in mock-applause, and there was an expression of such gloating triumph in her eyes that Julie was terrified.

Alice moved round the couple and stared down at their entwined bodies as they lay on the cream sheepskin rug. Slowly her smile faded. Her dress began to fade as well, the turquoise colour deepening to a shade of light green.

Then the dress lost its shape and became tattered. Pieces of cloth fell away from Alice's exquisite body, leaving her naked except for the green shreds which still clung to her. Only they weren't shreds of cloth. They were tendrils of seaweed, and they bound themselves tightly round her slender arms and tiny waist.

Julie moaned again and struggled against Peter's weight, but he didn't move. He seemed to be in an exhausted stupor and she could have screamed at him in her impotent fury at his masculine indifference to her comfort.

Alice raised her neatly pencilled eyebrows and shook her head, but for once a good-looking man was of no interest to her, she was intent upon her victim, Julie.

There was a physical lump of fear in Julie's throat; she knew that soon Alice's flesh would begin to tear and bruise. Hypnotised by the apparition she lay rigid and motionless, unable to close her eyes and shut out whatever horror Alice had in store for her.

Quickly the face began to disintegrate, but this time the blood from the cuts inflicted by the Cornish rocks flowed freely and dripped down onto Julie's face. Alice crouched at her cousin's head. 'See!' she hissed. 'She what you did to me.'

'No! It wasn't me. I . . .'

'Fantastic!' mumbled Peter, his weight still fully on her. Alice smiled, and as she did so three of her teeth fell from her mouth. She whimpered again, and now Alice's face was within two inches of her own. She kept her eyes on her cousin, waiting in frozen terror for what she sensed would be the ultimate horror.

Alice hesitated, then gave a small cry herself and her hands flew to her face. Paralysed Julie waited, her lips parted in a silent scream. For a moment Alice remained in the same position then, almost in slow motion, her hands came down and as they did so, her right eyeball came out of its socket and made its way down her bruised and battered cheek before falling with a ghastly plopping sound into Julie's open mouth.

It was too much for her sanity, and as Alice faded silently away so Julie began to scream aloud. She screamed and screamed at the top of her voice, shaking in every muscle, her mind scarcely able to apprehend the gruesome reality of what had happened.

Peter leapt off her, instinctively groping for his clothes. 'What the hell's the matter? I didn't rape you. You wanted it, and you enjoyed it. You . . .'

Julie ignored him. She got up and ran to the kitchen where she stood gagging over the sink. Filling a glass tumbler with water she rinsed it round and round in her mouth before spitting it out with great force.

She studied the water, but it was clear and uncontaminated. Her tongue moved round her mouth in a tentative exploration, and almost immediately encountered it. It was like having a small, peeled grape behind her front teeth and she screamed again, spitting furiously into the sink trying to dislodge the ghastly object from its position. It wouldn't be moved.

She rushed round and round the kitchen in demented circles, her fingers poking into her mouth. They could feel the eyeball, feel its glassy-damp surface, but they couldn't grasp it. It was immovable, stuck there like a large, sticky sweet.

Peter stood in the doorway watching. 'Have you gone mad? You'll wake your children, not to mention the entire street. What the hell's the matter?'

She gagged again and rushed up to him, gibbering, and

pointing inside her mouth. He peered into it, his dark eyes no longer tender and loving but apprehensive and bewildered. He wanted to get away, fast.

'There's nothing there!'

She poked the handle of one of her wooden spoons into her mouth, determined to prize the grisly object off her palate, but all she did was make herself retch and the spoon handle slid round the eyeball, completely ineffective.

She ran up to Peter again, flinging her arms round him. 'Help me!' she cried. 'In God's name, help me!' He backed away from her, fastening his trousers and fumbling with his shirt buttons. She looked like a mad woman as she shrieked. Her hair was tangled, her eyes wide with some invisible horror.

The marks of his lovemaking stood out sharply on her breasts and thighs, and her shuddered to remember how carefully he had caressed that flesh, how much he had desired to conquer her, to prove that she wasn't immune to his charms. Now he wished that he had never set eyes on her. She was obviously insane. He remembered Alison telling him about Julie's brother who had been put into a mental hospital, and wished that he'd paid more attention.

'I can't!' he shouted, pushing her away so that she struck her hip against the sharp edge of the draining board. 'There's nothing there. You're imagining it. Keep away from me.'

'It's her eye,' she moaned. 'In my mouth, her eye.'

He stood rooted to the spot, unable to believe his ears. 'You need a doctor,' he whispered. 'You're mad, completely mad.' Without taking his gaze off her he edged slowly out of the kitchen and into the hallway. Once there he found enough courage to turn his back on her, and then hurtled out of the house, leaving the front door open to the biting wind. He didn't care who saw him

200

or what they thought. He had only one desire now, to get away.

Julie knew the moment that he'd gone because abruptly the small, slimy, mucus-covered lump in her mouth vanished. Cautiously, unwilling to raise false hopes, she moved her tongue round and round. There was nothing there. It was only then, as sanity slowly returned, she realised that she was standing naked in the middle of her kitchen.

Chairs were overturned; a glass lay smashed in the sink. Still trembling violently she went towards the living-room to gather up her clothes.

Melissa was standing halfway down the stairs. She looked at her mother, stark naked, love-bites on her throat and breasts, and her eyes were as old as time. 'Whore!' she said with a peculiar smile. 'Self-satisfied, goody-goody, Julie, is a whore. Was it worth it? Did you enjoy him?'

With a muffled cry Julie ran away from the dainty, beautiful child still spewing forth filth, and scrambled into her clothes. She spent the rest of the night wide-awake on the settee, terrified lest Melissa joined her or Alice returned, but neither did and finally it was morning. Time to try and pick up the pieces; attempt to blot out the macabre events of the night and start coping again.

Melissa entered wearing a long, cotton nightdress. Her hair was tousled, just as Alice's used to be, and Julie waited tensely but the child merely yawned and rubbed her eyes. Relieved she drew back the curtains and surveyed the pouring rain.

'Grandma will think she's being buried at sea!' exclaimed Melissa, but dispassionately, not with the glee such a comment would normally have brought forth. Julie ignored her entirely, certain that further gloating about the previous night would quickly follow. She was wrong. Melissa was strangely subdued. There was none of her usual sparkle in evidence, and she pushed her cereal round the bowl scarcely eating a mouthful.

Once or twice she looked at her mother with a kind of fearful despair, as though she carried a great burden that she was unable to share. All at once her resemblance to the Alice that Julie remembered seemed to fade, and Melissa appeared both young and troubled.

She was also more affectionate than ever before, occasionally taking hold of Julie's skirt and rubbing the material against her face like a comforter; except that the Melissa of old had never needed comforters.

If Julie's night of horror hadn't been so vivid in her mind she might have puzzled more over this change in behaviour, but all the time, every second of the day while she worked about the house, her mind was re-playing the nightmare that Alice had inflicted on her.

Even now she could recall the viscidity of the eyeball, and the way her tongue had slithered round it so ineffectively. At the memory her stomach heaved again; quickly she turned her attention to Isabelle, unaware of an abrupt look of anticipation that briefly lightened Melissa's features, bringing back the similarity to Alice.

By nine-thirty the rain was still falling heavily and Julie decided not to attempt the trip to playgroup. They would all get soaked, and since Melissa was so lethargic it didn't seem worth making the effort.

At eleven o'clock – the time of the funeral service – the children were both playing in the living-room, and Julie bent her head in a brief prayer for her mother-in-law. She could still remember the time when the Firmagers had welcomed her into their family, and despite the cooling of affection once their grandchildren were born she wished that she could have been at the church. Without experiencing the usual trappings of death it was difficult to believe that Allan's mother was no longer alive.

The day passed very slowly. The rain never let up and

202

the house was permanently dark. Julie made sure that all downstairs lights remained switched on, for the shadows reminded her of night and the torment that night could bring.

After lunch she telephoned Alison's house. Peter answered. However, as soon as he heard Julie's voice he hung up on her. She had only wanted to enquire about Alison, but she understood very well why he didn't want to speak to her. She knew that for a brief time last night she had been out of her mind with fear, and Peter had witnessed it. If their positions had been reversed she wouldn't have wanted anything more to do with him.

By four o'clock she and Melissa were getting restive. Even television couldn't hold the child's attention; she spent most of her time sitting on the living-room window sill, peering out through the rain, her face pressed tightly against the glass.

'Daddy won't be long now,' Julie reassured her at five o'clock. Then, seeing the child's pale, worried face decided to telephone and find out what was going on. Funerals didn't take all day, and Allan had left them early the previous afternoon. His father must appreciate that he was needed by his own family now.

The telephone rang for a long time before Mr Firmager senior answered it. He sounded old and tired, but when he recognised Julie's voice he became stiff and formal. 'Allan left some time ago,' he said curtly.

'How long?'

'About an hour.'

'An hour! It doesn't take twenty minutes to get back here. He must have had an accident. I'll ring the police.'

'He had a lot on his mind. If I were you I wouldn't act too hastily.'

'That's ridiculous! How can you know whether he's had an accident or not?'

'He'll be with you quite soon enough I imagine.'

Before she could ask him what he meant the line went dead. He had hung up on her. Puzzled and worried Julie turned away, nearly falling over Melissa who was hovering beside her.

'Daddy's on his way,' she said. Melissa stared, her eyes so deep a shade of violet that it was once more like looking at Alice. Julie was jolted back to reality. Melissa wasn't a small child, and she couldn't be missing her father. Melissa was a living, breathing part of Alice. She had no existence of her own, she merely represented the dead cousin and mirrored her reactions.

At this thought the subdued fear in Melissa's eyes became even more frightening. It wasn't one troubled little girl standing before Julie, it was Alice – a very troubled Alice.

What could Alice possibly have to fear? she wondered. Nothing came to mind, but the ever-present sense of doom that had been pressing down on her deepened.

Outside it continued to rain, and now the wind had risen so that the drops were hurled against the windows at the front of the house with unusual force. There was a soft moaning sound as the branches of the tall poplars that lined their road bent and shook with the force of it.

The darkness outside seemed somehow to be creeping into the house itself. Julie's head started to throb. As she struggled to lift Isabelle into her high chair for tea she wondered if she could possibly be going to have a migraine. Her skull felt ready to split in two, and the walls of the house appeared to be closing in on her.

A storm, she thought, that's what it feels like; as though there's going to be a terrible storm. But it wasn't like the approach of a winter storm, it was like one of those frightening, humid summer storms that close in on a warm day until everyone longs for them to break and be over.

At five-thirty she lifted Isabelle down, cleaned her face

and put her into her playpen. Melissa had refused her marmite sandwiches, declined a plateful of strawberry ice cream – normally her favourite – and then followed her mother into the living-room. Her eyes followed Julie's every move. Occasionally she would bite at her lower lip as though undecided about some momentous decision.

Finally, at six o'clock there was the sound of Allan's key in the door. Melissa's eyes cleared. She moved over to her baby sister's playpen and busied herself by throwing the soft toys at Isabelle's head. Whatever had been troubling her was over. She withdrew, knowing that for the rest of her life she was merely required to be a spectator, speaking only if her father needed prompting.

Julie rushed out to meet him. He was standing by the front door, rain dripping from his short car coat, his face in darkness.

'Darling, what kept you so long? I was worried sick. When I rang your father he told me you left there over an hour ago.'

'Yes,' he said very softly. 'I had a lot to think about. I drove around for a while.'

'And it didn't occur to you to let me know?'

'No, Julie, it didn't.' His voice was now so soft that she had to step nearer in order to catch the words. He had a wild look about him, staring at her as though she were a stranger. She felt a moment's unease and stepped back.

'Have you eaten? I could always make you something quick.'

'I'm not hungry.' His voice was flat, peculiarly emotionless. He continued to stare at her and she laughed nervously. 'Well, at least take off your coat. You're dripping water all over the carpet.'

'It doesn't matter. It's only rain.'

'Yes, but . . . Never mind. How did your father cope?'

'Very well.'

'Was it dreadful?'

205

'That's probably an understatement.'

All the time that he was speaking she noticed how he kept his hands behind him, almost as though he were hiding a present from her, but the look in his eyes belied that theory. For the first time ever Julie felt afraid of him.

'What's the matter? Why are you looking at me like that?'

'Like what?'

'As though I've done something wrong. Look, if it's this family squabble again can we leave it until the girls are in bed? Melissa's been waiting for you for ages, and so have I.'

She moved forward to kiss him, but was stopped by the look of malevolence in his eyes.

'Missing her Daddy was she?' His mouth twisted into a sneer.

'Yes, of course.'

'Liar!' His tone was soft and pleasant.

Julie was aghast. 'What did you say?'

'I said "Liar!"'

'Darling, you're not well. I'll make you a cup of tea.'

'I'm perfectly well,' he said gently, then took two steps towards her. Instinctively she moved away, but when she tried to escape into the kitchen he quickly blocked the entrance. She was left with no choice but to continue walking backwards into the living-room, followed inexorably by Allan. Allan with a slight smile on his lips and his hands still behind his back.

Julie didn't know why she was petrified, or what he held behind him, but her one comfort was the thought that the children were in the living-room. He was unlikely to cause trouble in front of them. With her eyes fixed on his face she stumbled over one of Isabelle's wooden blocks on the carpet, her left knee buckled and she fell to the ground. As she went to rise Allan's right foot shot out and he kicked her savagely in the chest. She gave a startled scream of pain.

'Shut up and stay there.' he warned her, his voice still uncannily gentle. She wished that he would rant and rave, it was his quietness that made him terrifying.

'I don't even know what it is I've done wrong,' he parodied in a high-pitched voice, before giving a snarl of anger.

'What are you talking about? Allan, what's the matter?' Once again she tried to rise, but he kicked out and she froze, aware that she mustn't antagonise him further.

'Don't you recognise your own words? Your innocent response to my parents' antipathy towards you?'

She shook her head.

'No? Well, I'm not surprised. After all, your life must have involved so much lying that even the truth becomes distorted. Actually, I don't think you know much about truth. All you know about is deceit. You excel at that.'

Julie swallowed hard. 'Allan, let me up.' She made her voice as stern and brisk as a nurse dealing with a recalcitrant patient.

'No.'

'Yes.' This time she got to her knees before his shoe smashed against her face. She felt her top lip split open and the warm blood begin to trickle down her chin.

'Allan!' Her voice was thick, distorted by the injury. 'The children are watching!'

Very slowly he turned his head and met Melissa's unblinking stare as she stood with one hand resting on Isabelle's playpen, the other hanging loosely by her side. When she nodded he switched his gaze to Isabelle. She was making cooing noises, then she dribbled and toppled trying to reach a rattle on the playpen floor. His face reflected his revulsion.

'Ah yes! My lovely daughters. I mustn't make a nasty scene in front of my precious daughters! You bitch! You two-timing little bitch! What a bloody fool I've been.

207

When I think of the months I've been consumed by guilt over Alice. I felt so sorry for you. No one could have been more understanding than you, and that made everything worse. How you must have been laughing at me behind my back.'

'You did it very well; all those tears over what we'd lost through Alice; all those moments when you assured me you understood and forgave. You should have been an actress. Your talent was wasted on an audience of one.'

'But . . .'

'Shut up! Did you realise how much my guilt tormented me? Yes, *my* guilt. *I* felt guilty, but you didn't, did you? Oh no; you carried on in your own sweet way and continued to be understanding about poor, dead Alice.'

He shook his head in disbelief. 'You of all people, Julie. Gentle, loving, Julie. Bitch! Cow! Slut!' With each epithet he kicked out, and this time she protected her face but felt a terrible stab of pain in her chest and knew that a rib was broken.

There was a laugh from Melissa, then the sound of her hands clapping in delight. 'Stop it, Allan!' Julie screamed. 'What's your father been saying?'

'My father?' His voice was light again, almost conversational, and she did wish that he wouldn't keep his hands hidden. 'My father didn't say anything. It was Dr Baxter. You don't know him of course, he was our family doctor for years. More than that, he was a friend. It was quite by chance it came out. It happened when he was leaving. He came up for a last word, unfortunately for you.'

'Why? What did he say?' She was totally bewildered.

'He congratulated me. He actually congratulated us *both* on our courage over Isabelle! Thats quite funny isn't it!' He laughed hysterically.

'I don't see why.'

'You will. He remarked on how few people were willing to adopt handicapped children. He even told me what a wonderful woman you were!'

'Adopt? We didn't adopt her!'

'No, we didn't did we? But you see he couldn't know that. All he knew was that I'm sterile.'

Julie drew in her breath sharply, scarcely noticing the stab of pain in her chest. She shook her head from side to side. 'No! It can't be true. He'd have told you before. How can he say that now?'

'It happened long ago, before I met you. I had mumps very badly and my mother was left with the task of telling me what had happened, but she opted out. She hoped that the doctor might be wrong, that he was being pessimistic. Disgraceful I know; cowardly too, after all she let me marry you under false pretences, although she'd honestly convinced herself that the good doctor was wrong. However she did feel guilty, until she mentioned Melissa to Dr Baxter.

'She was so excited you see, so pleased to prove him wrong. Fortunately his incredulous reaction to her news gave her time to re-think, and she hastily explained that Melissa was adopted. After all, who wants to wash their dirty linen in public?

'When Isabelle came along she couldn't believe that you were continuing to deceive me, but she kept silent. She didn't know what else to do, and once again she told Dr Baxter the same story.'

'She should have told me . . .'

'Well she didn't, and now she's dead, so you tell me this. Who fathered Melissa, Julie?'

'You did!' she shouted. 'If anyone fathered her it was you. There wasn't anyone else, it had to be you. But we both know that Melissa isn't normal. Perhaps she didn't need a father in the biological sense. I don't understand her any more than you do, but I swear to you there was no other man.'

'Do you know I'd be inclined to believe you there. As

you say, Melissa isn't normal, but then there's Isabelle. Isabelle isn't normal either; however, that's quite different. She must have had a father, unless you were visited by the Holy Ghost one night and forgot to tell me!' Again he gave a terrifying giggle.

Stunned by his revelation Julie's mind darted frantically from one explanation to another, and all the time Allan was standing there with the smile still on his lips but murder in his eyes.

She turned towards Melissa, saw her smiling face, and then she understood. She turned frantically to her husband.

'Allan, please listen to me. All this is Alice's doing. She's had it planned right from the beginning. That must be why she picked you, why she made us fall in love. You mustn't . . .'

'Shut up about Alice! Alice is beautiful. She's beautiful, sensual, affectionate and honest. Above all else she's honest. You told me that. You said that Alice never lied.'

'Except by implication.'

'Stop splitting hairs. We're not talking about Alice, we're talking about Isabelle. Who is Isabelle's father?'

Terrified she stared up at him. She shook her head. 'I can't tell you. Please, Allan, don't make me.'

'You'll tell me,' he snarled. 'Sooner or later you'll tell me.' Once again his foot shot out, this time catching her in her side.

She cried out in agony.

'Tell me his name,' he whispered.'

'No.'

Again and again he kicked at her. Blood began to stain her clothes and her face became red and swollen. She cringed at his feet, one front tooth hanging by a thread distorting every word she uttered, but he was implaccable.

The tears streamed down her face as she realised that she had to tell him or die; and she didn't want to die, not now that she knew the reason for everything.

'It was Russell,' she gasped. 'Russell fathered Isabelle. That's why she's like she is.'

'Russell!' Allan's face went blank with shock. 'Your own brother?'

'No! It's not as bad as it seems. You see . . .'

'SHUT UP! I'm glad it was Russell. I've always hated him, and now I know exactly how much he'll suffer when you're dead; and make no mistake about it, Julie, I'm going to kill you.'

'Allan!' She put one torn and bleeding hand on his trouser leg. 'Allan, please don't kill me. I'm sorry. I'll move out. I'll take the girls with me. You needn't see any of us again, but for pity's sake don't kill me.'

'I have to.' He looked down at her bent head with an almost tender expression. 'You see, once you're dead Alice and I will never be apart again. She explained that to me while I was driving round this evening. I could hear her voice quite clearly, although she wouldn't show herself.

'Things didn't work out like she'd hoped when you and I married, she admitted that. It proved difficult for us to meet, but she assured me "kill Julie and we'll never be parted," so that's what I've got to do.

'I can't live without her, therefore you have to die. You do understand that? Quite apart from your betrayal you still have to die.'

'NO! She's lying to you. She lied before and she'll lie again.'

'Alice never lies, remember?'

'Then she's changed. Allan, this is what she wants. Don't let her destroy us. You'll be locked away. Alice won't visit you in prison. How can you hope to get away with it? Be reasonable, Allan.'

'Reasonable! After what you've told me you expect me to be reasonable?'

'Allan, I love you. I always have. I've never loved anyone but you, and that's the truth. Russell was different. I can't explain, but it wasn't the same as the way I feel for you. Believe me, you're the only man I've ever loved.'

For a moment he looked disturbed, and she thought that she was getting through to him. His expression began to change to one of puzzlement. She scarcely dared to breathe, wanting him to choose to let her go without any further pleading. It would be so easy to tip the balance against her again that she didn't want to risk another word.

'She made love to Uncle Peter last night!' stated Melissa, her voice crystal clear in the sudden silence that had descended.

Allan's eyes fastened back on Julie's face. He saw the look of guilty horror on it, and also the realisation that she no longer had any chance. Melissa had done what she had been sent there to do. Julie's fate was sealed.

He continued to stare at her upturned face. Flecks of blood and foam flew from her mouth as she breathed, then her tooth finally fell from the gum and dropped on the carpet at his feet. She looked hideous. A grotesque, blood-splattered figure from a nightmare. She was abhorrent to him, not only in appearance but in behaviour.

At that moment, Isabelle yelled because Melissa had tugged on her hair. Allan turned, saw the baby's bloated, dull face, listened to her slobbering cries and felt the bile rise in his throat as he realised afresh that she was the result of Julie and Russell lying together. A sin against God and nature, and he had been forced to share the punishment.

'Goodbye, Julie,' he said gently and finally brought his hands out from behind his back. In them, there gleamed a large spanner from the tool box that he kept in his car boot. As he raised it above his head Julie screamed again, beginning to drag herself away across the carpet, but

212

Alice's voice filled the room urging him on, a voice that both he and Julie could hear.

Then the madness descended on him and he began to strike out blindly, raising the spanner again and again. As Julie's blood bubbled from her nose and mouth the clammy chill of death began to invade her body. Through a pink-tinted mist she made one last hopeless attempt to speak to Allan; but as she opened her lips there was a final gush of blood and then nothing more.

Allan looked down at the huddled bundle of blood-stained clothing that only ten minutes earlier had been his wife and gave a smile of relief and satisfaction.

It was only when he heard Melissa give an uneerie, complaisant laugh that he came to his senses. He blinked in puzzlement at the bloody trail where Julie had dragged herself along the carpet, then as his eyes came to rest on her he gave a deep groan of horror.

Melissa sniggered. 'Now what?' she asked pertly. He swung round on her, startled to hear Alice's voice coming from Melissa's lips.

'I said now what?' she repeated.

'I don't know. I thought you . . . I mean Alice . . . I imagined . . .'

'Yes?'

'That you'd make it right.'

'Wrong!' There was no denying the note of triumph behind the statement.

'But . . .'

'Imbecile! You're a stupid, inept . . .' Alice's voice was growing stronger, but for some ridiculous reason Allan's daughter seemed to be fading. She was very pale, her features smudging as her eyelids drooped.

He didn't wait any longer. He had to get away, and he stumbled out to the telephone in the hall. He needed help. There was only one person who could possibly understand; lifting the receiver he began to dial.

213

Chapter 14

When Russell's mother called him to the telephone she looked mildly surprised. 'It's for you, dear. I *think* it's Allan, but he sounds most peculiar. I hope there isn't anything wrong.'

'He's probably broken down somewhere and wants me to go out in this filthy weather and take him home. He's useless at mechanical things. Useless at everything come to that!'

His mother smiled indulgently, but once she had gone Russell's features lost their casual amusement and with a worried frown he picked up the receiver.

'Russell here.'

'Thank heaven you're in. You must come over at once. There's been . . . That is we've had . . . Oh, God!' After that all Russell could hear were muffled sobs. He felt the first stirring of apprehension, but didn't dare ask any questions while his mother was within hearing distance.

'Sure. I'll come right out,' he said easily. When he hung up his brother-in-law was still crying.

'I'm going over to Julie's; Allan's fused every light in the place!'

'But . . .'

'It's O.K. I don't mind helping. See you.' She watched

214

him go, surprised that he didn't even stop to put on a raincoat. Surely, she thought, a few fused lights weren't exactly an emergency? However, the thought was a fleeting one. Russell often over-reacted, and she had long since learnt to ignore his minor inconsistencies.

Her son drove as fast as he dared in the appalling conditions. Alice hadn't appeared to him for over a week now, and with every day that she failed to materialise the worry had grown that if she wasn't with him then she was busy elsewhere.

He hoped to God that he was in time, and that no major disaster had occurred. He hoped, but Allan's hysterical distress hadn't been caused by any ordinary domestic crisis, and normally Russell was the last person he would have called upon for help.

Pulling into the drive he tooted the horn so that they could open the door for him. The rain was coming down like stair rods and he realised that in his haste he'd left his raincoat behind. Despite the horn the door remained obstinately closed, and he was forced to hammer on it repeatedly before the sound of footsteps reached him through the thick wood.

'Who is it?' called Allan, his voice high and shaky.

'It's me, Russ. Let me in you fool, I'm getting drowned out here!'

'Yes, yes of course. Sorry.' After much fumbling and muttering the door swung open and Russell stepped into the hallway. The bulb there was dim and the living-room was in darkness, but he could see that Allan's face had a greeny-white pallor and he was perspiring heavily.

'What's the matter? You sounded pretty distraught; is Julie all right?'

Allan stared at him without answering.

'Well, is she? Or is there something wrong with the girls?' Still his brother-in-law failed to respond.

Russell felt very cold. 'Julie!' he called loudly. 'Julie,

where the hell are you?' Allan touched him lightly on the elbow.

'She's through there,' he whispered, nodding his head in the direction of the living-room.

'Through there? Why isn't the light on?' For a moment Allan was silent, and then he gave a short, hair-raising giggle. 'I thought it better to leave it off.'

Russell stared at the other man. The giggle had increased his fears and without another word he strode swiftly across the hall carpet and switched on the living-room light.

For the rest of his life he carried a picture of the scene that met his eyes that horrifying evening in March. Again and again over the years he would find his mind returning to the dreadful carnage he witnessed that night.

There was blood everywhere. On the walls; over the chairs; all across the carpet where she had tried to crawl away, leaving bloody hand marks behind her. Russell had never realised that the human body contained so much blood. Finally his eyes took in the huddled figure of his sister and then he turned to Allan, ashen-faced.

'Why?' he croaked.

Allan ignored him and laughed hysterically. 'I've done it,' he shouted loudly. 'Alice, I've done it! We're free!' Then he waited, his head tilted to one side, but there was no reply.

'ALICE!' Now his voice was anxious. 'She's dead. It's over. Alice, where are you? Come and help me. I've done it for us; now we can be together for eternity.'

Again there was a terrible silence until, far away, both he and Russell heard her familiar tinkle of laughter, then Allan saw a faint outline of her body and heard the final words she would ever speak to him.

'Fool!' she jeered. 'Poor, ignorant, opinionated little fool! Goodbye, Allan. As you say, it's finished at last, and now I can leave. Farewell, Russell; try not to mourn too much!' While they stared at her she gave one brief, feline smile and then vanished.

Bereft of her support Allan started to moan. The room had begun to smell of blood and when he looked at his spanner he could see fragments of flesh clinging to it. Julie's flesh. With a scream he hurled it away from him, then his eyes darted round the room until the smell overwhelmed him and he retched in revulsion.

After a time he noticed Isabelle, her hands groping for specks of dust caught in the light from the standard lamp, but Melissa was no longer standing next to her. Instead she was lying in a crumpled heap on the floor. With a groan Allan approached the body. Tentatively he put out a hand and felt again the strange, boneless form that he had felt one night an eternity ago.

While he crouched beside her the flesh began to shrink beneath his touch, collapsing inwards as the body tissue slowly turned to a thin, milky fluid that then oozed out from every orifice. Petrified by the sight he was unable to move, instead he sat beside the disintegrating mass until all that remained was a strangely small piece of surface skin.

With trembling hands he picked it up and showed it to Russell, who backed away shaking his head and refusing to touch it. Despite his sister's description of Melissa's first dematerialisation he had not been prepared for the horror of the reality. Allan giggled at Russell's expression before walking out of the room, the skin held between the fingers of his left hand.

Russell remained in the living-room, trying to assimilate the full hideousness of the nightmare into which he had been plunged. Suddenly Isabelle rubbed her fists over her face, leaving smears of blood on her cheeks and nose; blood that must have been sprayed over her during the murder.

217

At that moment Allan returned, still giggling but without his ghastly burden. 'She won then,' Russell murmured. Allan stared blankly for a moment and then re-commenced his hysterical laughter.

Ignoring his brother-in-law Russell went to his sister's body and knelt down beside it. She was unbelievably battered. Her face had been smashed out of all recognition, but he knew the small mole on her neck and the tiny birth mark behind her left ear. He finally stood up, discovering immediately that even the knees of his trousers were covered in blood. With a shudder he turned to Allan.

'Why?' he demanded again. 'Why did you do it?'

'I had to,' he responded tonelessly. 'It was the only way to keep . . .' His voice tailed off.

'What harm had she ever done you?' shouted Russell. 'She was a good wife and mother. You never deserved her, I knew that, but she wouldn't listen to me.'

A gleam of intelligence crossed Allan's features. 'She lay with you,' he said in conversational tones. 'She lay with her own brother, and then passed that idiot over there off as mine.'

'Who told you that?'

'She did.'

'Julie? But why?'

'Because I found something out today, something quite unusual. It put a different complexion on everything. Oh yes, quite a different complexion.' And he smiled once more.

'What was this discovery?'

'My old family doctor let slip the fact that I'm sterile. He thought my children were adopted, and congratulated me on my Christian attitude towards the mentally handicapped. Unfortunate, don't you think?'

'Oh my God!' breathed Russell. 'So that's why Alice chose you.'

218

'The thing is,' continued Allan, 'what can I do? I mean, will you help me clean up? I don't want anyone to find out.'

'What! Clean up this slaughterhouse? You're completely round the bend. We've got to call the police.'

'I had to do it. It wasn't only because she'd betrayed me, you have to understand that. It was because of Alice.'

'I don't doubt that for one moment. How specifically does she fit into this hideous picture?'

'She threatened to leave me unless I . . . But it was all lies! *She* betrayed me too. She's gone; gone for ever. Russell, you must understand. You loved her once. I know you did, there's no point in denying it. What did you do when she left you? How did you . . .'

'You brainless idiot! You've got it all wrong. Everything's wrong. You've murdered your wife for nothing. Alice won't come back, she's done what she wanted, there isn't any reason for her to return. You were simply a tool in her hands. You bloody, bloody fool!'

Allan started to sob. 'But Isabelle? That's true isn't it? She is your daughter?'

'Yes, Isabelle's my child, but that's the only thing you've got right, and for that you've committed this . . . this unbelievably ghastly murder. If it weren't for the fact that the law will punish you I'd kill you myself here and now.

'Look around you! Look at Julie. Go on; look at what you've done to her.'

Allan's eyes followed Russell's round the room, and then he began to whimper. Russell suddenly felt faint. Reaction was setting in. He could scarcely bear to stay in the same room as his sister and the terrible stench of death that filled the air.

Again Isabelle made a gurgling sound; at the sight of her blood-streaked face and hands he gagged and rushed to the kitchen sink, leaving Allan collapsed on the floor whimpering like a child.

After he'd been sick Russell took a few sips of cold water and several slow, deep breaths. He knew that he had to hold on to his sanity. If he lost control now he might never regain it, and he needed to stay sane. He had to, he owed that much to Julie.

At last, feeling marginally more composed, he went back to his brother-in-law. 'What's happened to Melissa, Allan?' Allan chewed on his bottom lip and regarded Russell thoughtfully. 'She's in the bin.'

'She's what?'

'Don't worry; *I'm* quite sane, you know. She's in the bin, behind the kitchen door. No one will ever realise. Go and see for yourself. You wouldn't come with me earlier would you?'

Russell walked unsteadily to the kitchen and hesitantly lifted the bin lid. There was the usual collection of kitchen rubbish. Potato peelings, used tissues, soiled kitchen paper and even some bloody scraps of meat, but there was nothing resembling Melissa.

Then, as he was about to shut the lid, he saw her. She was crumpled beneath an empty corned beef tin; a translucent piece of dried-up skin that demonstrated more clearly than anything else that Melissa had never existed except as a part of Alice. Once her usefulness was over Alice had withdrawn from the shell she had used so skilfully, until finally only the outer wrapping was left.

As Allan rightly said, no one would ever know. All the same Russell picked it up and set light to it, flushing the ashes down the sink. Now there was nothing. It was as though Melissa had never been born. He gave a short laugh as he realised the truth of this. Then he remembered Julie, and the laughter died.

Quietly he went into the hall and dialled 999. There was nothing more he could do. The police would have to take over. He gave the briefest of details and hung up.

In the living-room Allan was trying to tidy the cushions. He was mumbling to himself as he worked, yet Russell was convinced that he was still sane. Allan knew what he'd done. What he didn't understand was how he had failed Alice, or why he had lost her.

'I've phoned the police, Allan.'

'Yes, I suppose that's best. They'll know what to do.'

'What will you say?'

'I'll tell them the truth, of course.'

'They won't believe you.'

Allan glared at Russell. 'Don't worry, I shan't mention your incestuous relationship with your sister, or Alice. After all, I don't want them to think me mad. No, I shall explain what my doctor told me after mother's funeral, and how I came straight home then killed Julie in a frenzy of hatred and shock. I should think they might deal quite leniently with such provocation, wouldn't you?'

'I hope not. What about Melissa?'

'Melissa? Well, that's difficult isn't it? I mean, they won't find Melissa, so I don't think I'll mention her.'

'But they'll search everywhere. You ought to have some story prepared.'

'There's nothing I can say. One minute she was there, the next she wasn't. That's the truth. I can say that if you like.'

'Yes, I think you should. They'll probably imagine she ran out into the night. Look . . .'

At that moment there was the sound of a police siren followed almost immediately by an urgent banging on the door. Still trembling Russell let them in, and then retreated to the kitchen. Later on, he watched as a young constable was sick into the sink, and even later he saw them take Allan away in handcuffs, but still he sat there until they were ready to talk to him.

He described the telephone call fetching him over, the sight that met his eyes, Allan's garbled tale of adultery and his subsequent call to the police. Yes, he said, there was another little girl but he hadn't seen her at all. No, his brother-in-law hadn't said where she was, and he himself had been too distraught by the scene to think of asking. Perhaps, he added, she was at a friend's.

The police took his address and telephone number and then helped him collect up some baby things for Isabelle before driving the pair of them back to the Pask home. They were gentle and kind, and he thanked them for their help.

Despite their offer he decided to tell his mother himself, so they left a policewoman with him while he did so. In the end she succumbed to hysterics and had to be put to bed. Then his father came home and it all began again. Throughout the long, agonising hours Isabelle sat cheerfully playing with an old tea-towel, grinning senselessly at everyone who caught her eye.

The following day Allan was charged with the murder of his wife, Julie, and remanded in custody for seven days. When he next appeared he was also charged with the murder of his eldest daughter, Melissa. This charge he strenuously denied, which meant there had to be a trial.

It was then that Russell decided to go and see him. He owed Allan that much at least. It might even stop them all from being exposed to the horror of a long and sensational public trial.

222

Chapter 15

They sat at opposite sides of the table. A warden stood by the wall, within hearing distance, but that scarcely mattered. He wouldn't understand half of what he heard.

Russell was surprised and relieved to see that Allan was looking far more like himself. He seemed calm and composed, and there was no longer the fanatically haunted gleam in his eyes that was the hallmark of Alice's victims.

'Why did you come? he queried, accepting the cigarette Russell held out.

'To explain.'

'Explain what?'

'Anything you want to know.'

Allan held out the cigarette for a light and then inhaled deeply. 'All right,' he said at last. 'Tell me about the summer that Alice died.'

Russell's mind turned back the clock with effortless ease. In truth he had always found it easier to recall the days before Alice died than the ones that followed.

'Well, it was very hot. I know people often say that we don't get summers like we used to, but that particular one was extraordinarily hot. We all spent most of our time in swimming gear, lazing around on the beach or in Alice's garden.

'There was a small apple orchard that her father owned. We frequently used to lie there and fall asleep, or read. It was all very peaceful and civilised – on the surface.'

'You *were* in love, weren't you? You and Alice? Despite your previous denials.'

'Yes, we were in love – but not with each other. It was far more complicated than that. You see, we were both in love with Julie.'

The cigarette in Allan's fingers shook and ash fell to the table. He blinked rapidly and stared at Russell. 'What is this? Some kind of sick joke?'

'I wish it were, but it's not: this is the truth. This is what really happened that summer.

'First of all, you have to understand our family a little better. I was adopted. My mother – Mrs Pask – didn't seem able to have children, and so they adoped me. After that, as often happens, she did eventually become pregnant and therefore although Julie and I grew up as brother and sister we always knew that we weren't actually related. There was no blood tie.

'At first I suppose our feelings were simply those of any brother and sister who are close, but by the time that Julie was fifteen we knew, or at least I thought we knew, that we were in love.

'We didn't tell anyone; there wasn't any need. We had plenty of time, and we were together every day. Either our love would grow or it would fade, we were content to wait. Julie was, after all, very young.

'When we went to Cornwall we decided not to tell anyone there either. For one thing they'd have kept teasing us, and for another Alice could never keep a secret, and so no one knew but us, and that was fine.

'I made a show of being keen on a girl who lived next door to Alice. Quite often she and I would go off to the pictures or a nearby cove. We kissed and cuddled a lot, but that was all. I don't know how deeply she felt, but for me there was nothing. She was useful, a diversion to complete our deception from our cousins, and it worked well.

'I *was* surprised at Julie's lack of jealousy. I mean, if it had been the other way round I'd have gone mad wondering what she was getting up to, but Julie was never interested. I put it down to trust, unfortuntely I was only fooling myself.

'All through those weeks, Alice flitted from one boy to the next. She slept around, we knew that, but on her terms. She was incredibly beautiful. I wondered why I wasn't attracted to her myself. Finally I decided that it was because of an inner coldness. I always felt that Alice could be smiling and kissing even as she mocked her boyfriends in her mind. They say that promiscuous women are often cold, and that's what I sensed in Alice. She had a cold core that no one would ever touch.

'One day, towards the end of the holiday, I decided I'd had enough of Leonie – the neighbour's daughter – and I whispered to Julie to steal away and meet me at the cove we'd all been using that summer. She smiled and agreed, but she wasn't as excited or delighted as I'd expected; I do remember that.'

He stopped, his mind going back to that conversation, the strange look that he had surprised in Julie's eyes before she lowered her lashes and promised to be there.

'Go on!' Allan sounded tense and impatient.

'Sorry! Well, as it turned out I was a bit late getting to the cove, my aunt sent me to the post office first. As I walked over the sand towards the rock where we were to meet I could hear Julie's voice and realised she wasn't alone.

'At first I thought it was a boy with her, and then I realised it was only Alice so I decided to spring a surprise on them. I crept round the base of the rock and tiptoed up behind them. I wish to God I hadn't. If only I'd called out first, given them some warning, then everything would have been different; but I didn't know that at the time. How could I possibly have envisaged that one tiny decision to have a bit of fun would shatter three lives for ever. Fate is very unkind.'

'I don't believe in fate. We make our own destiny.'

Russell sighed. 'Perhaps you're right. Anyway, you can guess what I found. Alice was lying spread out on the rock. She only had on the bottom half of her bikini, it was a red and green one, and there was Julie – my Julie – bending over her, stroking her flesh and kissing her on the breasts.

'I was hypnotised by the sheer horror of the situation. I couldn't go back, yet I couldn't go on. I wanted to be sick, and I must have made some sound because Julie twisted round, then gave a scream of fright. She looked absolutely devasted.

'Alice was far more composed. She sat up and smiled sweetly at me. "I'm introducing your sister to the delights of real lovemaking. Do stay if you like, you might learn a thing or two," she said.

'I ignored her, turning my attention to Julie. I couldn't believe what I was seeing. I shouted at her, reminding her that she was *mine*, and that what she and Alice were doing was perverted and evil, but she never answered me. She remained absolutely silent; even when she began to weep it was soundlessly.'

'What about Alice?' asked Allan. 'What did she do?'

'At first she just laughed, but when I continued ranting on she stood up and shouted at me. "Yours!" she jeered. "How can she be yours? She's your sister!"

'Naturally I explained. I thought she'd understand, being adopted herself, but instead she smiled all the more and her eyes, those incredible eyes, widened and sparkled with delighted anticipation. She waited until

I'd finished stumbling through my explanation then she turned her back on me and walked to the top of the rock. "You can't marry Julie," she called over her shoulder, "you share the same father. You were born on the wrong side of the blanket, Russell, and your poor mother agreed to bring you up because she herself was childless."

'I thought she was lying. I was certain it was another of her tricks and I told her so. I remember yelling that she was a liar, and she told me to ask my father if I didn't believe her.

'When I turned to Julie she was shaking her head, obviously as stunned as I was. Yet – and I think this was the breaking point for me – I could see a look of relief in her eyes, as though at last she saw a path to freedom without hurting my feelings.

'I walked up to Alice and caught hold of her shoulders. I shook her, calling her all the names I knew, but she kept on laughing. I heard that laugh day and night for three years after she died, and even now I can recall it precisely. The harder she laughed the harder I shook her; then her feet slipped a little and she gave a squeal and clutched me round the waist.

'It was only then that I decided to murder her. The sea was half-way round the rock and quite deep at the end where we were standing. Also there were several smaller rocks already hidden by the water. I released her shoulders and unclasped her hands from my waist. She looked up at me and grinned. "Thank you, kind sir," she mocked, but I kept hold of her hands and began to force her towards the edge of the slab.

'She suddenly realised that I was going to kill her, and immediately she fought like a demon. She kept screaming for Julie to help her, but Julie stayed where she was. She didn't help either of us, she just sat there and waited.

'It was over quite quickly. As a larger wave rushed

227

towards us I shoved her with all the force I could muster. She gave one final high-pitched scream and then fell backwards. I heard her head hit another rock, and when I peered down she was floating in the water, her hair trailing out round her face.

'I turned away at once and took hold of Julie's hands. She felt icy cold, but she followed me meekly off the rock up the beach to the sand dunes where the sea never reached. She didn't say anything, merely stared blankly a head.

'I kept shouting at her, asking her if she'd enjoyed making love with another girl, but she wouldn't answer. In the end I threw her down and virtually raped her. I was determined to blot out all her memories of Alice's touch and impose myself on her.

'At first she whimpered protests, but then she seemed to understand that it was a way of cleansing herself and she co-operated. Julie is – was – always too compassionate. If she sensed a need in people she did all that she could to fill that need. I don't know if it was a weakness or a strength but it never left her.'

'And after?' prompted Allan. Russell jumped as he came back to reality.

'After? Well, that was difficult. We had to provide ourselves with alibis, join in the search for the missing Alice, and then wait while the police and pathologists tried to work out how she'd died. It took a long time but in the end we were safe. Accidental death they said.'

'Did Alice tell you the truth?'

'What about?'

'Your father.'

'As a matter of fact, yes, she did. It was all very distressing, both for my parents and for me.'

'But not for Julie?'

Russell swallowed hard. 'No, probably not for Julie. We never made love again until just before you two were

228

married, although I never ceased to love her the way I had that summer. When she finally gave in to my years of wordless but unceasing pursuit there was no love in it, not on her side. It was one stupid moment of weakness on her part. I was very low, haunted by Alice, and she decided to comfort me in the only way that she knew would help. The pregnancy was a terrible shock to us both.'

'I see.'

'In the end she miscarried the child, as you know, and we were both relieved.'

'But not so relieved that it never happened again! How do you explain Isabelle?'

'It was virtually the same story. I was depressed and almost blackmailed Julie into making love again. She didn't want to. Of course I know now that Alice was behind it all. We were both driven by forces we didn't understand. It was never Julie's fault though. You must believe me.'

'She had an affair with our neighbour the night of my mother's funeral,' said Allan tonelessly.

'I don't believe you!'

'Melissa told me.'

'Melissa! There was never any such person.'

'I could see from Julie's expression that it was true. How do you explain that? Compassion again?'

Russell looked confused. 'How can I say? I don't know what your marriage was like by then. Perhaps she needed comfort and he was there. We'll never know now will we.'

'No, and it's pointless to speculate because you'll always say your beloved sister was guiltless. You're as besotted today as you were as a boy. Love's certainly blind in your case.'

Russell looked furious. 'It isn't that. Julie was a victim. She liked everyone and she tried to make people

229

content. There's nothing wrong with compassion. Not that you'd know; you're a cold fish, I never cared for you.'

'Nor I for you. I did love your sister though, at the beginning.'

'Before Alice?'

'That's right, before Alice.'

For a few moments both men were silent. Russell started to rise from his chair, there seemed very little point in staying longer. Allan put out a hand.

'Don't go, there's one thing puzzling me. You say that Alice never lied, but she does now. On the night before our wedding she came to me for the first time. She said "Marry Julie and we'll always be together." But we weren't.

'Then, the other night, she told me "Kill your wife and we'll be together for eternity." Why did she lie to me like that? What was she doing? Getting her revenge on you?'

Russell went pale. This was even worse than he had feared. 'No! She's been having her revenge on me for years. Don't you see, she was very clever, she never did lie to you. "Marry Julie and we'll always be together." It was true, they were – Alice and Julie were – Melissa made sure of that.

'Then the promise. "Kill your wife and we'll be together for eternity." *That* was her final goal, and you allowed her to achieve it. She and Julie, together for all eternity. You misinterpreted her words, as you were meant to, but taken literally they were the truth.

'I thought that all she wanted was Julie's death, but apparently it went deeper than that. She wanted Julie. Perhaps she really was in love with Julie, it would explain her casual attitude to the men in her life, and she manipulated us all so that she could come back and get her. How well she succeeded!

'You weren't important; no man was ever important.

230

You, and even I, were simply the means by which she could achieve her end. Collect Julie, to keep her company for eternity.'

Allan's head shook violently. 'I don't believe you.'

'I don't suppose you want to, but it has to be the truth. Think about it. There is no other explanation.'

'Do you think Julie loved Alice?'

Russell moistened his dry lips. 'I hope and pray she did, otherwise she's condemned to never-ending purgatory. There was a part of her that I felt she always kept private from everyone. I put it down to modesty, but upon reflection yes, she possibly did prefer Alice to men. It would explain why she kept so much calmer than I did when Alice returned to our lives.'

'There were some signs,' murmured Allan. 'I used to think she was frigid. Loving, but not sexual; although naturally I blamed my own obsession with Alice. There's another thing that's important. It concerns Melissa. Just before she was born the nurses told me how they lost the baby's heartbeat. That must have been because the original child died and Alice managed to slip a part of herself into the physical body at that precise moment.'

'I suppose so. I'm genuinely sorry you got caught up in this, Allan. It was your unknown sterility that made you the ideal candidate. That was Alice's trump card, and she played it with her usual exquisite timing.'

'I loved Alice. I really loved her.' Allan tried, not very successfully, to keep his voice calm.

'I know. Do *you* honestly believe that Julie loved her too?' He was desperate to be reassured.

Allan hesitated. 'At the end Julie said that she'd only ever loved me. I think now that she was telling the truth, in which case no, she couldn't have done.'

'Perhaps she meant that you were the only *man* she'd ever loved.'

'But she'd once loved you.'

231

'No, she was fond of me. I misinterpreted her feelings.'

'I think you're wrong about her and Alice.'

'Yes, well you would! You'd do anything to torture me even now when you're . . . I'm sorry. I shouldn't make things worse for you. About the trial . . .'

'There won't be one. Knowing the truth about Alice, realising how I wasted my life, there's no point in going on.'

'But . . .?'

'Thank you for coming, Russell. Goodbye.' The dismissal was pointed, and with one awkward hand-shake the men parted for the last time.

That night, to the embarrassment of the prison authorities, and the disappointment of certain more ghoulish members of the public, Allan Firmager hanged himself in his cell.

The police closed their files and a lot of public money was saved. After three months they even stopped searching for Melissa. They accepted that she would most probably never be found, and naturally she wasn't.

For the next few months Russell carried on normally. He supported his parents valiantly, and even found himself a job. All the time, day after day, he consoled himself with the knowledge that at least Julie was now at peace with herself; no longer forced to act out a lie contrary to her nature.

Then, one night, he was awoken by the smell of sandalwood and knew with horror that Alice was back. He sat up quickly, and there she was, standing beside his bed with her arm round Julie.

'Look!' she murmured seductively. 'See how well I care for her,' and her hands moved over his half-sister as gently and tenderly as any man's.

He was prepared for that, and he looked at his beloved Julie to assure her that he understood. She stood motionless. Her body was plainly becoming aroused, but her eyes were those of a soul in torment, and when Alice twisted and moved her slight form closer to her lover Julie gave one terrible hopeless cry of fear and distaste before their bodies fused and they slowly vanished from his sight.

Now, at last, he knew. Knew that Julie hadn't loved Alice, had possibly even loved him. He knew too that Alice's desire for Julie wasn't because of love, however misguided, but because of her awareness that this desire caused Russell, her murderer, the man who had cut short her life so ruthlessly, the greatest amount of pain possible.

Nothing else could have broken him completely. This did. As he absorbed the realisation that Julie was condemned to spend eternity in Alice's arms, never free of her unwelcome lover's embraces, his mind spiralled down into darkness, trying to retreat from the knowledge.

He cried out, begging Alice to release Julie, but all she did was allow him further glimpses of her intimacy with his half-sister. He tried to scream, but no sound came out, and Alice's violet eyes watched with cold satisfaction as he began to gibber and gabble until finally all hold on sanity was lost and his mind retreated from this ultimate horror.

At last Alice gave a whispered sigh of happiness. Her revenge was complete, and Julie – who had always loathed the side of her nature that Alice had disclosed that far-off summer – was now hers for eternity.

Death, mused Alice, had been far kinder to her than life.

In the morning Russell's mother found him huddled silently on the bed, legs tucked up in the foetal position, eyes wide with an expression beyond human understanding.

People came, looked, and departed again. He was put on a stretcher and taken away by ambulance. No straps were needed to secure him for he had no awareness of what they were doing. He was locked in his own world; condemned, as Alice had hoped, to endless years of unremitting torment.

He died in the mental hospital of pneumonia at the age of eighty-six years, by which time there was no one left to mourn him. He was buried with only a vicar and two male nurses to attend his passing: two nurses who never knew what demons had visited their patient night after night, but who both hoped that he had finally obtained peace.

If he had, then it was for the first time since that far-off summer when Alice died.